You're About to Become a

Privileged Woman.

INTRODUCING
PAGES & PRIVILEGES.™

It's our way of thanking you for buying
our books at your favorite retail store.

— *GET ALL THIS FREE* —
WITH JUST ONE PROOF OF PURCHASE:

◆ Hotel Discounts up to 60% at home and abroad

◆ Travel Service - Guaranteed lowest published
  airfares plus 5% cash back on tickets

◆ $25 Travel Voucher

◆ Sensuous Petite Parfumerie collection ($50 value)

◆ Insider Tips Letter with sneak previews of
  upcoming books

◆ Mystery Gift (if you enroll before 6/15/95)

You'll get a FREE personal card, too.
It's your passport to all these benefits– and to
even more great gifts & benefits to come!

There's no club to join. No purchase commitment. No obligation.

As a *Privileged Woman,* you'll be entitled to all these *Free Benefits.* And *Free Gifts,* too.

To thank you for buying our books, we've designed an exclusive FREE program called *PAGES & PRIVILEGES™.* You can enroll with just one Proof of Purchase, and get the kind of luxuries that, until now, you could only read about.

*B*IG HOTEL DISCOUNTS

A privileged woman stays in the finest hotels. And so can you—at up to 60% off! Imagine standing in a hotel check-in line and watching as the guest in front of you pays $150 for the same room that's only costing you $60. Your *Pages & Privileges* discounts are good at Sheraton, Marriott, Best Western, Hyatt and thousands of other fine hotels all over the U.S., Canada and Europe.

*F*REE DISCOUNT TRAVEL SERVICE

A privileged woman is always jetting to romantic places. When <u>you</u> fly, just make one phone call for the lowest published airfare at time of booking—<u>or double the difference back</u>! PLUS—

you'll get a $25 voucher to use the first time you book a flight AND <u>5% cash back on every ticket you buy thereafter through the travel service</u>!

FREE GIFTS!

A privileged woman is always getting wonderful gifts.
Luxuriate in rich fragrances that will stir your senses (and his). This gift-boxed assortment of fine perfumes includes three popular scents, each in a beautiful designer bottle.  Truly Lace...This luxurious fragrance unveils your sensuous side. L'Effleur...discover the romance of the Victorian era with this soft floral. Muguet des bois...a single note floral of singular beauty. This $50 value is yours—FREE when you enroll in *Pages & Privileges*! And it's just the beginning of the gifts and benefits that will be coming your way!

FREE INSIDER TIPS LETTER

A privileged woman is always informed. And you'll be, too, with our free letter full of fascinating information and sneak previews of upcoming books.

MORE GREAT GIFTS & BENEFITS TO COME

A privileged woman always has a lot to look forward to.
And so will you. You get all these wonderful FREE gifts and benefits now with only one purchase...and there are no additional purchases required. However, each additional retail purchase of Harlequin and Silhouette books brings you a step closer to even more great FREE benefits like half-price movie tickets...and even more FREE gifts like these beautiful fragrance gift baskets:

L'Effleur ...This basketful of romance lets you discover L'Effleur from head to toe, heart to home.

Truly Lace ...A basket spun with the sensuous luxuries of Truly Lace, including Dusting Powder in a reusable satin and lace covered box.

ENROLL NOW!

Complete the Enrollment Form on the back of this card and become a Privileged Woman today!

Enroll Today in *PAGES & PRIVILEGES*™, the program that gives you Great Gifts and Benefits with just one purchase!

Enrollment Form

☐ *Yes!* I WANT TO BE A *Privileged Woman*.

Enclosed is one *PAGES & PRIVILEGES*™ Proof of Purchase from any Harlequin or Silhouette book currently for sale in stores (Proofs of Purchase are found on the back pages of books) and the store cash register receipt. Please enroll me in *PAGES & PRIVILEGES*™. Send my Welcome Kit and FREE Gifts -- and activate my FREE benefits -- immediately.

▼ DETACH HERE AND MAIL TODAY! ▼

NAME (please print)

ADDRESS   APT. NO

CITY   STATE   ZIP/POSTAL CODE

PROOF OF PURCHASE

**NO CLUB!
NO COMMITMENT!**
*Just one purchase brings
you great Free Gifts
and Benefits!*
(See inside for details.)

Please allow 6-8 weeks for delivery. Quantities are limited. We reserve the right to substitute items. Enroll before October 31, 1995 and receive one full year of benefits.

Name of store where this book was purchased_____

Date of purchase_____

Type of store:

    ☐ Bookstore   ☐ Supermarket ☐ Drugstore

    ☐ Dept. or discount store (e.g. K-Mart or Walmart)

    ☐ Other (specify)_____

Which Harlequin or Silhouette series do you usually read?

_____

Complete and mail with one Proof of Purchase and store receipt to:

U.S.: *PAGES & PRIVILEGES*™, P.O. Box 1960, Danbury, CT 06813-1960

Canada: *PAGES & PRIVILEGES*™, 49-6A The Donway West, P.O. 813, North York, ON M3C 2E8

PRINTED IN U.S.A

"Tucker, you think every man has designs on me—"

"Because *I* have designs on you." Grinning, he moved closer. "You think I'm panting after you like a hungry wolf, that I'll do anything to get you into bed."

Harley took a step back and felt the kitchen sink behind her. "No, I don't." But her pulse was racing.

"Well, I am, and I would." He took her face in his hands and kissed her, deeply and passionately. "Just tell me what it takes."

"You're crazy." Heart pounding, she pushed him away. "Men don't say things like that. They finesse you—"

"They buy you flowers and take you to dinner. Spend lots of money. Then they bring you home, turn off the lights and engineer some seduction. A month later you're history."

"Except in your case it's the next morning," she pointed out. "Your track record isn't good, Tucker. You're the one likely to bolt." *Bolt at the first sign of love,* she finished silently.

Dear Reader,

By popular demand, Rebels & Rogues returns to Temptation! Over the years we've received lots of positive fan mail about this popular series. You told us how much you *love* stories that focus on the hero—and want more. Well, we've listened. Rebels & Rogues books will appear in the lineup several times a year.

This month's Rebels & Rogues title is written by new author Patricia Ryan. *The Return of the Black Sheep* is about the rebellious Tucker, who left home at sixteen. Now he's back, but ready to run from his growing attraction to gorgeous house sitter Harley.

Patricia Ryan is definitely a rising star in the romance world. Last year she was a Golden Heart Finalist in the Romance Writers of America's annual contest—*The Return of the Black Sheep* was voted Best Short Contemporary. A former editor and illustrator, Patricia is currently working on her next Temptation romance.

Look for a new Rebels & Rogues story in August: #551 THE LAST HERO by Alyssa Dean.

Happy Reading!

Birgit Davis-Todd
Senior Editor, Harlequin Temptation

THE RETURN OF THE BLACK SHEEP

PATRICIA RYAN

Carol and David

Happy reading! —
Pat Ryan

David &
Carol —
Set aside
sermons &
dissertations
for candlelight
& Eden
(if you want
quiet, remember
cows love
watermelon.)
Thanks, Kate

Harlequin Books

TORONTO • NEW YORK • LONDON
AMSTERDAM • PARIS • SYDNEY • HAMBURG
STOCKHOLM • ATHENS • TOKYO • MILAN
MADRID • WARSAW • BUDAPEST • AUCKLAND

For Rich, with love

My warmest thanks to
Carol Backus, Rina Najam, Kathy Schaefer,
Bev Lewis, Barbara Millet
and all my LCRW and NJRW friends
for your encouragement and support,
but most of all to Pam, for everything.

ISBN 0-373-25640-X

THE RETURN OF THE BLACK SHEEP

1

HARLEY ANN SAYERS awoke to the crash and tinkle of glass.

She lay still in the dark, struggling to hear anything above the sounds of her own ragged breathing and the blood pounding in her ears. A door closed softly downstairs. Footsteps crunched in the glass. A man cleared his throat.

Someone's in the house.

She swallowed hard, her mouth suddenly dry. She sat up and reached toward the night table, her hand shaking violently as it groped for the phone. No phone; of course not. This wasn't her apartment, this was Raleigh Hale's house. Mr. Hale didn't like telephones, and he didn't think they belonged in the bedroom. Great. Just great.

A sound that she couldn't identify—a dull thump, thump, thump—provided counterpoint to the groan of the floorboards from his footsteps. The floors always creaked underfoot in this two-hundred-year-old house, even through the Oriental rugs.

Harley got up, located her robe in the moonlight from the open window, and put it on over her short summer pajamas. Trembling, she fumbled with its sash, tying it in a double knot, then tidied her loose hair with an unsteady hand and crept into the hallway. He hadn't turned any lights on downstairs. Did he know she was here? Probably not, considering the noise he made.

She could hardly breathe, she shook so hard. She paused at the top of the stairs to think. The only phone was in the study, at the front of the big house. *He* was in the solarium, at the back. Maybe, if she avoided the really squeaky floorboards, she could slip into the study and dial 911.

But first, a weapon. She entered the closest room and looked around. Tucker Hale's room, unused but unchanged for over twenty years. A museum in memory of a dead son.

The moon, filtered through half-closed blinds, painted luminous stripes across hundreds of books and record albums shelved in floor-to-ceiling bookcases. Arranged in groups among them were dozens of model airplanes, cars, and sailboats. Nothing with which to defend herself. On the floor, leaning against the walls, she saw two guitars . . . and a baseball bat.

She gripped the bat with one hand and the skirt of her robe with the other and crept downstairs.

Her heart began to hammer. He was playing the piano. He played surprisingly well, his choice of music very beautiful and very familiar—one of her favorite pieces: Beethoven's *Moonlight Sonata*.

Why, after breaking into Raleigh Hale's house at one in the morning, had this guy headed straight for the solarium and sat down at the piano? Was it possible he was someone who belonged here—maybe Mr. Hale, himself? He was supposed to be sailing in the Caribbean all summer, but maybe he'd had to cut his trip short, and came home without his keys, and didn't want to wake her.... Wishful thinking, she knew.

She'd better get a look at him before calling 911. Cautiously she padded to the entrance of the solarium. Her shaking worsened when she saw him, barely illuminated by the moonlight. He sat at the grand piano with his back to her, motionless as he played. She squinted at his dark form.

He was big, as she had suspected from his footsteps, with a broad back and wide shoulders. It looked like he was wearing a baseball cap. Medium-brown hair, unkempt and overgrown, hung down almost to the collar of his gray sweater.

This isn't Raleigh Hale. Get out!

Suddenly he stopped playing. He rested one hand on the keys and rubbed the back of his neck with the other. She heard him sigh. Slowly, deliberately, he closed the piano, leaned his elbows on it, rubbed his hands on his face, lifted and replaced his cap . . .

And turned to look directly at her.

She gasped, paralyzed with fear and infuriated with herself. She should have called the police. No—she should have run while she had the chance. Too late now. He'd catch her in a second.

The man at the piano just sat and stared, his eyes wide and curious in the dark. He looked at the bat, at her face, at her white terry cloth robe and bare feet, then back at her face.

Don't show fear. Fear draws aggression. And don't shake. He'll see you shaking and know how scared you are. She held the bat with both hands in a threatening posture, prepared to swing.

She could see him a little better now. She could see that he was unshaven and that his black cap had the white image of a leaping fish on it. He wore jeans, and his loose sweater had a hole on the shoulder, revealing a patch of white T-shirt.

He reached for something, some kind of stick. Harley raised the bat. *"Put that down!"* Her voice quavered. *Get a grip!*

"Easy." The stick was curved at the top: a cane. That explained the dull thump she had heard earlier. With one hand on it and the other on the piano, he rose to his feet. Harley cursed inwardly. He was well over six feet tall, long-limbed and square-shouldered. She, at five-foot-four and a hundred ten pounds, would be no match at all for him.

"Sit down!" She swung to emphasize the command, and nearly threw herself off-balance. *"Now!"*

He made no move to obey her, but leaned on the cane and regarded her with an expression of puzzled amusement. "If you're going to work me over with that, do me a favor and lay off the bad leg." His deep voice had a raw edge to it.

He took a halting step toward Harley, supporting himself with the cane. She saw his left leg drag a bit. That was good, but he still looked dangerous. His forearms, revealed by the pushed-up sleeves of his sweater, were cabled with muscle; he was lean, but strong. And that cane, in the hands of someone like him, could make an effective weapon.

Harley took a deep breath and tried for a menacing tone. "Just stay where you are." Another swing, this one more controlled.

"Or you'll pop me out of the stadium?" A mild grin, another awkward step.

"Or I'll pop you in your leg."

The grin faded. She could see his eyes clearly now. They were brown, and in the silvery moonlight they looked enormous. A nasty scar meandered down his left cheek, disappearing into the dark stubble on his jaw. "You wouldn't do that."

"Try me."

His gaze rested on the bat, and his eyes grew even wider. He took another step and reached for it, saying, "Hey, that's—" But before he could grab it from her, she whipped it away.

She hauled back and slammed it with all her strength into the shin of his right leg, the good one. The impact jolted her, and she heard him grunt as he went down, his cane clattering on the slate floor. For an agonized moment, he curled into a ball, clutching the leg. Then suddenly he bellowed an oath so blistering that Harley drew in her breath, stunned by what she had done.

Leave now. She started to turn, then paused. Suddenly he didn't look like such a threat anymore, and she was beginning to realize that perhaps she wasn't entirely defenseless, after all. The man rolled onto his back, holding his right leg with both hands and growling, "Damn, damn, damn, damn, damn." He groaned, released the leg, and stretched out, breathless, on the floor. "That was my *good* leg!" he gasped.

"Not anymore," she said.

He looked her in the eye, astonished. The look disarmed her and made her feel guilty. Why should she feel guilty for disabling an intruder? He said, "Wow, you are one cold-blooded piece of work. I can't believe you *did* that!"

"I always do what I say I'm going to do." She stood over him, holding the bat, feeling confused and light-headed.

"How commendable." He sat up and massaged the shin, shaking his head. "That was some swing."

"Adrenaline." Seeing him brace his hands on the floor, she added, "Don't get up."

He raised both palms in a pacifying gesture. Oddly, he still looked amused, despite his obvious pain. He even smiled at her. . . .

Right before he snaked out his long arm, closed his fist around the bat, and yanked it out of her hands in a blur.

Harley, you fool! she thought, backing up. His smile became a cocky grin, as if to say his control of the situation had never really been in doubt. He hefted the bat in his hand, testing its weight.

Get out now! She turned and sprinted toward the front door. Halfway through the dining room, she heard a rattling sound behind her, something rolling toward her on the floor. She stopped and turned. The baseball bat had taken a crooked path and come to rest against a leg of the mahogany dining table. She could see him through the entrance to the solarium, still sitting on the floor.

"You can have it back," he said, as Harley picked it up. "I just wanted to look at it. That's all I wanted in the first place, before you attacked me."

"Why?" Slowly she walked toward him, holding the bat across her chest with both hands, confident now that she could get away any time she wanted to. She stopped just outside the doorway to the solarium, leaving him at a safe distance.

"I saw the initials on it."

She flipped the light switch and the frosted sconces lit up, bathing the solarium in their golden glow. She examined the bat. Near the handle, burned into the wood, were the letters T.H. and a child's crude drawing of a rocket ship spewing clouds of exhaust.

"That's my bat," he said.

His bat? Harley looked at him quickly and retreated a step. He was crazy. Either that or trying to pull a fast one. "Tucker Hale is dead," she said.

The expression slowly drained from his face. "Wow," he whispered. A muscle twitched in his jaw. "He told you that?"

"He?"

"R.H. My father. He told you I was dead?"

People close to Raleigh Hale called him R.H. "Your—Mr. Hale said . . . He didn't say it in so many words, but . . ." She took a breath, trying to remember. "I saw pictures of you— of *Tucker*."

There were two photographs on Raleigh Hale's desk. One, framed in silver, showed a young boy about ten at the wheel of a large sailboat, the name *Anjelica* painted across its stern. He wore a white polo shirt and chinos, and he grinned excitedly as he wrestled with the big wheel. In the other, framed in ebony and mother-of-pearl, a graceful white sailplane lay aground in the middle of a grassy field. Next to it, his hand resting on one slender wing, stood the same youth, older by five or six years. He had gotten tall, and wore a work shirt and patched jeans, his long hair caught in a disheveled ponytail.

"And I asked him about you," Harley continued. "About his son. What he did, where he lived . . . and he said, 'Tucker's gone.'"

"And you just assumed—"

"But then I asked someone else. A woman named Elizabeth Wycliff. She said something happened a long time ago and I shouldn't—"

"Liz Wycliff? She's an old family friend. She still teaching at Columbia, or has she retired?"

"She just retired last month," Harley said. "She was my statistics prof." So. He knew who Elizabeth Wycliff was. That didn't prove anything, but . . .

"You go to Columbia?"

Harley nodded. "M.B.A. program. It was Liz who got me this job. She introduced me to your—to Mr. Hale."

"What job? You work here?"

"I'm house-sitting while he's on vacation."

"Vacation . . ." He rubbed the back of his neck again. "Damn." After a moment, he asked, "So what did Liz tell you?"

"Not to talk to Raleigh Hale about you. About Tucker. Not to mention his name. Not to open up twenty-year-old wounds."

"Twenty-one," he said. "I left twenty-one years ago." He stared at the floor, eyes unfocused. "I was sixteen."

"Look . . . I want to believe you. But you broke in here in the middle of the night like some kind of—"

"I didn't think anyone was home. I knocked, but no one answered."

"I'm a sound sleeper. Until I hear glass breaking." He reached into his back pocket. Alarmed, Harley raised the bat. "What are you—"

He produced a little white card and held it out to her. "Identification."

She remembered the way he had grabbed the baseball bat. He could just as easily grab her arm. "Throw it." He flicked it toward her and it spun to the floor at her feet. She kept her eyes on him as she bent to retrieve it. It was a business card: "Hale Aviation." There was an address in Alaska, and a phone number.

He said, "My driver's license is in my wallet, which is in there." He nodded toward a duffel bag on the floor next to the piano bench. "Also a pilot's license and a library card. If you require a major credit card, I guess I'll have to take my business elsewhere, 'cause I've never had one of them."

She had no intention of passing by him to get to that duffel bag. He might be lame, but he was clearly still quick and powerful. "Take your hat off," she said.

After a moment's pause, he removed the cap, set it on the floor, and ran a hand through his disheveled brown hair. He looked up at her and smiled. "I guess I *have* been forgetting my manners."

She studied his rugged face, looking for similarities to the teenage Tucker, or perhaps to the elder Hale. He did have the same somewhat-patrician nose as Mr. Hale. Long and straight. Through the stubble she could make out a cleft chin and smile lines. Tiny grooves between his dark eyebrows. The scar still bore faint stitch-marks. It had healed some, but had not settled into looking like a real part of his face, as old scars do. This one might not even show that much, over time. She wondered what had caused it. And his limp.

He was watching her study his face, calmly and patiently, his own eyes on hers. Despite the depth of their color, they had an almost childlike transparency, undermining his laid-back machismo. Like when he thought his father had told her he was dead. He probably thought he had looked pretty stoical, but Harley had seen the hurt in his eyes.

Was Raleigh Hale this man's father? Mr. Hale had a commanding presence and aristocratic good looks. She could sense some of that in this man. They had a similar build, and some of their facial features were the same, but their coloring was different. The older man had fair skin and the kind of white hair you could tell had once been blond; the man claiming to be his son was darker. Also, Mr. Hale's eyes were ice-water blue, and Tucker's . . . Already she was thinking of him as Tucker, she realized.

Then there was the way he spoke. A hint of something. A distant, deeply ingrained upper-crust flatness that he shared with Raleigh Hale and Elizabeth Wycliff. You can take the boy out of Hale's Point, but you can't take Hale's Point out of the boy.

As she inspected him, she saw him inspecting her, his gaze resting on her mouth, her hair, her hands gripping the bat.

"You're trembling," he said.

"You would be, too, if a ghost woke you up in the middle of the night."

"Ah! So you admit I'm the long-dead Tucker Hale."

She thought for a moment. "Tucker Hale's room is just like he left it. Tell me what's in there."

"You mean all my old stuff's still there?" Harley nodded. "Not just Rocky, but everything?"

"'Rocky'?"

He nodded toward the baseball bat. "Rocky the rocket bat. Fastest bat in the East. Is Spiro still there? The dartboard with Agnew's picture on it?"

"It's still there."

"The models? The cars and boats and planes? Are they still—"

"Everything's just like you left it. It's real creepy." Just knowing about the dartboard and models wouldn't have convinced her. But he had called the baseball bat "Rocky." When he did that, although she couldn't say just why, she knew in her heart that he was Tucker Hale.

He began positioning himself to get to his feet. It looked like a pretty challenging endeavor. "So I take it I'm free to stand now, without risk of further bodily harm."

She cringed. "Listen, I—I'm sorry if I hurt you. Are you— Is it very bad?"

Straining, he managed to chuckle. "Nothing another operation couldn't fix. Course, that's what they said three operations ago."

"What? Did I—I mean, are you going to have to have another operation 'cause I . . ."

She dropped the bat and held out her hands to help him up. He let go of the cane and took them. He had large hands. They felt warm around hers, and a little rough. Rising to his feet, he said, "Of course not. Can't you take a joke?" He didn't let go of her hands.

"I've never been able to. No."

He grinned and shook his head, then turned her hands palm up and rubbed his callused thumbs over them as if trying to soothe away their trembling. His touch only made it worse, just when it had been getting better.

He looked up. "I'm sorry I scared you." She knew he was. She saw the remorse in his eyes. And something else. Something that made her extract her hands from his and cross her arms, one hand automatically pulling closed the collar of her robe.

"You can put your hat back on now."

He leaned down and swooped his hat off the floor, then tossed it across the room like a Frisbee. It landed neatly on top of the duffel. "Funny thing. At home, I can wear a hat indoors and not think twice about it. But here—" his gaze took in the huge, trailing Boston ferns, the piano, the Ming urns "—it simply isn't done."

He picked his cane up off the floor. Leaning on it, he again reached into his back pocket, this time for a pack of Camel cigarettes. He shook it until one slid out halfway, then brought the pack to his mouth, took the cigarette between his lips, and returned the pack to the pocket—all one-handedly, while the cane supported his weight. It looked like a well-practiced maneuver.

Harley said, "Sorry, but that's another thing that simply isn't done here. Smoking. Your father doesn't allow it in the house."

"But he smokes." He brought forth a pack of matches. Again with one hand, he opened it, bent a match until it was doubled over, and thumbed it against the striking area. When it flamed, he lit the cigarette.

"No, he doesn't. Not anymore, anyway. Look, I know you're his son, but he left me in charge of the house. And when it came to smoking, he made it crystal clear—"

"Well, that hasn't changed, at least. He always did like to make things crystal clear." He took a relaxed draw on the cigarette, clearly with no intention of putting it out. "I can't tell you how sick I got of his rules. By the time I turned sixteen, I'd heard enough about what is and isn't done to last me a lifetime."

"Okay, fine. You don't like to do as you're told. No problem, except this is my job I'm talking about, and I *am* expected to do as I'm told. He told me not to allow smoking in the house."

"Did he tell you how you're supposed to enforce that edict if someone absolutely refuses to obey?" He brought the cigarette to his lips again.

"He didn't have to." She reached out and snatched the cigarette out of his mouth, then marched with it around the piano to the French doors leading to the patio. She didn't look back at him, but she could hear him following her. "I told him I was going to keep cigarettes out of this house. And—"

"And you always do what you say you're going to do. Right?" He sounded amused.

"Right." It was cool for mid-June, even considering the hour, and the air was swollen with moisture. It would rain soon.

She crossed the brick patio to the pool, crouched down, and dipped the cigarette in it. It extinguished with a sizzle.

"When did he put the pool in?" He was standing silhouetted in the open door of the solarium.

"I don't know. I never saw this house till two weeks ago."

"It's a big sucker. Olympic-size?"

She nodded. "Seventy-five feet." She walked over to him and handed him the soggy butt. He accepted it with a bemused expression. "It's all right if you want to smoke out here. Just not in the house."

He leaned against the doorframe, scrutinizing her, his gaze lingering on her mouth. When he met her eyes, there was something that looked almost like shyness hiding in them. "You're not from Hale's Point. I'd hear it in your voice if you were."

"I'm from . . ." That was a rough one. "All over. But I live in Manhattan now, on the Upper West Side. Except I'm subletting my apartment for the summer."

"What's your name?" Seeing her hesitate, he added, "We're going to be living in the same house. I should know your name. I think Emily Post would agree."

"Are you planning on staying here? What, till your father comes back?"

"That's not an answer."

A kind of panic seized Harley. She had no way of contacting Raleigh Hale, but she doubted he would approve of his estranged son just showing up in the middle of the night and moving in. Perhaps it would help to remind Tucker what it was like to live under his father's many rules. "If you think you want to stay here, then you should know there are a few other things your father's kind of picky about."

Wearily he said, "Why doesn't that surprise me?"

"He said no eating or drinking anywhere except the kitchen, dining room, or breakfast room. No dogs or cats allowed in the . . ."

Shaking his head, Tucker turned and walked back into the solarium. With a sinking feeling, Harley noticed that his limp had worsened considerably since her attack with the baseball bat. He picked up his cap and put it on, then slung the duffel over his shoulder.

"I honestly can't imagine why I came here," he said when she joined him. He shrugged his big shoulders. "Sorry I disturbed your sleep."

Bewildered, she walked behind him as he made his halting, pained way out of the solarium and through the house to the front door. He wasn't staying? What was going on?

Shivering, she followed him onto the porch and halfway down the steps. It really was getting chilly, and she could feel minuscule drops of rain, like pinpricks, on her face.

"Where are you going?"

"Back to La Guardia. Then home, I guess."

"Home? But you just—"

"Just got here and I'm just going home. I know when to cut my losses. I haven't forgotten that much in twenty-one years."

Harley looked around. "Where's your car?"

"Don't have one. I hitched from the airport."

"You *hitchhiked?*"

"And I'll hitch back."

"La Guardia's seventy-five miles away. Let me drive you."

"You're not dressed."

"I can get—"

"I don't want to wait. I'm outta here."

"But it's the middle of the night, and it's starting to rain. What if no one picks you up? What about your leg?"

"I'll survive. I'm *damn* good at that."

She considered his battered body and wondered what, exactly, he had survived. She thought about his bad leg, and grimly speculated on how much damage she had done to the good one with that bat. Was he in a lot of pain, but just too much of a tough guy to show it? "Tucker—"

"I wonder if R.H. knows just how lucky he is to have you watching after things for him." The statement might have been taken as a compliment under different circumstances. As it was, his words, soft-spoken though they were, just made her feel that much colder. "You couldn't be more eager to carry out his dictates. Your enthusiasm blows me away, it really does. You must love rules almost as much as he does."

Despite the implied criticism, there was no real rancor or arrogance in his tone, as if he knew she wasn't responsible for her nature. Harley felt numb.

"Loving rules is something I can't relate to," he continued. "My guess is you need them like you need to breathe. Any hint of disorder, anything messy or unexpected in your life, just won't do." Harley wanted to tell him he was wrong, but she knew he would see that for the lie it was. "That's why you're incredibly relieved that I'm leaving. I'm very messy and very unexpected, and you're not entirely sure what the old man would think about my staying in the house. God knows, you don't want to displease R.H. Everyone who knows my father craves his approval. I've been there." He looked up at the enormous, whitewashed brick house, each window fitted with its own crisp, green-and-white-striped summer awning. "But I can't go back."

He descended another step and turned to face her, their heights almost level now. "He's lucky to have found you. You're orderly and right-thinking and good at giving commands. You're him! You're Raleigh Hale, only— How old are you?"

"Twenty-three," she replied woodenly.

"Only forty-five years younger, and..." He hesitated, then lifted a hand to her face, trailed his fingertips lightly along her jawline, and traced her lower lip with his thumb. "You have a much, *much* nicer mouth."

With a gentle pressure under her chin, he tilted her face toward his. He was suddenly very close to her. When he closed his eyes, so did she. Then she felt his warm mouth on hers, the rough sandpaper of his stubble grazing the soft skin around her lips.

In a moment, the kiss was over. It had been fleeting, scratchy-sweet. A goodbye kiss between two people who had only known each other for ten strange minutes in the middle of the night and would never meet again. Harley was breathless, and her legs felt weak.

"Goodbye." He shrugged. "Whatever your name is."

She took a steadying breath. "Harley."

He smiled and reached out to touch her cheek. "Harley. Thanks."

He turned and made his awkward way down the porch steps, then disappeared into the darkness without once looking back.

HARLEY RACED UP AND DOWN halls and in and out of rooms, slamming windows shut against the sudden, torrential rain.

It was like a living thing, a monster, rattling the sashes and soaking her with its spray as she struggled to keep it out of Raleigh Hale's home. She grabbed a pile of towels from the linen closet and went from window to window, drying off woodwork, varnished floors, and the furniture she had so painstakingly polished the day before. She saved her own room for last.

Tucker is out in this. According to the clock on her night table, it was 3:17 a.m. He had left two hours ago. During most of that time, the rain had been no worse than a light drizzle, yet even then, she had worried about him. And now...

Through the closed windows she could hear the crashing of storm waves on the beach below the house and the scraping of wind-whipped branches against the roof. And, of course, the driving rain. She thought about his limp, about the obvious pain he was in, pain made all the worse by her attack with the baseball bat. A wave of guilt overcame her. How far had he gotten? Had he gotten a ride? The only logical road for him to have taken didn't see a lot of traffic at night. And on a night like this... She pictured the road, bleak and deserted. No gas stations, no 7-Eleven stores, no shelter of any kind.

She took her rain-dampened robe off and began to get dressed without thinking about why. She looked in the mirror, at her mouth. The skin surrounding it still felt raw from the contact with his prickly stubble. She ran a finger over the sensitive skin, her mind unfocused. When she snapped out of it and saw herself in the mirror, she suddenly realized why she had gotten dressed.

TUCKER HALE LEANED BACK against a chain-link fence, hunched over, and pulled up the collar of his denim jacket. He smiled ruefully. He had just left a dry house that he had traveled thousands of miles to get to—and the most attractive woman he had seen in a long time—so that he could stand out here in this hellish rainstorm in the middle of the night and get soaked to the bone. It was as if the rain were beating on him with a thousand little fists. Harley and her baseball bat couldn't have done any worse.

Harley. Until he'd heard her call the old man "Mr. Hale," he thought she might actually be some new half-sister from a second wife. Or even the second wife herself. Rather young for a stepmother, he thought. And rather . . . Well, he would have had a hard time calling her "Mom," that's for sure.

She was very pretty in an offbeat kind of way. Not a classic beauty, but she did have classic lips. Wide, full, naturally red lips. Incredible. Great hair, too—bronze shot through with gold, thick and shiny, a sexy, sleep-tangled mane. She had a sweet, all-American voice. It was hard to pin down her origins, but he doubted she was a native New Yorker.

She had guts, too, facing him down with that bat. She'd been scared, but that hadn't stopped her. Too bad she was such a martinet. He sensed in her the kind of officious, regimented thinking that had driven him away from R.H. and Hale's Point two decades ago. She really did remind him of his father: everything by the book, nothing left to chance.

He wasn't only soaked to the bone, he was chilled to the bone, as well. God, his legs hurt—both of them now, not just the one. Every step made his right shin throb and sent a jolt of fire up to his left hip. Why hadn't he stayed in Hale's Point? Or at least let Harley drive him, or better yet, called a cab? It was that old bolting instinct. That urge to flee.

He shook his head. What was the matter with him, anyway? Kids hitchhiked—kids too broke to get around any other way. He had no business being out here. He was thirty-seven years old and far from broke. His net worth probably exceeded that of his father at this point, and none of it, he reminded himself proudly, was inherited.

It was beginning to look like he'd be spending all night out here. Cars were few and far between, and in this downpour, he'd be invisible.

Headlights. The hell with it. He wrapped his arms tightly around his chest, lowered his head, and closed his eyes.

Could you sleep standing up in a rainstorm? He tried to remember all the worst places he had slept. The hospital was pretty bad, with his leg in traction. But that wasn't half as bad as that roach-infested oven of a cell in D-Block, with a 320-pound bunkmate who'd murdered his brother-in-law by suffocating him with a pillow while he slept. And then there was the time his pals had talked him into climbing that mountain in the Canadian Rockies and they'd had to rig up their sleeping bags so they hung vertically off the cliff face. *That* had been a trip.

A horn honked somewhere.... Funny thing was, he'd slept like a baby that time. He could still remember the feeling, suspended high above the Rockies in the sharp, cold air, drifting, drifting....

Honk. "Tucker!"

He opened his eyes and raised his head. A car had pulled over. Its door stood open. Inside, it glowed with light.

She was there, beckoning to him.

2

TUCKER BEGAN STRIPPING the moment the front door closed behind him. Leaning on the hall table for support, he tossed his cap, cane, duffel, and denim jacket onto the tiled floor. Then, in one swift motion, he whipped his sodden sweater and T-shirt over his head and flung them on top of the jacket.

Harley's eyes grew wide at the sight of his bare chest—more in horror, he realized, than in appreciation. The ragged gashes carved into his flesh between his left shoulder and the bottom of his rib cage were an alarming sight—even to him. His back, on that side, was almost as bad.

He took the towel she handed him, quickly dried his face, hair, and upper body, and draped it around his neck. Then he undid the button fly on his jeans. "Hope you don't mind, but I've got to get out of these."

She turned around and headed toward the back of the house. "I'll make up your bed."

"I can handle that. Don't worry about it."

"I don't mind." Clearly Harley just wanted an excuse to get away from him while he undressed. That was okay. Still, he wondered whether it was the nudity or the scars that had unnerved her.

He kicked off his wet, heavy jeans and added them to the heap on the floor. In the car, Harley had told him that the sensible thing was for him to come back to the house, catch a few hours' sleep, and book a flight when it was convenient. Exhausted, drenched, and in pain, he had thanked her for her trouble and agreed to do the sensible thing.

He wrapped the towel around his hips, bent to retrieve his cane, and followed Harley to the maid's room, next to the kitchen. The maid wouldn't be back until September, so he had decided to sleep there, instead of in his old room, in order to avoid the stairs. He didn't think his leg could take any more abuse than it had already suffered tonight.

She was bending over the narrow bed, making crisp hospital corners in the white cotton sheets.

He said, "I want to be able to bounce a dime off that sheet, Private."

Her face stained pink when she saw that all he had on was the towel. She *was* uptight! Then her gaze dropped to his disfigured left leg, and she quickly returned her attention to the bed.

"I'm going to take a hot shower before I turn in," he said. He flipped the light switch in the little bathroom off the maid's room, then turned on the water in the claw-footed tub, adjusting the knob to get it scalding.

"I'm done here," she said, turning to face him, her arms folded across her chest. Her hair was pulled back in a ponytail, and she wore a white sweater and new jeans with an ironed-in crease; she looked like a schoolgirl. Except for her face. The hot color in her cheeks brought out the green in her hazel eyes. Even her lips seemed to blush a darker red.

He was staring at her. He should say something. "Thanks for everything, Harley."

"No problem. Good night."

"Good night."

HE COULDN'T MOVE. He lay on his back in the white sand and stared at the hot-pink sky, green palms and blue waves slapping the shore.

A shadow fell over him. It was her. He saw her lips, those amazing lips. She knelt down and leaned over him, and he thought she was going to kiss him, but instead, she said, "Does it hurt?"

He looked down. It was Alaskan snow he lay on now, and it burned, it was so cold. The reason he couldn't move was the jagged pieces of metal that pierced him all along his left side, pinning him down like an insect in a case.

"Does it hurt?" she repeated. He was consumed with hurt. Pain was all there was and all there ever would be.

"No," he said.

She stood. "Liar."

She was gone. He tried to sit up, to reach for her, and the metal tore at his flesh.

"No!" he gasped. He sat up in bed, sweating and shaking. "No," he whispered.

He looked around. The maid's room. Hale's Point. Oh, yeah. He rubbed the back of his neck. "Wow." He couldn't even sleep without pain. Even in his dreams it pursued him.

There was a digital clock on the night table. It was 8:05 a.m. Outside, the waves still lapped and retreated, but they didn't sound right; too loud and too regular, just like they were in the dream.

His bed stood against the back wall, a window within reach. He pulled the curtain back and pried apart the slats of the blinds, squinting against the bright sunlight. He could see all of the brick patio and most of the pool. The patio was scattered with teak furniture, including a large round table under an enormous square canvas umbrella. The pool took up a good part of what had been, in his boyhood, a flat expanse of broadloom lawn. The lawn ended fifty yards from the house in a low stone wall bordered with roses, lavender and creeping thyme.

Beyond it, the rocky shore and Long Island Sound. From a gap in the stone wall, a hodgepodge of boulders set into the sandy precipice served as a kind of stairway to the beach. It was the Hales' beach, which included a crescent-shaped jetty that sliced into the Sound—the point for which Hale's Point was named. Some twenty acres of woodland, also Hale property, abutted the beach—prime North Shore real estate, entirely undeveloped except for the half acre or so immediately surrounding the house and stable, the latter of which R.H. had long ago converted into an eight-car garage for his collection of vintage sports cars. The Hales had fended off lucrative offers for the land for two centuries.

He had loved the beach as a boy, but with his leg all but useless, he couldn't even think about climbing down there.

The sound he had taken for waves came from the pool, where Harley glided smoothly and swiftly through the pale blue water. Her arms curved in perfect arcs: her movements were graceful, but eerily mechanical. Every third stroke, like clockwork, she took a breath. Her pace never varied or slowed as she swam lap after lap.

He lay back down and threw an arm over his eyes. How long had it been since he had swum? Ten years? Fifteen?

He rolled over and tried to get to back to sleep, but the splashing kept him awake. Her pace was maniacally, irritatingly perfect.

Finally, the splashing stopped. Tucker sat up and parted the blinds again. Still in the pool, she reached onto the smooth concrete deck for something—a black stopwatch—clicked it, and checked her time. Then, pushing against the deck, she propelled herself up and stepped nimbly out of the pool.

She was compact and sleek, a healthy animal. For a woman her size, she had long legs, and they looked like they meant business. She wore a black swimsuit, one of those unlined Lycra racing suits, as revealing as skin. He could see the contours of her breasts as clearly as if she were nude; they were small, high, and firm, their nipples hard in the cool morning air.

He turned away from the window, feeling like a Peeping Tom. Then he took another shower to get the kinks out, combed his wet hair back to get it off his face, and put on a pair of baggy shorts and a T-shirt. He forgot what their original colors had been. Most of his clothes were army surplus—khaki, olive drab, and navy—so they had probably started out militarily neutral before fading, like everything else he owned, into a kind of used-up noncolor.

He grabbed his cane and followed the aroma of freshly brewed coffee to the kitchen. She stood at the stove, cocooned in her white terry-cloth robe, holding a saucepan full of gray paste, which she spooned into a bowl.

The paste had pieces of something in it. When she saw him, she tilted the pot so he could get a better look. "Oatmeal with raisins, apples, and sunflower seeds. I made enough for you."

"Thanks, but I'm trying to cut down." She looked a little confused, then rolled her eyes. "You don't have any glazed doughnuts, do you?" he asked.

"That's what you eat for breakfast?"

He nodded, taking a seat at the big pine table and leaning his cane against it. "I've been known to have them for lunch and dinner, too."

She joined him at the table. "You are what you eat."

"I beg to differ. I saw you get out of the pool just now, and I know for a fact you're not gray and lumpy." She glanced at him and then spooned some oatmeal into her gorgeous mouth. "Do you swim every morning?"

"A hundred laps. But usually I swim at six. I set the alarm two hours later today 'cause I was up half the night." Her skin shone, her eyes glittered. She looked invigorated and happy. He figured she was probably just jazzed on endorphins, but she looked sensational. She looked like she'd just had great sex. The thought made him want to get up and untie the double-knotted sash on that terry-cloth robe.

Instead, he said, "A hundred laps? You count them?" She nodded. "Doesn't that kind of take the pleasure out of it?"

"My morning swim is for exercise. And my afternoon run. My evening swim is for pleasure."

She was too much. "What happens if you suddenly find yourself enjoying your morning swim? Do you have to stop and take a break and think about something really annoying so you can get back in there and finish off your hundred laps in the right frame of mind?"

She chewed slowly, watching him from across the table. "Are you mad because of the baseball bat?"

"What?"

"First the oatmeal, now my swimming. Are you mad because I—"

"You really think I'm mad at you? You weren't kidding when you said you couldn't take a joke. Honey, you've got some serious chilling-out to do."

They sat in silence for a minute, and then she said, "I've been wondering about something. It's none of my business, I know, and you don't have to tell me—"

"Shoot."

"What are you doing here? I mean, after twenty years—"

"Twenty-one," he corrected.

"Twenty-one. I think I've got a pretty good idea why you left. My guess is it had something to do with rules and expectations, and what is and isn't done. A father who thought he knew everything and a son who *knew* he knew everything."

Her insight amused him. "It's a little more complicated, but that's it in a nutshell."

She looked at him over the top of her coffee cup. "You've had no contact at all with your father for twenty-one years?" He shook his head. "So what's this all about? Why are you back?"

He rubbed his long fingers over the scarred pine, composing an answer. After a few seconds of watching him, she rose and went to the stove to refill her bowl. The oatmeal had congealed into a solid mass, and she had to use her fingers to push wads of it off the wooden spoon. "Forget it, Tucker. I didn't mean to pry. I ask too many questions, I always have."

"No, it's okay. Mostly I'm just here for R and R. I've got some healing up to do, and I thought this might be the place to do it." He shrugged. "Maybe it is, maybe it isn't." There was more to it than that, of course. He could have rested up in his own home instead of the one he had fled twenty-one years ago. If she was thinking these same thoughts, she didn't voice them.

Her gaze took in the scar on his face and dropped toward his injured leg, but the table hid it from her view. "What happened to you?" she asked, taking her seat.

Tucker wanted a cigarette. Badly. He reached into the pocket of his T-shirt before remembering: R.H. did not permit smoking in the house, and his personally appointed agent prided herself on making sure those orders were followed.

Rising, he brought his cup over to the counter to refill it, not needing the cane, since it was just a couple of yards. Her stopwatch was lying next to the coffeemaker, and he picked it up, shaking his head. You needed one to time a swim meet, but not for your morning exercise. Unless, of course, you were the kind of person—like R.H. and, apparently, Harley—who didn't believe something was real unless you could count it.

"I got hurt," he finally said.

"Fair enough. I'm out of line."

"No, you're not." He spoke softly, turning the stopwatch over in his hands, his back to her. "You're just being polite. You're trying to make conversation. You're asking me about myself. But the truth is, you don't really know me, and you don't really care."

He set the watch down and turned to face her and found her jaw set and her eyes glittering. "It's okay." He tried to make his tone gentle and nonthreatening, but realized even as he spoke the words, how condescending he sounded. "I have no problem with that. But I'd rather you didn't go through the motions of pretending you did."

She gripped the table with both hands. "Don't tell me what I feel. You don't know me any better than I know you, and you *don't* know what I care about."

He held up both palms. "Look, honey, I just—"

"And *don't* call me honey. I don't like it."

"All right . . ." A second ticked by as they stared at each other. "Sweetheart."

She stood and stalked out of the room. "It's a *joke*," he said to her back. Groaning, he slumped against the counter and rubbed hard at the back of his aching neck. "You know. *Jokes?* Those things you laugh at? Well . . ." he mumbled, "not you, but . . . normal people?"

HARLEY LOOKED DOWN on Tucker from the window of his old room, the cleaning basket in one hand and the pull cord of the wooden blinds in the other. He lay out there on the patio, faceup on a lounge chair, asleep in the early-afternoon sun. Or probably asleep. She couldn't see his eyes under the aviator sunglasses he wore. He still hadn't shaved. He hadn't done anything all morning except read the paper, smoke some cigarettes, eat the peanut-butter sandwich she'd made him, and sleep. Well, that was his right. He said he'd come here for R and R—rest and relaxation—and considering his torn-up body, he could probably use it.

He obviously wasn't after a suntan. He hadn't removed his T-shirt, and although he was wearing shorts, he had the open newspaper spread over his legs like a blanket. One hand rested on his flat stomach, the other on the ground. For a guy who didn't seem to do much, he looked to be in great shape. Even through the T-shirt, she could make out the well-defined muscles of his chest and shoulders.

Last night, when she had seen him in that towel, her heart had raced, and she had actually blushed! Those incredibly wide shoulders, those narrow hips. His arms and legs went on forever, powerful and sinewy. It was the kind of body you'd see at the Olympics, crouching at the edge of a pool, waiting for the crack of a starter's pistol.

His beauty made his scars that much more shocking. Whatever had happened to him looked like something you wouldn't expect to live through. He had said he was damn good at surviving, and she suspected he knew what he was talking about.

In order to make room for the cleaning basket on his desk, she had to push aside a stack of magazines two decades old, topped with an unusual paperweight: a big cat, leaping, cast in chrome—the hood ornament from a Jaguar. What an appropriate bauble, she thought, for a boy with everything, a child of immense wealth, brought up in one of the most exclusive communities in the world—a community named after his own family.

He sprang from privilege, she from deprivation. Looking at them now, anyone would think it had been the other way around. In fact, although she hated to admit it, in some ways he reminded her of her parents. Like them, he was a square peg in a round hole, although not so extreme. He did, after all, own his own business. Her aimless, self-destructive parents could never have managed that.

Her efforts to lead an orderly, right-thinking life amused him. A bohemian blue blood like Tucker Hale might laugh at her straight-and-narrow path, but only by keeping to it

could she ensure that she would be spared in adulthood the
poverty and tragedy that she could not escape as a child.

She withdrew a feather duster from the cleaning basket and
flicked it over the hood ornament and the magazine on top—
a *Rolling Stone*. Curious, she thumbed through the rest: one
or two each of *Car and Driver, Sail, Sailing World,* and
Sports Illustrated, and about a dozen *Playboys*.

A framed black-and-white studio portrait sat on the desk,
and she touched the duster to it: a beautiful young woman
with black hair and large dark eyes holding a baby in her
arms. The infant Tucker and his mother, she guessed. Tucker
had her eyes. In the photograph, she wore her hair pulled
back. Ornate earrings with dark stones in them dangled from
her ears. An equally striking ring graced her left land—a large
cabochon stone with what looked like two little hands, one
on either side, holding it in place. Nestled next to it she wore
a simple gold band, presumably her wedding ring.

Harley scanned the room. Until now, she had avoided
coming in here. She had thought it a kind of shrine to a dead
son, and it had given her the creeps. Now that she knew it
was, instead, a shrine to a wayward son, it intrigued her.

In addition to the Spiro Agnew dartboard, the walls were
festooned with sports pennants and posters. There were po-
litical posters, too. One showed a drawing of a hand holding
flowers, and the words War Is Not Healthy for Children and
Other Living Things. And above the bed—an antique four-
poster with an incongruous-looking batik bedspread—hung
a huge black-and-white photograph of Sophia Loren standing in water, her clothes soaked and clinging. *Hmm*.

She turned to the shelves. The trophies that served as
bookends were all topped with sleek male figures in swim
trunks, crouched and ready to spring. Precisely the pose in
which she had, moments ago, envisioned Tucker's built-for-
speed body. So he *had* been a swimmer. As she dusted the

trophies, she glanced at their inscriptions: 1500-Meter Freestyle, First Place . . . 200-Meter Butterfly, First Place. . . .

There were innumerable model boats, planes, and cars. Three long shelves bulged with record albums. And books—yards and yards of them—ranged in shelves all the way up to the ceiling. She glanced at some of the titles, wondering what the teenage Tucker liked to read. *The Electric Kool-Aid Acid Test, Huckleberry Finn, The Kama Sutra. Hmm.* She picked up the last one, a small hardcover; its spine made a cracking sound when she opened it.

"Find anything interesting?" His voice made her jump. He stood in the doorway, leaning on his cane.

"No," she lied, then made a show of dusting and replacing the book.

He came up behind her and slid it out of its place, smiling when he saw the title. "I haven't read *this* for a while." He held it out to her. "You'll like it. It's all about control." She had changed into the blue spandex bike shorts and cropped white tank top that she would run in later, and as he returned the book, she saw his quick, appreciative glance.

She backed away. "What are you doing up here? I thought you couldn't walk up the stairs."

"No, I can make it up a flight of stairs. It just . . ." He shrugged.

"Hurts?"

"It's a bit of a challenge. I try not to do it too often. I came up 'cause I saw you at the window."

Oh, no. She turned away and ran the duster mechanically over the models. *He wasn't asleep. He saw me staring at him.*

"Wow," he whispered, his gaze taking in the room and its contents. He seemed particularly interested in the poster above the bed. "Sophia! You're still here! *¡Mamma mia!* I'm a happy boy. Maybe I'll sleep up here, after all."

Harley couldn't help smiling. "She does have beautiful eyes."

"Everyone's got beautiful eyes. But Sophia has those lips! Look at them!" He smiled at her. "I've always been a sucker for great lips." He looked at her mouth, and Harley didn't know where to look, so she turned away, shook some furniture polish onto a rag, and went to work on the oak bookcases.

After a minute of silence, she became curious and turned to find him standing at his old desk, staring at the photograph of himself as an infant in his mother's arms, his expression solemn. When he realized Harley was watching him, he looked away and continued examining the room.

"My guitars! Both of them! This is my favorite—the twelve-string." She heard the bedsprings creak as he sat. While she polished, her back to him, he adjusted the instrument, then began to play. She didn't recognize the tune, but it was nice, with a kind of country-blues flavor. From that he drifted into a bit of something very baroque and complicated and then some lively Spanish guiter.

When he paused, she turned to face him, saying, "You're good. That was—" The compliment stuck in her throat when she caught sight of the shin of his right leg, which had become badly bruised and swollen overnight. "Oh my God. Did I do that?"

He glanced down. "Isn't that what you were trying to do?" On his left leg, the flesh from midthigh down was gouged with ugly, barely healed wounds and surgical incisions, and the muscles were atrophied. The right was merely insult to injury, but it had been her insult, her responsibility, and she felt it keenly.

"I'm really sorry," she said.

He resumed his strumming. "Forget it. You were defending yourself."

She tossed her polishing rag into the cleaning basket. "That needs ice."

"I think it's a little late for that," he said as she strode out the door.

In the kitchen, she filled a plastic bag with ice cubes, wrapped it in a clean dish-towel, and brought it back up to Tucker. He chuckled when she knelt before him and held it gingerly on the shin.

"Does it hurt?" she asked.

"No."

"Liar." The oddest expression crossed his face when she said that. "What did I say?" she asked.

He shook his head as if to clear it. "Nothing." He set the guitar down on the bed next to him. "It's kind of nice, having someone tend to your wounds like this. I'm not used to it."

"It's no secret that you've spent time in a hospital recently. You must have had lots of people tending to your wounds there."

He shrugged. "Let's just say I'm not used to people doing it unless they're getting paid for it. No one's ever fixed me for free."

She lifted the ice to check the shin; it looked the same. She replaced it anyway. "That can't be true. What about your mother?"

A pause. "I don't know. I guess so. She died when I was five."

"Five? I'm sorry." She glanced toward the photo on the desk, and Tucker followed her gaze. He grabbed his cane and stood, the ice pack falling to the floor, then walked over to the desk and picked up the photo. "She was beautiful," Harley said, and he nodded. "I was noticing her jewelry. Very unusual. Exquisite earrings."

"Italian, late Renaissance."

"Late Renaissance. So they're what, like four hundred years old? Your mother wore four-hundred-year-old jewelry?"

"She had pieces much older than that," he said. "She collected antique gold jewelry. Byzantine, Egyptian, pre-Columbian... She had an Etruscan bracelet from the seventh century B.C."

Harley fingered her little silver hoops and wondered what four-hundred-year-old earrings felt like in your ears. "And the ring?"

"That was my mother's most prized possession. Kind of an engagement ring."

"Kind of?"

"My parents never had any real engagement. Not much of a courtship, either. They met and got married. It was love at first sight. After the wedding, R.H. told her he wanted her to have a proper Tiffany diamond to go with the wedding band, but she told him about this emerald ring she knew of that was locked away in a private collection. Roman, first century A.D. She loved it more than anything she'd ever seen. So he went to see the collector in London and bought it for her."

"Your father never remarried?" Tucker hesitated, and she quickly added, rising to her feet, "If you want me to shut up, just—"

He shook his head. "No, that's all right. Liz gave it her best shot, in her own understated way, but he never remarried."

"Liz Wycliff?"

He set the photo back down. "Yeah, they've been friends since childhood. Everyone always assumed they'd end up getting married, but then one Christmas he came back from the Greek Islands with a bride." He nodded toward the picture of his mother. "Anjelica Koras. The only impulsive thing he's ever done."

Harley picked up the polishing rag and went back to the bookcases. "Your mother was Greek?" That explained the warm brown eyes, so unlike his father's.

He nodded, opened one of the desk drawers, and absently rummaged through it. "They met at a party on her father's yacht and they got married in Athens a month later. Much to her father's dismay, I'm told."

"Much to Liz's, too, I imagine."

"I understand she took it well." He leaned his cane against the desk and sat down, then untied the twine from around a pack of letters and flipped through them. "But that's the Hale's Point way, after all. Go about your business. Mustn't let them see you care."

"Maybe she didn't," Harley offered.

"But she did." He retied the letters. "She always loved him. Everyone knew it, but it was rarely mentioned. She was very tasteful about it, kept her distance from him until a couple of years after my mother's death. Even then, they never became more than friends, as far as I knew. His choice, not hers."

"Do you know whether she ever told him how she felt? Tried to force the issue?"

He laughed. "Don't you know, it's terribly bad form to declare yourself. Much better to spend decades hanging around waiting for the object of your misguided affection to open his eyes and notice you. She immersed herself in her work, got an apartment on Central Park West, got tenure at Columbia. But she never married." He looked at her. "Or has she? I haven't seen her since I moved away, and she might have kept her maiden name."

Harley put the polishing rag back in the basket and wiped her hands on a clean dustcloth. "No, it's *Miss* Wycliff. She never married." She shook her head. "She turned sixty-five last April. I baked a cake and brought it into class. She told me she'd blow out the candles, but she wouldn't make a wish because, statistically speaking, they were a waste of time."

He looked sad, and that intensified his resemblance to his mother. She saw that his eyes, although brown, weren't dark and opaque, like some brown eyes. They looked like the chunks of amber she kept in her jewelry box—transparent and luminous, with streaks of gold and rust.

"Thoreau said the mass of men lead lives of quiet desperation," he said. "Same goes for women." He fanned out a stack of what looked like report cards, then tossed them in the trash.

She rose and retrieved them. "Your father might not like you throwing these out."

"You got *that* right. He loved report cards. They take a person and reduce him to a list of grades. What could be neater?" While Tucker sorted through the papers in the desk, Harley moved behind him to covertly inspect the cards. They were from the Wilmot Preparatory Academy for Boys; he had earned straight A's until the first semester of his junior year, when his grades took a nosedive. There didn't appear to be any report cards after that.

She returned them to the drawer and sat on the bed. "So you were sixteen when you ran away from home?"

"Yeah, but I don't think of it as running away, exactly. I think of it as extricating myself from an impossible situation."

"That's got a lot more syllables, but you're saying the same thing."

He gave her a look, weary but amused. "Then how about *bolting*? I bolted. I felt the bars close in and I got the hell out of here."

"Like you did last night." She didn't smile, and neither did he.

"Like I did last night," he agreed. "The bolting instinct takes over when I start to feel cornered or penned in. What's wrong with that? What virtue could there possibly be in putting up with a lousy situation that I could just as easily walk away from? I know it's the Hale's Point way to grin and bear it, but it's not my way, and it never will be." He closed the drawer and rubbed the back of his neck.

"What impossible situation were you facing at sixteen that was so bad you felt you had to—"

"Military school. He'd decided to send me to military school." He opened another drawer and began pawing through old photographs.

"Seriously?"

"Very seriously. Incredibly seriously. He showed me the brochure. This granite fort up on the Hudson where you wear a uniform and get your head shaved and do predawn maneuvers before class every day. Can't you just picture me there?" He laughed and shook his head.

"Why?"

"You saw the report cards."

"I—"

"I caught you looking. The last one, the one where I started cutting classes? I was spending too much time with the guitar and not enough with the books, he said. He couldn't stand my getting bad grades, because my grades defined me in his eyes. Bad grades, bad kid."

Harley kicked off her sandals and reclined on the bed, leaning on one elbow. "I don't know, it's just . . . You'll have to forgive me if the horror of your situation kind of escapes me. To those of us who weren't brought up with the advantages you had, your complaints come off as—"

"Whining. Poor little rich boy." He stood and took a sailboat model from the shelf. The word *Anjelica* had been painted in tiny, painstaking letters across the stern. "Yeah, I know. The best schools, a beach for my backyard, lots of toys, and lessons in everything. R.H. believed in a sound mind in a sound body. I can play any kind of sport there is, or fake it with the best of them. I can talk to anyone from just about any Western European country about any damn thing they want to talk about, in their own language. And I can climb into just about any kind of machine that moves and make it get from point *A* to point *B*. I learned to sail before I could read and I had my own speedboat before I could shave. A glider license at fourteen, a pilot's at sixteen. I had stuff galore, my life was filled with stuff."

"My heart goes out to you. How could you have stood it for sixteen whole years?"

He grinned despite himself, put the sailboat back, and picked up an airplane—a World War II bomber. "Thing is, after a while I started to wonder if there was more to life than stuff. I started to get passionate about things that R.H. couldn't understand. It was okay if I dug sailing and flying, 'cause he did, too. But music didn't mean that much to him, so he decided it shouldn't mean that much to me. Certainly not so much that it would interfere with my grades."

"I don't understand how music could have interfered with your grades."

"We were playing at a couple of the local clubs—"

"We?"

"I had this . . . this friend." He turned the airplane over in his hands and inspected it with a distant expression. "This guy Chet. We met while we were both taking flying lessons. Turned out he played guitar, too. Anyway, this was back when there were still a lot of coffeehouses around, and it was great for untried talent. If you hung around long enough, you got to go onstage. After a while they started actually booking us. R.H. thought it was unseemly. It was okay to take piano lessons, he said. Every well-rounded man should be able to appreciate music. But to actually spend the time and energy to get good at it, and then get up in front of an audience . . . There was something terribly low-class about that. It was not the Hale's Point way."

"Hence the military-school threat . . ." Harley prompted.

"Hence the bolting. Chet, too. We put our thumbs out on the expressway one night and never looked back."

"Where did you go?"

"New York. The Village. We played in clubs for a while. Almost got a record deal, but it didn't work out, and we ended up quitting that scene and getting real jobs. Then we went to Miami, but that . . . didn't really work out, either. Things kind of fell apart there. Then I ended up in Alaska."

"Chet stayed in Miami? Did you have a falling-out? What happened?"

He put the airplane back, his expression grim. "Wouldn't interest you." Somehow Harley suspected that it would. Summoning a more lighthearted demeanor, he turned and bowed formally in Harley's direction, supporting himself with the cane. "My adolescence in a nutshell. Your turn now."

Right. "In a nutshell? I had a lot less stuff and a lot less angst."

"You got through your adolescence without angst?"

"Oh, there was angst, just not your fancy, wanting-to-be-fulfilled kind. It was more your garden-variety, struggling-to-survive kind." She bowed her head, indicating she was done.

"That's it? That's not a very vivid description."

"How about this—unrelenting squalor. Is that vivid enough?"

"Come on—I'm serious."

"Unfortunately, so am I." That was as much as she would tell him. The rest was none of his business. Or was she just ashamed? It didn't matter, since she had no desire to relive it just to satisfy his curiosity. He walked over to the bed and looked down at her, his expression thoughtful. "Come down to the kitchen and have a Coke with me."

"Can't. I've got to get ready for my afternoon run. Besides, we don't have any sodas. Just juices and mineral water."

He grunted and sat on the bed near her feet, bedsprings squealing. She tried to curl her legs up to make room for him, but he rested a strong hand on one of her calves to still her. "That's all right, I've got room." The hand traced a warm path down to her ankle and then wrapped around first one small foot and then the other. "Your feet are cold. They shouldn't be cold on such a hot day."

The warmth from his hand felt wonderful. Nevertheless, she sat up, and he took the hint, removing the hand. She said, "You know, I can't help but wonder.... It strikes me that the real world must have come as something of a shock to a poor little rich boy from Hale's Point."

He grinned. "Rebel without a charge card. Once I realized there wouldn't be any big music career, and moved to Miami, I decided to start saving up for an airplane so I could go into the air cargo business. Took a few years to get the bread together. I drove a forklift, pumped gas, patched roofs, cut sugarcane. I caught fish, I cleaned fish, I canned fish—I still can't stand the sight of it."

"What did you do in your spare time?"

"I worked some more. Usually I was holding down two full-time jobs, sometimes one full-time and two part-time. Till I'd gotten together four thousand dollars for a used Piper Comanche. Man, I was proud of that plane."

"And now you've got your own aviation business in Alaska," she said.

"I'm really just a bush pilot. Only now I've got a bunch of other pilots working for me, 'cause there got to be too much business to handle alone."

"I'm afraid I'm a little fuzzy on the definition of 'bush pilot.' Do you fly people or cargo?"

"Both. Mostly cargo. Alaska's full of remote, inaccessible areas, and they rely on us to fly in all their food, medical supplies, lumber, everything. And then we handle all kinds of passengers—surveyors, explorers, guys who want to parachute onto the North Pole in their skis . . . all kinds."

"Do you like it?"

He squinted into the sunlight from the window, his eyes igniting from within. "No. Not anymore. I mean, I like that it's my own business, and it's a simple one. Doesn't take some great high master of business administration to figure out how to make money from it. No offense."

"None taken."

"Everyone tells me I should be reveling in my success, but I don't know—it's worn thin on me. It's taken the pleasure out of flying, for one thing. I used to think it'd be great, being able to fly for a living. Buying that first beat-up old plane was the biggest rush in the world. Now I buy a new one just about every year and don't think twice about it. I've got six of them. Seven, including my Cessna Skywagon." He grinned self-consciously, as if he'd forgotten something. "Scratch the Skywagon. It's just six."

"What happened to the Skywagon?"

He reached over her for the guitar, took it and his cane, and started toward the door. "Some of it's in my leg."

Harley stared openly, first at his leg, and then, to see if he might be kidding, at his face. She could tell he wasn't kidding.

"There might be some left in my chest, I've lost track. The rest is scattered over the side of a mountain halfway between Anchorage and Fairbanks." Standing at the door, he said, "Sure you won't join me downstairs?" She shook her head. He turned to leave. "Don't forget your stopwatch."

3

TUCKER SAT ON THE LOW stone wall overlooking the beach, having a cigarette and watching Harley returning from her run. The late-afternoon sun, low in the sky, cast the boulders on the rocky beach into sharp relief. The sea air mingled with the lavender and thyme growing along the stone wall to create a familiar perfume, the scent of his mother, who had planted this border. It was Harley's scent, too, he realized, breathing it in. At least, the lavender part. Her shampoo, or maybe her soap.

As she approached, he noted that she ran barefoot and kept to the wet, pebbly sand at the water's edge. He watched the muscles in her legs flex and contract; grace came from strength, and she was obviously well-conditioned. Fanatically so, it seemed.

She was driven and she was humorless, but there was something about her. As she crossed the property next door—the Tilton place, or used to be—she waved to someone hidden from his view by a stand of gnarled pines. She passed by Tucker without looking up and seeing him, and then, instead of stopping, she disappointed him by continuing east. Her ponytail bobbed with each step, and from time to time she squirted water into her mouth from a white plastic bottle that she carried. As she ran out onto the jetty, her stride never altering, he lit a new cigarette off the old, stubbed the butt out on the stone wall, and slipped it into the pocket of his T-shirt.

From behind the stand of pines, a man emerged, obviously the person Harley had waved to. Tucker stood to see him better, squinting through his sunglasses. He was young, about twenty, tanned, with sun-streaked hair. His feet were bare and he wore a white polo shirt and khaki shorts, in the deep pockets of which tennis balls bulged. The Tiltons used to have two clay courts in the backyard; looked like they still did. The young man stood next to a boulder at the water's edge, also watching Harley.

She ran to the tip of the jetty, turned, and took the return trip in an impressive, all-out sprint. When she got to its base, where it joined the beach proper, she slowed her pace to a brisk walk, checked her stopwatch, and pressed the side of her throat to take her carotid pulse. The young man pulled three tennis balls from his pockets and began to juggle them. Harley smiled, then noticed Tucker for the first time, standing at the top of the makeshift boulder stairway. She waved to him and he nodded. The young man looked up at him and frowned, dropping a ball. Tucker knew he didn't look reputable enough—with his black aviators, cigarette, and three-day growth of beard—to be mowing Raleigh Hale's lawn.

Harley propped first one foot and then the other on the boulder, leaning over to stretch her hamstrings. While she warmed down, she and the boy talked, both of them glancing from time to time in Tucker's direction. Her stretching took longer than Tucker thought strictly necessary, and when she climbed up to the yard and rejoined him, he merely nodded again in response to her smile.

"Who's the guy?" he asked.

"Déjà vu," Harley said. "Those were Jamie's first words just now." When she repeated the phrase, it was with a stiff-jawed Hale's Point accent: "'Who's the guy?'"

Tucker couldn't help smiling. "So you *do* have a sense of humor."

"Of course I do!" She sat in the grass, extended her legs straight out in front of her, grabbed her sandy feet with both hands, and pulled. "I just can't take a joke. There's a difference."

He chuckled and shook out another cigarette. She closed her eyes, and he took the opportunity to appraise her shamelessly. Her skin had a ruddy glow and was glazed with a sheen of perspiration. The wisps of hair that had sprung loose from her ponytail clung in damp curls around her face.

When she opened her eyes, he said, "This Jamie, does he live next door?"

She nodded, shifting position so that the soles of her feet were together, and leaned over to touch her forehead to her ankles. It looked effortless; she was limber. "His name is Jamie Tilton."

Tucker thought back. "Oh, man, I know who that kid is! Mrs. Tilton was pregnant with him when I left here." He glanced down at the beach, where Jamie stood knee-high in the surf, juggling. "Wow."

"He just graduated in the top of his class at Princeton."

"What law school is he going to?"

"Harvard." She looked up. "How did you know he was going to go to law school?"

"They all do."

"'They'?"

"Rich boys who don't have to work, but feel the need to make themselves—" now he adopted his own exaggerated imitation of the Hale's Point accent "—useful to society."

"Are you saying there's something wrong with that?"

He sighed. "No. There's nothing wrong with that."

"Because there's nothing wrong with that."

"That's what I just said."

She crossed her legs, put both hands on her waist, and twisted back and forth. "He's a very nice person, he's been very friendly to me—"

"I'll bet he has." Harley rolled her eyes. "You think he wouldn't jump at the chance to get into your spandex?"

Still twisting, she said, "Not every man on the face of the earth thinks about sex constantly." Tucker just laughed. "Anyway, he's not interested in me." With every twist, her breasts strained against the white cotton of her tank top.

"Don't be so sure."

"I *am* sure. He's in love with the au pair. His stepmother told me. He just talks to me to make her jealous."

"Stepmother? What happened to Mrs. Tilton? The first Mrs. Tilton. Well, technically, the second Mrs. Tilton. There'd already been a first Mrs. Tilton."

"Well, now there's a third Mrs. Tilton. No, she must be the fourth Mrs. Tilton, 'cause there was an in-between Mrs. Tilton." She stood, shaking out her arms and legs. "In answer to your question, Jamie's father divorced the first, second, and third Mrs. Tiltons, each time in favor of a younger Mrs. Tilton. Jamie says it was his hobby, collecting wives."

"'Was'? Has he finally found one he's happy with?"

"He died a year ago of a heart attack."

"Younger and younger wives will do that to you." Tucker had liked the second Mrs. Tilton, but had thought her husband petty and self-important, and was not sorry he was dead. Back down on the Tiltons' piece of beach, two young women and a fat toddler had joined Jamie. "Which one's the Widow Tilton?"

Harley squinted. "The dark-haired one. Mimi. She's really nice, I like her." She was very slender, with close-cropped hair and delicate features. She stood ankle-deep in the water, holding up the skirt of her flowered sundress. The other woman—a copper-penny redhead in a yellow bikini—

squatted next to the child and quickly undressed her down to her pink disposable diaper. When she stood, Tucker saw that she was no more than eighteen or nineteen, but very tall, with a nonstop centerfold body. She had pale, freckled skin, and her hair was a blazing mop of corkscrew curls. Jamie couldn't seem to take his eyes off her.

"Is that the au pair?" Tucker asked, and Harley nodded. "Nice." From the corner of his eye he saw her glance at him, then back at the au pair, who was folding the child's clothes and looking around for a place to put them.

Then Harley actually said, "If you like that type."

Tucker laughed. "I've got news for you, hon—Harley. Half of the human race likes that type. Very much." Actually, Tucker, unlike some men, did not find redheads irresistible, no matter how buxom. Harley's reaction to his interest, her obvious displeasure, intrigued him much more than the au pair herself. "What's her name?"

A slight pause, Harley shielding her eyes and scowling at the beach. "Brenna."

"Brenna. Irish?" She nodded. "Does she speak with a brogue?" She grimaced and nodded again. "Outstanding."

Down on the beach, Mimi called out, "Brenna, don't let Lily eat sand!" The little girl sat on the damp sand at the water's edge, cramming a handful of it into her mouth. Jamie hooted with laughter.

Brenna dropped the clothes and ran to the child, shrieking, "Sorry, missus!" Lily, finding the sand less tasty than she had anticipated, was screwing up her mud-streaked face in preparation for crying. "Lily, Lily, Lily," Brenna cooed. Lily jutted her lower jaw and looked up at the au pair with teary eyes. Brenna calmed her down, cleaned her off, and carried her through the water toward her half brother.

Jamie took the child, lifted her onto his shoulders, and held her by her chubby feet as he cavorted in the waves for her amusement. Even at this distance, Tucker could hear her delighted laughter. "Has the kid made his move yet?"

"You mean has he told Brenna how he feels?" Harley shook her head. "She's only been with the family for a month, and Mimi says he wants to give her time to get to know him better."

"Uh-huh. I can tell you right now, it's not going to happen. He's going to tough it out in splendid Hale's Point fashion, giving her space, waiting for the right moment, not wanting to crowd her, and meanwhile every tomcat on Long Island will be howling on the fence by the back door."

"Mimi says they're already howling."

He chuckled. "I can believe it."

Harley bent to swat the sand from her legs and feet. "If she's so great, why don't you take a shot at her yourself?" It was poorly feigned nonchalance. Some women were good at pretense, but Harley wasn't one of them.

"I'm out of practice," he answered. "She'd hurt me." Harley shot him a quizzical look, then smirked when she saw his grin. Still, he was only half joking. "I've spent most of the past year in and out of the hospital. Mostly in. Kind of took me out of circulation, you know?"

"Weren't there any attractive nurses?"

"As a matter of fact, there *was* one I kind of liked. But a body cast tends to cramp your style. Our relationship never progressed beyond the sponge-bath phase." He nodded toward the redhead on the beach. "That one scares me. A girl like that could put me right back in traction." He smiled. "Of course . . . it might be worth it."

Harley brushed her hands together. "I say, take the risk. Go for it. Only, you might want to shave first." Tucker's hand automatically went to his face. His stubble felt like hundreds of little pins, even to his roughened hands. "Or else," she continued, her expression smug, "the first kiss is as far as you're going to get." She picked her water bottle up off the grass and turned toward the house, saying, "I'm going to do some upper-body work. Catch you later."

Unwilling to accept the dismissal, he followed her.

On the back outside wall of the house was a showerhead with a towel slung over it, and below it, a concrete slab with a drain. It hadn't been there when he was a boy, but it would have been handy, considering all the sand he used to track through the house after visits to the beach.

"Where do you work out?" he asked.

She turned the water on and adjusted the temperature. "Your father had a gym put in upstairs, right off his bedroom. Used to be a sitting room, he said. Now it's got weights, treadmill, NordicTrack, flywheel rower. Two whole walls are mirrored. He said he put it in after his first heart attack." She rinsed one foot off under the spray.

"He had . . . I didn't know he had—"

"Oh." She looked contrite. "I'm sorry, I should have realized. I should have told you. He had two. They were mild, he said." Shaking her head, she extended the other foot and rinsed it off. "Sorry."

"No, that's okay. He's . . . all right, isn't he? I mean, he's not an invalid, or—"

"Hardly." She took the towel and dried off her feet. "He's spending the summer in the Caribbean with a friend, sailing. He couldn't do that if he were an invalid."

"The whole summer? I didn't realize that. I thought he was just on a two-week vacation or something. What about his law practice?"

"He told me he retired three years ago."

Tucker had that off-balance feeling you get on the beach when an outgoing wave sucks the sand from beneath your feet. "Retired. Right. I should have known that. I should have figured—"

Harley put a hand around his arm, and the ground stopped moving. "Why don't you come upstairs with me," she said. "I can really use a spotter on the bench press."

STARS MATERIALIZED in the deepening sky as Harley, executing a languid backstroke, glided slowly from one end of the pool to the other and back again. This was her favorite part of the day, when everything was done and night was descending and she could relax a little bit.

She tried to put the past twenty-four hours out of her mind. Tucker Hale's unexpected arrival had tossed a bomb into her orderly life, just as he had warned her it would. She still didn't know when he would be leaving, and she doubted he had given it much thought, despite his abrupt departure the night before. He was both fascinating and irritating, and very hard to ignore, but she would try, at least for a little while. Right now he was inside—she saw lights on in the bathroom window of the maid's room, and heard water running—and she had the evening sky to herself.

She had killed the patio lights and switched on the pool lights, the underwater bulbs making the blue water glow from within. She usually took her evening swim in the nude, since the yard was so private. Of course, she couldn't do that with Tucker around. But there was no need for the racing suit, so she wore a simple white maillot.

She had backstroked several dozen laps when she heard the French doors open and close, and the sound of Tucker's cane on the brick patio. Pausing in the deep end to tread water, she saw him, a dark figure standing on the deck at the shallow end. He kicked off his moccasins and sat down on the edge of the pool with his feet in the water, an awkwardly executed maneuver. After a moment there appeared a small red glow as he lit a cigarette.

Abandoning the backstroke, she swam underwater to the shallow end, surfacing a few feet from the deck, and Tucker. She stood waist-high in the water, smoothing her wet hair off her face and pretending she didn't notice his brown eyes swiftly appraise her. He never leered, but several times she had caught him discreetly checking her out. She knew that some men found her tight, athletic build unappealing, but she also knew that Tucker Hale wasn't one of them.

He exhaled a plume of blue smoke. "You're a good swimmer."

"So are you," she said.

The frown lines between his eyebrows deepened momentarily and then vanished. "The trophies," he said. "Yeah, once upon a time." He glanced at his mangled leg. "No more."

Harley twisted her hair to squeeze the water out. "Did the doctors say you couldn't swim anymore?"

He took a drag before answering. "Actually, they said I *should* swim. Said it'd be good therapy."

She dropped her hair. "Why don't you, then?"

He shrugged. "I've had enough physical therapy. Months and months of it."

"Swimming?"

"No, there was no pool at the hospital. They had me do different things. It was a pretty grueling routine, actually. Machines, lots of weight work."

"Weights? I wondered about that." In the gym that afternoon, although he hadn't worked out himself, he had handled hundred-pound plates as if they were made out of foam rubber. That also explained his physique, so impressive for a man with such limited mobility. "You should stick with it."

He made a dismissive gesture. "I've gotten all the good I can out of that stuff. Months of it, and I still can't get by without that thing." He gestured to the cane next to him.

Harley approached the edge of the pool. He looked different, but she couldn't put her finger on it. Maybe it was just an illusion created by the shimmering light reflected from the pool onto his face. "Hand me that towel?" He did, and she draped it around her shoulders, which made her feel less vulnerable under his scrutiny. "Was it painful, the weight work? I mean, considering the extent of your injuries . . ."

He tensed, and that provided her answer. "It wasn't the pain," he said finally. "It was the lack of results."

"You might get better results with swimming," she said. "And I'll bet it wouldn't hurt as much."

"Harley, listen, I don't want to insult you or anything, but you really don't know what you're talking about."

"I know a little," she said. "I was on the swim team as an undergrad, and my coach was this woman named Eve Markham. She was from Palm Beach, your kind of people—old money. She swam in two Olympics—'64 and '68—and then she did swim therapy with Vietnam vets. They were amputees and guys with paralyzed limbs—major injuries. Then, during the time she was coaching my team, she also worked with physically challenged kids, and I used to help her out. She taught me a lot. Sometimes we'd go out for pizza afterward. Eventually she'd always get to talking about the wounded vets. She said the hard part wasn't knowing what kind of stroke or how many laps they should be doing, that was common sense. The hard part was motivating them, making them want to do it. Once they started swimming, really putting their hearts into it, they made terrific progress. Almost all the guys she worked with far exceeded what the doctors said was possible. She was famous for her results."

"That's real inspiring," he said dryly. "The key, of course, is the motivation part, making them want to do it. Apparently she was pretty good at it, and apparently you're not. Too bad she never shared her secret with you."

"She did," Harley said, and instantly regretted it. Quickly she added, "But it's . . . not something I would do." Her face felt warm. Rather than let him see her blush, she popped up onto the deck, stood, and pulled the towel over her head to dry her hair off.

She could hear Tucker struggling to his feet. "What did she do, hold a gun to their heads?"

"No. It doesn't matter, I just wouldn't do it her way. It's not my style, I couldn't pull it off." She tossed the towel aside and, wet and chilly, looked around for her robe. Tucker had it. He was behind her, holding it open for her. She slid her arms into the sleeves, and he closed and tied it for her, from behind.

"Double knot, right?" he asked.

"I'll do it."

But he did it himself. Even through the thick terry cloth, she felt his warmth. Her wet hair had gotten caught under the collar of the robe, and he pulled it out, his fingertips brushing the nape of her neck. Her heart was racing and she felt a little breathless.

"Wow, you're tense," he said quietly. He worked his fingers gently along the muscles of her neck. "You just swam, you should be loose."

With one hand against her sternum to hold her still, he kneaded her neck and shoulders with his long fingers. His hands felt very strong, and they seemed to know just where and how to rub.

"You're good at that," she murmured.

"I learned how in the hospital. Massage is the only good part of physical therapy."

As he worked, Harley felt a band of tension loosen, and her eyes closed. She decided it was dumb not to tell him. "What Eve did, to get them motivated, she told them that she was going to swim from one end of the pool to the other, and they'd have to swim after her. And whoever caught her could . . . you know . . . have her."

The massage stopped, his hands resting on her shoulders. "Have her, as in . . . *have her?*" Harley opened her eyes and nodded over her shoulder. He turned her around so he could look her in the face. "Really? And she meant it?"

"She always meant everything she said, and they knew it. She was just that kind of person. If she said she was going to do something, she'd do it."

"Kind of like you," he said. "What is it you said? 'I always do what I say I'm going to do'?"

She pulled away from his grip. "Yeah, well—"

"Did she ever have to . . . pay up?"

"No. She was an Olympic swimmer, remember, and these were injured men. She said once a guy *almost* caught her. He'd been a competitive swimmer himself, before he got drafted. No one else ever got close, but they all tried real hard. She was a beautiful woman in middle age, when I knew her. She must have been spectacular in her twenties."

Tucker grinned. "I think it's a great inspirational technique."

"I'm sure you do." Draping the towel over her arm, she said, "Thanks for the massage. I'm going to catch a hot shower, then read in my room for a little while and turn in." Tucker looked at his watch and frowned. "Yeah, I know, but I want to get back on schedule with my six-o'clock swim tomorrow." She was sorry she had said the word *schedule* when she saw the look on his face.

"This regimen of yours blows my mind," he said, picking up his cane. "You know, all this incessant working out is yesterday's news. It's a very eighties kind of a thing, driving yourself like that. Not a nineties scene at all."

He smiled, but Harley never quite knew how to take him. "I'm not *driving* myself, I just—"

"Sure, you are. You don't know how not to. Getting an M.B.A. is just one more example of it. M.B.A.'s are for people who want to spend their whole lives clawing up that ladder, maneuvering for the next deal, the next promotion, the next raise. What joy can there be in that? What satisfaction?"

"The pay's good."

"Money? Is that what it's all about?" He looked grim. "Maybe this has managed to escape you, but it seems to me I've heard about a million times that money doesn't buy happiness. Trust me, it's true."

"That's easy for you to say, isn't it, with that silver spoon hanging out of your mouth."

"I earned my own way," he said angrily; she had touched a nerve. "I started from scratch at sixteen and I worked for what I've got, so don't go tarring me with that brush."

"Well, earning my own way is exactly what *I'm* trying to do, so don't go condemning me for it!" Her voice had risen, and now she struggled to control it. "I don't deny that I'm driven. If you knew how I grew up, how I lived—" She stopped herself and took a breath. "It's just that I want something better, and I don't like people telling me I'm some kind of mercenary—"

"I wasn't saying that." His raw voice adopted a quiet, conciliatory tone. He took a step toward her.

She stepped back. "That's exactly what you were saying, and I resent it. I know what you think of me. You've got me all sized up."

"If I do, it's because you won't let me near you. You grill me about myself, my past, but you won't tell me a thing about yourself. I'd *like* to know how you grew up, how you lived—"

"No, you wouldn't." The words quivered in her throat. He seemed about to speak, but then just stared at her, his expression sober. When she spoke again, her voice emerged as a whisper. "You wouldn't. And I assure you I don't want to talk about it. Good night."

She turned, and he seized her with his free hand, gripping her by the shoulder as he came around to face her. "Don't freeze me out, Harley. Maybe we only just met, and maybe we have nothing in common, but that doesn't mean we can't communicate, for God's sake."

She twisted free of his grip and backed away from him. "'Nothing in common' meaning I'm so driven and you're so laid-back, right?"

"Well—"

"You know, I've been thinking about it, and for a guy who worked two and three jobs for years and built up his own business from scratch, I'm starting to think you've got a lot of nerve calling *me* driven."

He considered that, then shrugged. "I won't argue that I've been there. But that's not where I am now."

"Meaning?"

"Meaning I'm taking a vacation from all that—maybe permanently." He seemed to be growing exasperated. "You're right. I worked my butt off for more years than I care to think about. Then one night I crashed my airplane into the side of a mountain. Suddenly I couldn't work at all anymore. For a long time I couldn't do much of anything—couldn't hold a book, couldn't sit up in bed and watch TV, couldn't even feed myself. All I could do was think. *You* try doing nothing but thinking for a few months. It's a very useful exercise for shaking some of the chaff out of your life. You could use it— you've got plenty there to shake out."

Harley's voice rose, and this time she didn't try to tame it. "Yeah, well, maybe I don't need an airplane crash to help me set my priorities."

His voice rose, too. "Honey, there could be a nuclear holocaust and you wouldn't question your life! You'd still be out there, stopwatch in hand, timing things and measuring things and making sure everything was going according to plan."

"That's not fair."

"I never said it was." He was calmer now, weary. "It's the truth. The truth doesn't have to be fair."

"Very profound. You're full of insights and wisdom, aren't you? You know, I could do without lessons in life from a guy whose answer to difficult situations is to just *bolt*. Someone who didn't even bother to pick up the phone and call his own father for twenty-one years. Does he even know where you've been all this time? What you've been doing? God knows what he thinks. Jamie Tilton didn't even believe me when I told him who you were. He said he'd heard you were dead. Someone told him you'd died in Vietnam."

Tucker smiled as if this were preposterous. "I never went to Vietnam."

"Someone else told him you'd died in jail."

The smile faded. He didn't answer that one, she noted, just lowered his head, closed his eyes, and rubbed the back of his neck. "I shouldn't be here. I should have left last night, not let you bring me back. I've done nothing but irritate you." He looked from her eyes to her mouth, and frowned. Reaching out, he rested a hand lightly on her face and gently trailed his thumb over her upper lip. "In more ways than one, I guess."

It struck her then, why he looked different. He had shaved. For her? The thought made her legs feel weak.

His fingertips stroked her face with a feathery touch, from cheekbone to chin. He smiled again, but this time it was that shy smile that he had worn last night when he'd asked her name. "I've got to tell you, though. I mean, it may sound like a line out of a B movie, but it's true. You're really very beautiful when you're angry." He chuckled self-consciously, the delicate caress trailing down her throat and along one collarbone, coaxing shivers from her. "Really. Just outstanding. I wish you could see yourself."

Harley just stared at him, at a complete loss for words. Finally he withdrew his hand, said, "Good night," and went into the house.

THE BOOK HARLEY TRIED to read in bed was *Priorities for the Successful Manager.* She had already read the first two chapters, "Stress in the Workplace" and "Strategies for Coping with Stress." Now she turned to chapter three, "Learning to Live with Stress," and reread the first page twice without comprehending it.

She closed her eyes and leaned back against her mountain of pillows. What was that line from Thoreau that Tucker had quoted . . . something about living a life of quiet desperation?

"What am I doing?" she whispered.

She heard a creak and opened her eyes. Everything was very quiet. Then came another creak and a thump she recognized as the sound of his cane on carpeting. He was upstairs. Her door was closed. She waited, and then came two light knocks.

She cleared her throat. "Yes?"

A little pause. "Do you mind if I come in?"

She looked down at herself. It was a warm night, and although she had pulled down the covers, she had not gotten under them. She wore her favorite summer nightgown, sleeveless white handkerchief-cotton with a row of tiny heart-shaped buttons down the front. It was thin, but you couldn't see through it—not quite. Not in the dim light from the little bedside reading lamp, anyway. The left side had slipped off her shoulder, and she righted it, then smoothed the skirt so it covered her legs down to the ankles.

"No, come in."

The door opened halfway and Tucker paused in the darkened hall. She could see him—he still had on the shorts and T-shirt he had worn that day—but she couldn't make out his expression.

"What are you reading?" he asked, taking a few steps into the room.

She held up the book, and he frowned, coming closer for a better look. He leaned his cane against the night table, took the book from her, and turned it over, skimming the blurb on the back cover. "'Prioritization of strategies for minimizing job-related anxiety in order to maximize managerial effectiveness'? *This* is your bedtime reading?"

"Did you come up here to criticize my reading material?"

He sat down on the edge of the bed and laid the book on the table. Without looking at her, he shook his head. Absently he ran a hand over his now-smooth chin.

He turned to her. "I came up here to see if you'd let me spend the night with you." She stared at him, eyes wide in disbelief—not at what he wanted, which she had suspected, but at his breathtaking candor. "Pretty smooth seduction, huh?" That shy smile again, the lazy brown eyes staring back.

"That's probably not a good idea," she said.

He reached toward her with both hands, gently took her face between them, and looked her straight in the eye. "No, I think it's a great idea."

She laughed, partly from nervousness and partly because his sincerity disarmed her—but only momentarily. There were many reasons not to sleep with Tucker Hale, and she would spell them out, since he seemed to like the straightforward approach.

She forced a note of cool reason into her voice and said, "We haven't exactly been getting along real well."

He said, "Then we should try to get along better."

He shifted his hands, his long fingers twining through her hair to wrap around the back of her head. Her scalp tingled at his touch, little rivulets of pleasure coursing through her. He pulled her slightly forward as he moved closer. She thought, *I shouldn't let him kiss me*, but then she felt his warm lips on hers, and her will weakened. *It's just a kiss*, she thought, closing her eyes. *Just one kiss. Then I'll make him leave.*

He was surprisingly gentle, his lips barely grazing her own, which felt extraordinarily sensitive. Then he leaned into the kiss just a bit, his mouth moving slowly over hers. There was no irritation from stubble this time; his skin was smooth against hers.

He lingered over the kiss, softly coaxing her into returning it, which she did, at first tentatively, then with real warmth. As her resistance evaporated, she felt both apprehensive and excited. This sense of being overwhelmed by a man was new to her, and she found that a certain part of her, a part she had not known of before, welcomed it.

He was so large, so sure of himself. Everything about him was masculine, even the scent of his warm skin mingled with hints of tobacco and shaving cream.

Her heart pounded furiously. To react so strongly alarmed her, and she pressed her hands against his chest to push him away, pausing when she felt his own rapid-fire heartbeat.

When they finally drew apart, he was as breathless as she, and he looked surprised, as if the kiss, in its quiet intensity, had taken him aback.

His expression altered then, as desire replaced surprise. She saw an unmistakable, age-old need in his eyes, and a kind of panic seized her. She should have resisted him more firmly, she should have had more self-control. Now he would presume too much. His hands slid to her shoulders and he pressed her back against the pillows.

She said, "Tucker, this is nuts. We've known each other less than twenty-four hours."

He smiled, watching his own fingers stroke her throat from chin to sternum. "What better way to get acquainted?"

She threw her head back against the pillows, chuckling in exasperation, and he took advantage of her position to kiss her throat softly, all over. The left side of her nightgown had slipped down again, and his lips traced a path along her exposed shoulder. Easing his hand between them, he slipped the first little heart-shaped button out of its buttonhole.

She struggled to remind herself that this wasn't a good idea. "Tucker," she said, her voice unsteady. She put her hands on his shoulders. "This is pointless. You're leaving soon. I don't even know when. *You* don't even know when."

With his mouth near her ear, he murmured, "Then we should take advantage of the time we have." He took her earlobe between his lips and gently tugged as he unbuttoned the second button. His fingertips glided down the narrow opening of her nightgown, between her breasts, and then up again. When he rested his hand, palm down, on her upper chest, she knew he could feel her drumming heart.

With the other hand he gently kneaded her thigh through the thin cotton, then gathered a handful of the fabric and pulled, uncovering her lower legs. She felt his hand on her knee, and then he reached under her gown to stroke the bare flesh of her thigh. His breathing quickened, and she felt the muscles in his shoulders tense.

"Tucker…" she whispered. He answered the whisper with a kiss; this time a deep kiss, one of unmistakable longing. He took claim to her mouth with demanding force, pinning her back against the pillows as he explored her lips and tongue with his own. She realized her grip on his shoulders had tightened.

He slid his hand up her leg, pausing briefly at the top before continuing along the round contour of her hip, bare and smooth. Caressing the taut flesh, he breathed a low moan into her mouth.

Realizing she had let this go too far, she abruptly broke off the kiss. "Tucker..." He unbuttoned another button. "Tucker..." And another. "Tucker, *no*."

He froze, one hand on her hip, the other poised over a button near her waist.

She had evidently said the magic word.

"No," she repeated.

He considered this. "No for real, or no because that's what you're supposed to say?"

"For real."

His forehead came to rest against hers, as if some of the air had gone out of him. After a few moments, he said, in a quiet voice, "It could be really great."

She was actually tempted, which amazed her. Biting her lip, she shook her head, and again said, "No."

He sat back, his hand trailing from her hip to her thigh, where it stilled. Just as quietly as before, he asked, "Are you a virgin?"

Harley was tempted to lie, because, at twenty-three, her virginity was becoming something of an embarrassment. Opting for the truth, she said, "Yes."

His expression didn't change, she was relieved to note. He wasn't at all surprised or put off. "You shouldn't let that stop you. It could still be really great. I'd make sure of it."

With a small shake of her head, she said, "I couldn't. Not with someone I just met. Not the first time."

He nodded thoughtfully. "All right." Again he reached for the little heart-shaped buttons, this time to slip them back into their holes one by one, bottom to top.

She felt a need to explain. "It's just that I—"

"Shh, it's all right. Really."

He finished rebuttoning her gown, replaced the shoulder, and smoothed the skirt down to her ankles. Taking up his cane, he rose. "Oh, here." He picked up *Priorities for the Successful Manager* and handed it to her. "I lost your place. Sorry."

At the door, he said, "Good night, Harley."

"Good night, Tucker. I'll see you in the morning."

He looked momentarily distracted, as if there were something he wanted to say, but thought better of it. "Yeah. See you in the morning."

As the door closed behind him, she sank back against the pillows, closed her eyes, and released a long, shuddering breath.

4

IN THE MORNING he was gone.

Harley didn't realize it until after her six-o'clock swim, when she passed by the maid's room on the way to the kitchen. The door stood open and the room looked empty. She said his name, and upon hearing no answer, walked in. The bed was unmade and his guitar leaned against the back wall. Otherwise, there was no sign that he had ever been there.

She toured the house, then the property, looking for him, occasionally calling his name. She even checked the beach, in case he had managed to make his way down but couldn't get back up. No Tucker. He was really gone. He had left.

She went to the kitchen, turned on the radio, and made some coffee.

He might have said goodbye.

She thought about their argument at the pool yesterday evening, and his coming to her room later. He was right when he said she wouldn't let him near her. Brian had said the same thing during their brief relationship; that she was cold and ungiving, that she discouraged intimacy, not just sexually, but emotionally.

Was it true? She didn't *feel* cold. Her reactions—to Tucker, if not to Brian—were too warm, inappropriately so.

She took a sip of coffee. It tasted like acid.

Why inappropriately? Because, of course, *he* was inappropriate. He was a nonconformist, a man of exasperating honesty for whom compromise was impossible. After a miserable childhood of pitying looks and being thought odd, of being the outcast, all she wanted now was normalcy. She craved the mainstream; she had struggled for years just to fit in and be like everyone else.

She lifted her chin. There was nothing wrong with her. She had acted appropriately. She had no reason to feel guilty. Where was it written that you were some kind of ice goddess if you didn't jump into bed with a man you had just met?

She was glad he was gone. Still, she would have driven him to the airport. She had *told* him she would drive him to the airport.

For several minutes she sat at the table, willing herself not to cry.

THE RADIO SAID IT WOULD be a cloudless day of high, possibly record-breaking, heat and humidity. She liked hot weather, and decided to spend the day weeding and cutting back the perennial borders. She interrupted her work only briefly for a light lunch and a reapplication of sunblock, and then threw herself back into it, grateful to have something physical to do. It was dirty work and she wore comfortable old clothes for it: a chambray shirt, oversize tan walking shorts belted with a red bandanna, and her grungiest running shoes, plus sunglasses and a Walkman.

It *was* a hot day, brutally hot, but she immersed herself in her work, laboring mechanically and virtually without pause. The effort she had to expend just to muscle through the heat and keep going served to steer her mind from the subject of Tucker Hale, although from time to time his image seemed to waver on a ripple of warm air, then dissolve.

The sun burned like a blowtorch in the sky; everything she touched felt like it was about to burst into flame. Looking anywhere but at the ground made her feel queasy, so she just bent her head over her work, digging and cutting with an automatic relentlessness. She had never perspired so much, and her clothes were quickly soaked through. Sweat dripped onto the plants she was clipping and ran into her eyes, stinging them. She took the bandanna from the waistband of her shorts and tied it around her forehead, and that helped.

In the interests of mood management, she chose her most upbeat tapes for the Walkman, mainly Beethoven. The *Ninth Symphony* was perfect; it made her feel exhilarated and empowered. She made short work of the borders edging the front walk and got started on the driveway. Beethoven's *Seventh,* however, was a mistake. She had forgotten about that really soulful part halfway through that always filled her with sorrow. Instead of turning off the tape, as she knew she should, she turned the volume up. Then she put down her weeder and sat on the grass next to the blacktop driveway, suddenly very tired.

Harley checked her watch. It was 2:09 p.m. She had worked almost nonstop for over six hours. Her head throbbed and she felt slightly nauseated. At least she no longer sweated as she had; that wet, sticky feeling was gone. When she realized that was probably because she had drunk nothing all day but a little mineral water at lunch, she felt sheepish. She should have considered her fluids, as she did when she was running. She should have taken some breaks, and she should have worn a hat. She also should have quit hours ago.

She was so stupid.

Harley tried to stand, but things shifted and then she felt a sudden jolt of pain and something hard under her head: the driveway. She lay on her back, her body absurdly heavy. The blacktop felt very warm beneath her, almost hotter than she could stand, but not quite. She closed her eyes, took off her sunglasses, and draped an arm over her face. The beautiful, solemn music filled her ears and her mind, and she gave herself up to it, losing herself in its sadness.

Yes, she was very stupid. She would go through life being stupid and doing stupid things. So much for the theory that Columbia M.B.A. candidates were intelligent people.

After a while the driveway began to vibrate, as if there were a subtle tremor in the earth. Then the vibrations stopped, and presently a shadow fell over her.

She opened her eyes and squinted at the dark form blocking the sun; someone was crouching over her, reaching toward her. As she groped on the driveway for her sunglasses, a large pair of hands plucked the earphones from her ears, and silence rushed in to replace the music.

"I said, are you all right?" came the familiar, rusty voice.

Tucker? She dropped the sunglasses and just stared. The thought occurred to her that he might be an illusion conjured up by the heat. She reached up with a trembling hand to touch him, but her arm fell like a deadweight across her chest.

"Harley?" The hands cupped her face. She could see him clearly now. He looked distraught. "God, you're on fire. Honey, what's wrong with you?"

"I'm stupid," she murmured. Her eyes closed of their own accord. She felt his arms wrap around her. Her head rolled back like a newborn baby's, and he gripped it firmly with one hand and held it upright. Her eyelids were too heavy to open.

"Wake up, honey. I've got to get you inside, and I can't carry you. You've got to walk." Harley struggled to open her eyes, then forgot the point of her struggle and allowed herself to drift off again. "Wake up! Wake up!" he commanded. "You can do it!" Panting with the strain, she forced her eyes open. "Good girl." Tucker sighed.

She peered over his shoulder. Something large and dark stood on the driveway behind him, swimming on waves of heat. She concentrated, and it took form: a black convertible sports car, very smooth and shiny in the bright sun. She squinted to get it in focus, then shook her head, but that was a mistake; the world spun sickeningly, and she slumped against him. He held her tight and she clung to him, breathing in his now-familiar scent and listening to his heart pound. He felt warm and solid, the only solid thing in a spinning world.

"THIS IS *YOUR BED*," she objected as he whipped aside the covers with the arm that he wasn't using to hold her up.

"Consider it yours." It was all he could do to get her as far as the maid's room. No way were they going to make it up those stairs. Her legs gave out again, but he managed to steer her onto the twin bed as she was collapsing.

"That's all right," he said, more to himself than to Harley, who appeared to be senseless. He straightened her out so she lay on her back, untied her shoelaces, and pulled off her dirt-encrusted running shoes. "That's all right, hon. No more walking. You did real well."

He sat on the edge of the bed and wiped his brow with the frayed hem of his T-shirt—*damn*, it was hot—then untied the damp red bandanna that Harley had been wearing as a sweatband. Whenever he had a fever as a child, his nanny used to gauge it by kissing his forehead, insisting that the mouth was much more sensitive to temperature than the hand. He leaned over Harley and pressed his lips gently to her forehead; it felt like something out of an oven. Without meaning to or thinking about it, he kissed her lightly before drawing away.

He looked around the room. It did not surprise him that R.H. still hadn't installed air-conditioning. The old man had always condemned what he called "frivolous technology." Of course, "frivolous" was in the eye of the beholder. State-of-the-art gym equipment was apparently not frivolous. Neither were small airplanes, large sailboats, and fast cars, with which he had always surrounded himself. They were his passion—a passion that had rubbed off on Tucker—and owning dozens at a time was not frivolous. Owning more than one telephone—black, rotary dial— was.

Tucker remembered having seen a fan in the maid's closet when he stowed his duffel bag there. Now he set it up and turned it on, aimed at Harley. He removed her ponytail holder with the two big red plastic balls that prevented her from lying faceup, and spread her hair out on the pillow, a corona of bronze silk. Then he dampened a clean washcloth with cold water and laid it on her forehead, which caused her to mumble something incoherent and shake it off.

"Easy," he whispered. He blotted her face gently with the washcloth, noting how pale she was, although color was beginning to rise in her cheeks. Her beautiful lips, which had looked white, were red again. Was that a good sign? He felt helplessly out of his depth, here. He sighed and held her head still, the washcloth pressed to her forehead.

Phil Zelin would not be out of his depth here. Phil, the cabbie's son from Brentwood, the friend from the wrong side of the tracks whom R.H. had at one time not even permitted in the house, was a doctor now, some kind of great high Pooh-Bah of internal medicine. Tucker knew this because Phil was the only person from his youth with whom he was still in touch. About once a year, one of them would pick up the phone and call the other, and they would talk for a couple of hours, just like old times.

Tucker tossed the washcloth into the bathroom sink, went to the study, called the Stony Brook University Medical Center, and, after about five minutes of being transferred around, was finally put through to Dr. Philip Zelin.

"Sounds like heat exhaustion, all right," Phil agreed. "See if you can get some fluids into her. Mix a teaspoon of salt in a quart of water and make her drink some." Despite Tucker's distress, he found his friend's brusque professionalism amusing. Was this really the same Phil Zelin who had lifted his robe, dropped his bell-bottoms, and mooned all the school administrators at his high-school graduation? "And keep sponging her off. I just finished up my rounds—I can be there in half an hour."

Tucker mixed a glass of salt water and set it on the night table. "Come on, honey. You've got to drink this. Doctor's orders." He sat her up, cradling her against his chest, her head supported by his shoulder. "Come on. Wake up." Had she gotten hotter? Was that even possible? She was flushed all over now, her skin a deep pink. He patted her cheek, which was no longer clammy, but dry. No response. He put the rim of the glass to her lips. "Come on, Harley, drink. *Please.*"

He gave up and bathed her face and arms with the cool washcloth until the doorbell rang.

Phil greeted him with a warm hug and a slap on the back. "Trade you my house for that Jag."

Even after twenty-one years, Tucker would have known him anywhere. His lanky frame and dark, perpetually amused eyes hadn't changed, although now those eyes were surrounded by a pair of tortoiseshell glasses. The main difference between the teenage Phil and the pushing-forty Phil was the scattering of gray in his wiry black hair, now much shorter than the shoulder length he'd worn it in high school. And, of course, his natty attire—pleated linen trousers with suspenders, a striped shirt with rolled-up sleeves, and a loosened polka-dot tie—was a far cry from the tie-dye and faded denim of his youth.

Dodging further time-consuming conversation, Tucker quickly turned and led Phil to the maid's room.

"Your face has more character," Phil said as he followed behind. "And that leg of yours has a *lot* more character. What happened?"

"I got hurt," Tucker said.

"That part I already figured out, tough guy."

"She's in here," Tucker said, standing aside at the door.

Phil walked straight to Harley and thumped his black bag on the night table. He sat on the edge of the bed, took her head in his hands, and pried her eyes open. "She been comatose long?"

Comatose. The word snapped a memory into focus: a young doctor's moon face and the words, *Mr. Hale, you've been comatose for nearly a week.* He had thought, comatose, as in coma? Phil was looking at him, waiting for an answer. "Uh, in and out for a while. Completely out for the better part of an hour. Is she okay? Is she going to be okay?"

"How long she been flushed like this?" He took her pulse.

"Not long. Since I spoke to you."

Phil withdrew a stethoscope and blood-pressure kit from his bag, wrapped the cuff around her arm, and pumped the bulb. "You get any fluids into her?"

"No. That was hopeless." He bit off the impulse to ask again if she was going to be okay. If the answer had been an unequivocal yes, Phil would have given it. He hunched his shoulder to wipe his brow on his shirtsleeve, thinking, *Please let her be okay. Please.*

"Blood pressure's a little high," Phil said. "That's good, that's what we want." He opened the top two buttons of her shirt and listened to her chest with the stethoscope, then rolled her onto her side, pulled out her shirttail, and slid the stethoscope under it. "Lungs are clear." He sheathed an electronic thermometer and inserted it in her mouth. "Her clothes are damp, but she's dry, meaning she perspired heavily for a while and then stopped. Her body's cooling mechanism shut down and she overheated, just like a car." The thermometer beeped and he checked it.

Tucker looked over his shoulder at the digital readout. "Is that right?" he asked. "Her temperature's 104.8?"

Phil put away the instrument. "That's her temperature."

"So it's heat exhaustion?"

Phil glanced up at him. "No, she's graduated to heat-*stroke*." He stood.

Stroke? Heatstroke? "Does she have to go to the hospital?"

"Not if we can get her cooled down. Let's try a cold bath with the fan on." He quickly finished unbuttoning her shirt, opened it, then unclasped the front closure of her white bra and stripped her of both garments, revealing her from the waist up.

She had a beautiful body, her breasts taut and perfect, but Tucker had known that; what Lycra had not revealed, his imagination had filled in. It tugged at his heart for her to be exposed this way. She was a private person, with a highly developed sense of dignity. She would not knowingly have him see her like this.

When Phil unzipped her shorts, Tucker turned away. "I'll run a bath," Tucker said.

"Great."

In the little bathroom, he stoppered the claw-footed tub and turned the cold water on all the way, contemplating the discomfort he had felt when Phil undressed Harley. It wasn't just her vulnerability that had gotten to him. He was jealous of Phil for having the right, as a doctor, to touch Harley, to take her clothes off, to see her naked. Phil, of course, was merely doing his job. The problem, if there was one, was Tucker's.

The tub filled quickly, and Tucker turned the water off. Phil brought the fan in and handed it to him, then left again. While

Tucker was crouched under the sink plugging it in, he heard Phil's footsteps again, heavier this time, and the sound of water being displaced. He wrestled himself to his feet, turned the fan on, and carefully aimed it toward the tub and Harley.

It astounded him that she could remain completely unconscious through all of this. Immersion in cold water should jolt anyone awake, but there she was, as peacefully unaware of her situation as if she were asleep.

She had settled into an artlessly graceful pose, head back against the curved lip of the tub, arms crossed at the waist, lower body curled modestly toward the wall. She looked so lithe and fragile.

"The point of all this," Phil said as he knelt beside the tub and dipped a washcloth into the water, "is to lower her body temperature, and fast. If it keeps rising, she'll go into circulatory collapse." He looked up at Tucker to underline the seriousness of his words. "Shock."

"Shock," Tucker repeated dumbly. He lowered the lid of the toilet and sat, rubbing the back of his neck. "How will you know if she's—"

"You see how pink her skin is? Flushed?" Phil ran the wet washcloth over Harley's shoulders and upper chest, which were not immersed. "The blood is on the surface. If her circulation gives out and she goes into shock, she'll go gray, pallid—we've got to watch for that. Her blood pressure will plummet."

"What do we do then?"

"We find out how fast that Jag of yours can make it to the medical center."

Tucker mulled that over. "What's the worst that could happen?" Phil hesitated, as if weighing his words. "Don't be coy, Zelin. Just answer my question."

"I'm not being coy, Tucker, I'm just being careful. I've had years of experience explaining to people what's happening with their loved ones. It's not always an easy call. People tell you they want the unvarnished truth, but they really—"

"Relax. We're not talking about a loved one here—she's the house sitter." Not the whole story, perhaps, but Tucker wasn't in the mood to split hairs. He wanted answers.

"House sitter." Phil looked at Harley and then at Tucker. "I thought she was your—"

"Well, she's not. She's the house sitter, so tell me."

"All right, then." He wiped her face with the washcloth. "She *could* die. It's been known to happen."

Tucker lapsed into a stunned silence. Finally he swallowed and asked, "What's the likelihood of that?"

Phil felt her forehead. "Not as likely as brain damage." Tucker felt something slowly whirl inside him. He put a hand on the edge of the tub to steady himself as Phil continued, oblivious: "Which, in turn, is less likely than heart, liver, or kidney damage." Phil nodded to himself. "Which, in turn, is less likely than no permanent damage at all, in this particular case. In my opinion."

"No permanent damage," Tucker said. "That's the likeliest?" Phil nodded.

Tucker patted the pocket of his T-shirt, felt his sunglasses and nothing else, and sighed. Phil, recognizing the gesture for what it was, pulled a pack of Newports from his own shirt pocket and offered them to Tucker.

"You smoke?" said Tucker. "Still? You're a doctor. You should have quit by now."

"Absolutely. I couldn't agree more. You want one or not?" Tucker shook his head, and Phil lit one for himself with a monogrammed gold lighter.

"Uh, Phil . . ." Tucker hesitated. This was weird. Why was he doing this? "You mind taking that outside? You're not supposed to... She doesn't like... I'd rather you didn't smoke in the house."

Phil stared at Tucker, cigarette in one hand, dripping washcloth in the other. "*You'd* rather? You're a smoker—what do you care?" Before Tucker could formulate an answer, Phil nodded toward Harley. "And *she's* out cold, so she could care less. And the old man's in parts unknown, so he'll never find out. Besides which, it serves him right for hating me for no reason whatsoever way back when. I'll smoke in his house and give him a reason to hate me. He'll never know, but it'll make *me* feel better. I hate it when people hate me for no reason. Better I should have done something wrong." He nodded, happy in his logic, all of this making perfect sense to him.

Tucker looked at Harley, naked and unaware, remembering how she had snatched the cigarette from his lips and doused it in the pool that first night. She was powerless now, her authority gone. He didn't want to order his friend outside, yet it struck him as profoundly wrong to ignore Harley's will simply because she was incapable of exercising it at the moment. It was like taking advantage of her while she was at her weakest, and he found that impossible to do.

"Take it outside, Phil," he said, just soberly enough so that his friend knew he meant it.

Shaking his head, Phil rose and tossed him the washcloth. "I'll go out and sit in the driver's seat of that nice new Jag while I smoke this. Hope it doesn't slip out of my fingers." He paused in the doorway and smiled. "Nothing takes burn marks out of leather."

After Phil left, Tucker sat on the edge of the tub and dabbed the washcloth on Harley's face, throat, and shoulders. It struck him as an intimate thing to be doing—she was naked, after all, and he was bathing her—yet he felt only tenderness, not lust. This surprised him, since he had an active libido, and had never been good at reining it in. Witness the way he had tried to rush her into bed last night, when, as she'd pointed out, they had known each other less than twenty-four hours. His common sense should have told him that a woman as conventional and tightly wound as Harley, virgin or not, would never go for that. He had wanted her, though— badly—and desire had won out over common sense.

In spite of their differences, he found her very attractive. Her face was compelling, if not conventionally pretty, and he liked her sleek, strong little body. But it went beyond looks. It was her aura of health and purity that drew him to her, he decided. Opposites attract.

He dipped the washcloth and patted her dry lips with it, then touched them with his fingertips. Perhaps he sought in her what he had once enjoyed in such abundance but had lost—youth, strength, clear vision of the world. Is that what attracted him to her? Something did; something more, or at least different, from what had attracted him to women in the past.

This might not be a good thing. This felt complicated. Maybe the best thing he could do would be to pack up his duffel, toss it in the trunk of his new car, and head back to Alaska in the morning. No, he had to wait until Harley had recovered from her heatstroke. He would leave in a day or two.

He shook his head, bemused. Responsibility had never kept him from bolting before. It had also never made him into a member of the Hale's Point antismoking vice squad before. He stroked Harley's cheek, ran a thumb over a closed eyelid. He had been wrong, thinking of her as powerless just because she was unconscious. She was more in control than ever.

Phil's voice jolted him out of his reverie. "What's with the dealer plates on that Jag?" He had his black bag in his hand, and now he set it down on the floor next to the tub and withdrew the thermometer.

"I only bought it this morning." Tucker stood, and Phil took his place on the edge of the tub, slipping the thermometer into Harley's mouth. "I got up before dawn, thinking I might head home. Then I remembered I hadn't seen Liz Wycliff yet—you remember Liz?"

"Sure." The thermometer beeped. Phil checked the readout and shot a fist. *"Yes!"*

"Yes?" Tucker hovered anxiously, trying to see the numbers.

"It's down to 103.2."

Tucker closed his eyes and leaned back against the wall. "Yes."

Phil lifted Harley's right arm out of the water and took a pulse. "Got a towel?" He dried off the arm, draped it over the side of the tub, and wrapped the blood-pressure cuff around it. The results made him smile. "Looking good." He picked up the washcloth and went back to wiping Harley down with it. Tucker observed that his touch was coolly impersonal, and he found this reassuring. "So you wanted to see Liz."

Tucker took his seat on the toilet lid again. "Yeah. She was like a surrogate mom to me. I couldn't leave without seeing her. So instead of hitching to La Guardia, I hitched to the train station—"

"Hitched?"

"And took the train into New York. She's got this co-op on Central Park West—the San Remo. The doorman wouldn't let me up."

Phil gave him a sideways sneer, his eyes scanning Tucker from head to toe. "Can't imagine why."

"I know I need a haircut."

Phil expelled a gust of laughter. "It'd be quicker to list the things you *don't* need than what you do. You don't need . . . God, I don't know. Elevator shoes! There. You don't need elevator shoes. You could live without them. What you *do* need, as soon as possible, *is* a decent haircut, some decent clothes, a decent pair of shoes—"

Tucker chuckled. "Where have I heard that before?" He frowned, pretending to search his memory. "Those words, they're so familiar. 'Get a haircut, get some decent clothes, what are you, an animal in the zoo?'" He smacked his head as if the light bulb had just gone off. "Oh, I remember! It was your father, that's right! Standing on the front porch screaming at you with all the neighbors listening, and you giving him the finger and slamming the car door."

Tucker's legs felt too long for the little bathroom; they kept bumping into things made out of porcelain. He lifted the bad one with both hands and crossed it over the good one, then leaned back and tried to get comfortable, but it was a lost cause.

"Did I really give him the finger?" Phil laughed disbelievingly, although Tucker suspected his friend remembered the incident just as clearly as he did. "What a *punk* I was! *I'm* the one that should have been sent to military school." He opened one of Harley's eyelids, then closed it. "So the doorman, exercising superb judgment, wouldn't let you up."

"Yeah, but he buzzed her and she came down." He smiled, remembering. "She's . . . Well, she's older. I hadn't really expected that. But still beautiful. She's so great, you know? She's just great. As soon as I saw her, I realized how much I had missed her. When she saw me, she said, 'Good morning, Tucker. How nice that you're not dead. You may take me to breakfast.'"

"I'm all choked up. You realize this is supposed to be leading up to the Jag, which is the only part I really care about."

"So at breakfast I told her I wanted to buy a car to drive back to Alaska, and she said what kind, and I flashed on this hood ornament up in my room and said Jaguar, and she drove me to a dealer, and he had a black XJR-S right on the lot, and I bought it," he said, all in one breath.

Phil frowned as he patted Harley's forehead with the washcloth. "Now, when you say you just bought it . . . People don't just buy cars on impulse like that, especially not expensive cars. You've got to arrange for financing, there's paperwork—"

"I don't finance anything," Tucker explained. "I don't owe money. I wrote him a check, and he'll take care of the paperwork and plates and stuff by tomorrow, he said." He shrugged. "It's a done deal."

Phil stared at him. "You wrote him a check. You've got, like, a zillion dollars sitting around in a checking account just in case you suddenly get the urge to buy a—"

"I did have to make a phone call to transfer the funds. This is very bad form of you, you know. We never discuss money in Hale's Point."

"We do it all the time in Brentwood."

"You live in Hale's Point now, buddy. You're coming up in the world."

"And you, you who are lecturing me on decorum, live in . . . Elk something?"

"Moose Pass. *Near* Moose Pass."

"In a two-room cabin in the woods. That you built yourself from *trees*."

"The logs came from trees, yes. But it's really one room and a kind of a lean-to on the side, there."

"Is there enough room in the lean-to for the Jag?"

"No, I've got to keep the Jeep in there to keep the snow off it."

Incredulous outrage flared in Phil's eyes. "Is it me? Am *I* nuts? Because, you'll have to excuse me, but I'm having a really, really hard time picturing that exquisite, magnificent piece of British engineering covered in snow out in front of some two-room—strike that, one-room-plus-a-lean-to-for-the-Jeep hovel that you made yourself out of *trees!* In the middle of the *woods!* In Elk, excuse me, *near* Elk Pass, Alaska, for God's sake—"

"Moose. Moose Pass."

"Moose, elk . . ." He shrugged wearily. "The point is, I am very serious about this trade, and I want you to give it every—"

"What trade?"

"My house for your Jag. Remember?" He turned back to Harley, and Tucker could no longer see his expression.

"Right." Phil's oddball sense of humor was one thing about him that hadn't changed over the years. It had always amused him to propose some ludicrous idea, hammer away at it until everyone believed he was serious, and then laugh at their gullibility. Tucker rose and put on his sunglasses. "My turn for a break now."

Tucker retrieved his Camels from the glove box of the Jag and smoked two while he sat on the stone wall staring out at the Sound. That kid from next door, Jamie Tilton, was walking along the water's edge with the au pair and his little sister. He turned and saw Tucker, then shielded his eyes and peered first toward the west, then toward the jetty to the east. Probably looking for Harley; she would be due for her afternoon run about now. He looked again toward Tucker, frowning as if trying to make up his mind about something. Whether to come up and ask him where Harley was? Tucker made his mind up for him by stubbing out his cigarette and going back in the house.

He walked into the bathroom as Phil withdrew the thermometer from Harley's mouth. He looked up at Tucker and smiled. "Chicken's done. What'll we have with it?"

"Man, you are one twisted—"

"It's 102.2 and dropping," Phil announced triumphantly.

"All *right!*"

Harley moaned and her head rolled to the side.

Phil said, "Let's get her back into bed."

Tucker moved the fan into the bedroom and went to the linen closet to fetch a bath sheet. When he returned to the bathroom, Phil had Harley out of the tub and on her feet, although she was still insensible. His arms supported her against him and her head rested on his chest, as if they were dancing. Now that she was vertical, her nudity seemed more . . . nude, more sexual, especially in contrast with the fully clothed Phil. She still inspired Tucker's protective instinct, but now another, more fundamental instinct, as well. Tucker wished it were his arms embracing that warm, wet skin; his shoulder on which her head reclined. He felt a painful stab of jealousy toward his friend, but swallowed it down, composing his features into a neutral mask.

"You want to dry her off a little?" Phil said.

Tucker scrubbed the bath sheet over her back and legs in a cursory way. He would have loved to linger over the task, particularly as regards that small, firm bottom, but without the good Dr. Zelin in attendance, and with Harley's full knowledge and approval. He wrapped the bath sheet around her, and Phil carried her into the bedroom, laid her on her side on the bed, unwrapped her, and pulled the sheet up.

As he was doing this, Tucker happened to notice Harley's clothes in a jumble on the floor where Phil had tossed them, and he did a double take. On top of the pile, the last item removed, was a pair of black-and-white zebra-print string-bikini panties. He smiled. Zebra-print panties. Who woulda thunk it?

Phil said, "Are you listening to me?"

"Yes, Doctor."

"I said, keep sponging her off until she's down to about a hundred degrees. I'll leave you this thermometer. Take her temperature every half hour and call me if it goes up even a little." He went back to the bathroom for his bag and snapped it closed.

"You're leaving?"

"You don't need me here anymore. She's out of the woods. As soon as she can sit up and drink, start forcing fluids on her. She cooled off fast, so I think it's unlikely there's any kind of irreparable damage to the body tissues." Tucker sighed with relief. "Unlikely, but not impossible. Brain tissue is particularly susceptible to those high temperatures. When she can get out of bed, watch for signs of ataxia."

"Ataxia."

"Vertigo, disorientation. Call me if she can't stand by herself or walk. After she's been awake for a while, that is. At first, of course, she'll be disoriented. I'll stop by tomorrow to check on her." He slapped Tucker on the arm and headed out of the room. "I'll find my way out. You stay with her."

"You're a good friend, Phil. I don't know how to thank you."

From the doorway, Phil said, "You can thank me by getting a haircut."

Grinning, Tucker extended his right arm, the middle finger raised.

Turning away, Phil said, "He *should* have sent you to military school. Would have served you right, you punk."

5

HARLEY OPENED HER EYES. It was night. A dim lamp shone in the corner where Tucker sat reading a book. She was in his bed. She couldn't remember why, but she knew there was a good reason. It was very quiet, the only sound the soft white noise of the fan.

Even with the breeze from the fan, it was warm in the room. Tucker wore a pair of baggy olive-drab shorts and nothing else. His legs were crossed, the bad one over the good. There was a small movement, a rustle, as he turned the page. She could see the concentration in his face, the little frown lines between his eyebrows.

She wanted to ask him what he was reading. "Tucker," she said, but her mouth was dry, and it came out as a parched whisper.

He looked toward her, his eyes lighting when he saw that she was awake. He put down the book and uncrossed his legs by lifting one off the other with both hands. She could see his chest clearly now, the muscles hard and smooth on one side, torn by savage wounds on the other. The magnitude of his injuries suddenly struck her; the burden of living with them day after day.

She closed her eyes and began to drift, but his touch woke her up again. He sat on the bed next to her, pulled the sheet up, and tucked it around her shoulders.

"Not yet," he said softly. "You can sleep in a minute, I promise." His voice sounded raspier than ever. He was tired.

He lifted her into a sitting position, one long arm curled around her while the other poured water from a pitcher into a glass. She liked the feel of his arm against her bare back, his skin cool against hers. She could feel his muscles tense to support her weight.

He brought the glass to her lips and she drank, then he eased her back down again. She tried to remember what it was she had wanted to ask him when she had said his name.... His name ... it had always struck her as odd....

She said, "Tucker—that's a funny name."

He leaned over her, his arms flanking her on either side. For a few seconds he just looked at her, faint amusement in his eyes, then he smoothed some stray hairs off her face and pressed a wet cloth to her forehead and cheeks. "It's an old family name on my father's side. Saxon. It means a tailor—a tucker of cloth."

He picked something up off the night table, fiddled with it, and aimed it at her mouth, saying, "Under the tongue." While he held the thermometer in place, he said, "Harley's kind of a funny name, too." There came a beep. He withdrew the thermometer and said, "Down to 101 on the nose. Were you named after a relative?"

Harley tried to shake her head no, but it made everything start to reel. "A motorcycle," was all she managed to say before oblivion reclaimed her.

"WHAT HAPPENED TO MY clothes?"

Tucker opened his eyes. The room was yellow with sunlight. Harley sat up in bed, holding the sheet to her chest. Her color seemed normal, her hair was in delicious golden disarray, and she looked angry.

He wanted to laugh, but he knew that would probably be a mistake. He pried himself out of the chair in which he had fallen asleep, every bone in his sorry body complaining. The book he had been reading—Kerouac's *On the Road*—tumbled off his lap onto the floor.

"I said, what happened to my clothes?"

He pointed to the pile in the corner, zebra panties et al. "They're right there."

She glanced at the pile and then glared at him. She looked like a scruffy, mean little cat. "Who took off my clothes?" she asked more pointedly.

Tucker came to stand over her. She noted his state of undress—he still wore shorts and nothing else—and pulled her sheet up higher. He said, "Dr. Philip Zelin, M.D., of the Stony Brook University Medical Center Department of Internal Medicine, took off your clothes."

She squinted, as if trying to remember. "You weren't here?"

He poured her a glass of water. "Little hair of the dog?"

"You aren't answering me."

"That's a bad habit of mine. You've called me on it before."

"That's still not an answer."

"Here, drink this."

Her lower lip jutted and her eyes glittered ferociously. "Why aren't you answering me?"

He sat on the bed and she squirmed away from him. "Because you are so very, very beautiful when you're angry. Drink."

"What is that?"

"Straight vodka. I've been pouring it down your throat for days."

She swatted at him. "Get *away* from me!"

"First drink this. It's water."

She took the glass with the hand that wasn't holding up the sheet, but it shook, so Tucker steadied it while she drank.

"Excellent," he purred demonically. "My plan is working perfectly." He traded the glass for the thermometer. "Open up the hangar, here comes the airplane."

"That never worked with me."

"No? And I had such hopes for that one." He popped it in—*beep*—and popped it out. "Congratulations, Miss... What's your last name, anyway?"

"Sayers. *Ms.* Sayers."

"*Ms.* Sayers, you are, at long last, normal. Except, of course, for being named after a motorcycle."

HARLEY ALLOWED TUCKER to help her stumble up the stairs to her room, wrapped in the sheet, but then shooed him away, preferring to wash and dress unassisted—a challenging task. She was confused and uncoordinated, aware that she had been sick, but fuzzy on the details.

It was almost noon before she sat down to Tucker's offering of toast and ice water at the umbrella-shielded table on the patio, only to find she had no stomach for the toast. It was cooler than the day before, and overcast. She wore crisp cotton—a sleeveless pink shirt and white shorts—and her usual ponytail.

She pushed away her plate. "How did you know I was named after a motorcycle?"

He reached across the table to pour some more water for her. "You told me. At about 3:00 a.m. You don't remember?"

She shook her head. "About 3:00 a.m.? Was I awake all night?"

"No, you were mostly pretty much out of it."

"But *you* were awake."

"Yeah, up to a point. I remember the sun rising, so I guess it was past dawn by the time I conked out. I do know you were down below a hundred by that time."

"I had a fever? Was I sick?"

"Heatstroke."

She groaned and nodded. "Of course. I'm so stupid."

"You did keep mumbling something to that effect." He pointed to the toast. "You're not going to eat that?" She shook her head, and he picked up a slice and took a bite.

She was pensive for a few moments. "You sat up all night with me. You took care of me. Thank you."

"My pleasure," he said with a full mouth.

"And I'm sorry for being so creepy when I first woke up."

"That's perfectly understandable."

"Did you see me naked?"

He sighed, and this time he waited until he had swallowed, before speaking. "Yes."

She felt heat flood her cheeks. "How can you just say yes like that? You should lie to protect my feelings!"

His eyes widened and he laughed. "You *want* me to lie to you?"

"Of course! There's such a thing as being too honest, you know."

"No, I don't know anything of the kind. I don't lie." He took another piece of toast.

"Ever?"

"Not if I can avoid it."

"Well, try to *avoid* avoiding it with me sometimes," she said. "Try giving me the answer I want to hear, just to keep me happy."

"I don't *want* to keep you happy."

"You don't—"

"You're *magnificent* when you're angry."

"Good. This is your lucky morning, then, because there's something I'm really—" She reined herself in, not wanting to come off as shrewish, especially after the scene at the pool the night before last. "*Angry* may be too strong a word. Something I'm *curious* about."

"Shoot." He popped the last of the toast in his mouth and dusted his hands.

"How come you just sneaked away yesterday morning with no word at all? I thought you'd left, that you'd gone for good."

"Did you miss me?"

Yes. "No."

"I didn't want to wake you."

"You could have left a note."

"I don't leave notes. I'm bad about things like that."

"I'll bet you're not very good at saying goodbye, either. I mean, I just get that feeling."

He pulled a pack of cigarettes from his pocket and shook it. "You're right, I'm not."

"Are you going to smoke?"

"We're outside. I thought that wasn't a problem."

"It's just that I feel a little woozy. It's all right. Enjoy your cigarette, I'll go inside." She started to rise.

He quickly replaced the pack and reached out an arm. "Stay. Please." She sat again, and he said, "I have a question for you, too. I don't understand why you went out in the heat yesterday and pushed yourself till you dropped. I mean, you were out way too long, you drank way too little. You know better—you're a smart woman. What were you thinking of?"

You. "I don't know." He kind of shrugged, as if to say, is that all? She found she couldn't look at him. "I don't know. It was stupid. I have no explanation."

His candid brown eyes seemed to search her, looking for a better answer. Presently he said, "Fair enough."

Of course, Harley knew it wasn't fair. She made a practice of smoothing out life's rough spots with gentle untruths. So did everyone else she knew. Except Tucker Hale. He never lied. In their sparring, they used different weapons: her lies, his truths. She had yet to decide which weapon conferred the superior advantage.

"Here you are!" came a voice from behind Tucker, and he turned to see Phil, black bag in tow, rounding the corner of the house. "Can't you hear the doorbell from back here?"

"No," said Tucker. "It comes in handy."

Phil threw him a look and came straight to Harley, dumping his bag on the table and taking a seat next to her. Tucker made introductions as Phil proceeded, without ceremony, to wrap a blood-pressure cuff around her arm.

When he had his reading, he reached into his back pocket and tossed a Polaroid snapshot across the table toward Tucker. "What do you think?"

The picture showed the front of a large brick Colonial house surrounded by boxwoods.

"Twenty-eight-hundred square feet," Phil said as he took Harley's temperature. "I built it nine years ago. It's on that cul-de-sac at the end of Windward Lane. Four bedrooms, three and a half baths, master suite with Jacuzzi, finished basement with wet bar, new oak kitchen with Sub-Zero fridge, all new wall-to-wall. It's on half an acre, professionally landscaped." *Beep.* "Great, cool as a cuke."

Harley aimed a quizzical look in Tucker's direction. "He wants me to trade him my new Jaguar for his house," he explained.

She cocked her head. "Excuse me?"

Tucker said, "What you have to understand about Phil is, he's always had this peculiar sense of humor, and sometimes it's not too clear when he's joking and when he's for real."

"This is not a joke," Phil said, looping his stethoscope around his neck. "My house for your Jag, and I'll throw in the window treatments." To Harley he said, "You want to unbutton your blouse, please?"

After a moment's hesitation, she looked toward Tucker, who rose. "I think I'll go have a smoke."

He sat on the stone wall overlooking the beach. On the Tilton side, Jamie, Brenna, and Baby Lily frolicked in the surf. The current Mrs. T., Mimi, lay on a towel reading. Despite the gray sky, all of them wore swimsuits, with the exception of the baby, who was naked. Brenna's thong bikini was lime green with big pink polka dots.

After a few minutes, Phil joined him and delivered a favorable report on Harley's condition. Tucker looked back toward the patio, where she reclined in her chair, head back, eyes closed, and thought, *Thank God.*

Phil said, "That's some pool R.H. put in. There's an in-ground pool behind my house, did I mention that? Not Olympic-size or anything, but who needs that much water in their backyard?"

Tucker nodded toward the Sound. "As far as my father was concerned, there could never be too much water in his backyard."

"Guess not." Phil breathed deeply of the salt air. "I always loved this beach. I missed it when the old man wouldn't let me come over anymore. I'm near the beach now. Oh, that's another thing—the house is a five-minute walk from the Sound. Learned to sail so I could fit in with my neighbors and discovered I liked it. Got a nice little Flying Scot I call the *Pacemaker.* She's no *Anjelica*—just nineteen feet—but I'm crazy about every one of them. You should take her out while you're here."

"I'd like that."

"About the house," Phil continued. "I replaced the water heater two years ago, and added a deck the year before that."

"Doesn't Kitty have something to say in all this? She might not like you trading her home for a car."

A pained look crossed Phil's face. He glanced briefly toward Harley, motionless in her chair. "Let's go down and walk on the beach."

Tucker shook his head and indicated the leg. "Can't."

Phil looked him in the eye. "What happened?"

"Flew my plane into the side of a mountain."

Phil's eyebrows shot up. "You didn't see it coming?"

Tucker said, "My turn to ask a question. What happened with you and Kitty?"

Phil groped for his cigarettes. Tucker lit one for each of them.

"We're separated," Phil said.

Disappointment bloomed within Tucker. "What happened? You've been together forever." Tucker had introduced them when they were teenagers—the slightly bent cabbie's son from Brentwood and the cool blond heiress from Hale's Point—and was surprised when they took up together, stunned when he found out they were engaged. He even tried to talk Phil out of it, worried that their dissimilarities couldn't support a marriage. Yet, during his infrequent phone conversations with Phil over the years, his friend had painted a bucolic picture of the union. More than once he thanked Tucker for bringing her into his life, told him how crazy he was about her, how empty life would be without her.

"I made a mistake," Phil said, his voice practically a monotone. "About six months ago. There was this nurse." Tucker groaned. "It got back to Kitty. She took the boys and went back home, back to the castle." Kitty's parents owned the largest house in Hale's Point, a Gothic Revival monstrosity just down the road. "Now my lawyers talk to her lawyers. I haven't seen her since she left. She won't return my calls. She's . . . she's very proud."

"Of course she is," Tucker said. "Any woman would flip out, Phil. No wife likes her husband to have an affair."

"It wasn't even an affair. It was twenty minutes in a broom closet, for God's sake. Twenty minutes, and there goes my whole marriage—my whole life!" Suddenly Phil's proposed trade of his house for Tucker's Jag seemed not so much funny as poignant. He was losing almost everything—why not give away the rest? "It was the first time—how's that for irony? I was tempted, I was restless. I figured Kitty would never find out, no harm would come of it. Don't ever cheat on your wife, Tucker, no matter what the temptation. I mean, if you ever get married."

"They'll be flinging snowballs in hell when I make that mistake. Marrying, not cheating, although I'm not a big fan of that, either. You know how I feel about marriage. Fidelity is only one of its drawbacks, but it's a big one. If you get married, you're making a commitment. One person forever. If you stay single, you can have all the broom closets you want, and it doesn't matter."

"See..." Phil had that look on his face, that look that said, *Tucker, you moron, you just don't get it.* "The operative phrase in that sentence is 'It doesn't matter.' And that's where I guess we part company. Because I want there to be things in my life that matter—and there are. My kids matter. Kitty matters. I love her. I'll never be able to stop loving her." His voice was unsteady. "She *matters*. More than anything. I don't think I can live without her."

The depth of Phil's emotion awed Tucker. For a minute he didn't speak, letting his friend get his bearings. A movement from the patio caught his eye. Harley was stretching like a cat in her chair, back arched, arms and legs quivering. A strange kind of ticklish warmth filled him, as if someone were gently stroking his scalp. For a fleeting moment he had a sense of what Phil felt for the woman he had spent two decades of his life with, created children with, built his world around. It would be as if that warm tickle never stopped, just went on and on, filling him with contentment day after day.

What a gift to have it; what a tragedy to lose it.

Phil was still morose, but calm. Tucker said, "I take it you've said these things to Kitty. Told her how you feel, begged her to take you back."

"God, no. She'd only have contempt for me."

"*What?*"

"You know how she is. She's got this bizarre, other-worldly reserve. She hates displays. If the tables were turned, she'd never in a million years come crawling to me, and she'd think I was a spineless worm if I came crawling to her."

"My God, it's *catching!*"

"What?"

"The Hale's Point syndrome. Your upper lip stiffens and it keeps spreading until it reaches your brain, and that's when you're really in trouble."

Phil scowled. "You're not talking about the deer-tick thing."

"God, you're such an idiot! You and Kitty both!" He grabbed his cane, stood, and gestured with it toward the beach. "*And* that witless little Princeton snot down there. And venerable old Liz Wycliff, and, last but far from least, the king of restrained good taste and excellent judgment himself, my beloved sire, Raleigh Hale, Esquire!"

In the distance, Mimi looked up from her book. Jamie and Brenna shielded their eyes to peer at him. They almost certainly couldn't hear his words, but they were probably curious as to the cause of this unseemly outburst. He looked toward Harley, once again immobile, her eyes closed.

Phil sat staring at him. "Are you done?"

"No! No! Don't you understand? A pattern is emerging. This is fascinating, it really is. I can't be the only one who sees it."

Phil grinned. "You know, there *is* a psychiatric unit at the medical center if you ever feel like you want to discuss this with a professional."

Tucker used the fingers of one hand to help him track the relationships. Finger number one: "Liz is in love with R.H., but R.H. is carrying a torch for Anjelica and doesn't notice. Liz, a lifelong victim of Hale's Point syndrome, feels it would be bad form to clue him in."

Finger number two: "Jamie Tilton believes himself to be madly in love with the au pair, one Brenna."

Phil said, "Who? I don't know these people."

Tucker pointed to the beach. "See the blond kid? That's Jamie. See the redhead?" Phil emitted a feral groan that spoke volumes. "That's Brenna. Young Jamie, afflicted with the syndrome since birth, conceals his feelings from said Brenna, thus ensuring that he will eventually lose her to a man who knows how to take what he wants."

Finger number three, and now his delivery became more subdued: "You love Kitty. Kitty loves you." Phil made a face. "She's hurt, but she still loves you, you have to believe that. Kitty was born with the syndrome, she can't help it. You, by reason of your lowly birth—" Phil raised an eyebrow "—for which you should be extremely grateful, were spared it. However, now, in a bizarre twist, you have actually begun imitating the symptoms of the syndrome—aloofness, denial of emotion—because you believe that this is what your wife prefers. When, in fact, she doesn't *prefer* it at all, she just can't help it! She'd love it if you threw yourself at her feet and begged forgiveness and pleaded with her to take you back. It's what any normal person would want and expect of a loved one who had wronged them. It's also what she deserves, after what you did."

"Throw myself at her feet." Phil looked skeptical.

"Absolutely. Make some grand gesture. Have a thousand helium balloons made up with 'I Love You, Kitty' on them, and send them to the castle."

"A thousand helium balloons."

"*Something*. My God, are you willing to give up so easily?"

"It's not a matter of giving up. If I'm going to go out, I at least want to go out with some dignity."

Tucker shook his head. "Well, I think it's a damn shame. I say, do not go gentle into that good night."

"Wasn't it Dylan Thomas who said that?"

"Well, now *I'm* saying it." Tucker stamped his cane. It stuck in the soil beneath the grass, and he yanked it free.

"And it was about death, not divorce."

"What's the difference? The end of life, the end of love."

"Big talk from the king of the broom closets. Have you ever even had a serious relationship?"

"No, but I've got imagination." Harley rose from her chair, clasped her hands over her head, and bent from side to side. That warm tickle crept along his scalp again, and he smiled.

Phil followed his gaze. "She recovered quickly. She's a healthy young woman." He smiled, too. "Very healthy."

Something in Phil's tone, in the way he was staring at Harley, made a silent alarm go off in Tucker's head. He said, "What happened to that professional reserve I was admiring so much yesterday? Not to mention your undying devotion to Kitty."

Phil said, "Harley is cured. She's not my patient anymore, so I'm allowed to take an interest. And as far as Kitty is concerned, it's true that I'm deeply and undyingly devoted to her." He let out a long sigh. "I'm also lonely. It's been six months, and there's been no one. I know now that Kitty will never have me back. I just want . . . I want a warm body to reach over and touch in the middle of the night."

"Uh-uh. You know better than that. You're a doctor, for God's sake. You should know that you have to treat the cause of a problem, not just slap on a Band-Aid."

"There is no cure for my underlying problem, regardless of your optimistic advice. All I can do is treat the symptoms. And I've picked her—" he nodded toward Harley "—as my treatment of choice."

For a few seconds Tucker watched Harley stretch first one leg and then the other behind her while holding on to the back of her chair. Finally he said, "Pick someone else."

It took Phil a moment, and then he said, "So she's just the house sitter, huh?"

"Just pick someone else."

Phil was contemplative for a minute. Then he said, "Remember back when we were kids and we used to argue about competition? You used to say there was nothing wrong with a little healthy competition, and I said you were just an unrepentant jock, and competition led to wars and other sundry miseries?" Tucker answered him with a grim stare. "Well, you'll be happy to know I've come around to your way of thinking. And to prove that I'm willing to compete, I'm going to go after Harley. May the best man win."

"How come, all of the sudden, after six months, you want *her?*"

"How come, all of the sudden, *you* want her?" Phil countered. "Yesterday she was 'just the house sitter.' Now you've suddenly staked a claim."

"You hardly even know her."

"And you do? When did you meet her? Two, three days ago? And what makes you think she'd want anything to do with you, anyway? You know, I hate to point this out, but on the one hand here's this nice, sweet girl, an M.B.A. candidate and all, and on the other hand . . ." He gave Tucker the once-over and shrugged.

"I'm not a serial killer," Tucker pointed out.

"You're not a doctor or lawyer, either, which is probably what she's in the market for." He grinned cockily. "Doctor is my guess." Tucker snorted. "Seriously, does she know anything about you? Does she know your history? Does she know about . . . Well, does she know about Miami?"

Tucker sighed with irritation. Phil was bringing out the heavy ammo now. "What, are you threatening to tell her?"

"All's fair in love and war. It would tip the scales in my favor, that's for sure. She seems like a pretty straight arrow. A criminal record is a real turnoff to a girl like that."

Tucker gripped the cane with a white-knuckled fist. "I can't believe you'd actually—"

"Hey, relax." Phil stood and gave Tucker a friendly whack on the arm. "I wouldn't. Which is not to say I won't play dirty. I just won't play *that* dirty."

A woman's voice from the beach called, "Phil?" and the two men turned to look. Mimi, in a white beach cover-up now, walked toward the boulder stairway. "Phil Zelin?"

"Oh, that's Mimi Tilton," Phil said, and waved.

"You know each other?" Tucker asked as Mimi climbed up to them.

Phil smiled at her. "She's in the Historical Society with Kitty. Nice girl. Awfully young for widowhood, but it seems to suit her. While her husband was alive, she always looked kind of tired, but in the past year she's really bloomed."

Mimi joined them. When Phil introduced her to Tucker, she extended her hand and said, "So you're the black sheep I've been hearing so much about. You'll have to tell me which version of your death comes closest to the truth."

Tucker laughed, appreciating her candor and wit. She reminded him of Liz; not in appearance—she was slender, black-haired, and no more than twenty-five—but she had the self-possession of an older woman.

"Here you are," said Mimi, and Tucker turned to see Harley approaching. "I was worried about you. Jamie said you didn't run yesterday, and it's the first day you've missed."

Explanations were made, and Mimi cluck-clucked and promised to bring over a casserole later—the first time Tucker could remember having heard such an offer being made in Hale's Point.

Mimi said, "So, Tucker, it's a shame R.H. turned out to be gone when you got here. What are your plans now? Will you stay the summer anyway, or do you have obligations elsewhere?"

Phil answered for him. "He's got a business to look after, Mimi. He couldn't afford to take the whole summer off."

"Actually," Tucker corrected, "my top pilot's been running the business for a year now, and doing a damn good job of it. She wants me to sell it to her, and I'm thinking about it."

"*She?*" Phil said.

"Molly Little. Best pilot I've ever worked with. It's the nineties, pal," said Tucker.

"So, stay," Mimi said. "I'm sure Harley wouldn't mind."

Harley glanced from Mimi to the ground, and then looked up and met Tucker's eyes. He thought she would look away again, but she held his gaze.

Phil said, "Business or no business, that's just not Tucker's style, Mimi. A rolling stone like him? My guess is he'll be gone by sunrise tomorrow."

Harley still had not looked away from him. To Phil and Mimi, her expression probably appeared completely neutral, but Tucker saw something in it that surprised and pleased him. That distance, that safe remoteness that had always been there when she looked at him, had vanished. He realized that he had not been consciously aware of it up till now. Its presence had been subtle, like a haze in the sky that doesn't really register until it clears and the sun shines, bright and powerful.

Phil said, "Isn't that right, Tucker? Tucker?"

Tucker looked from Phil's irritated sneer to Mimi's knowing smile. "Actually, I, uh, I was thinking of staying on. Till R.H. comes back at the end of the summer, anyway. That is, of course, if Harley wouldn't—"

Harley's smile transformed her into a creature of extraordinary beauty. "Of course, I wouldn't mind. Please stay."

Tucker took a deep breath. "All right. That would be great. Thanks. I'll try not to get in your way. I'll pay for half the groceries and I'll split the housework with you fifty-fifty."

Phil guffawed. "*You're* going to do half the housework? I'm sorry, but I have a hard time picturing Mr. Bush Pilot Tough Guy in a frilly apron, pushing a broom across the floor."

"I've lived on my own for twenty years," Tucker said. "Trust me, I can push a broom with the best of them. Only the apron's leather, and there are pockets for my power tools."

"Do you cook, too?" Mimi asked.

"Just bear meat."

Harley said, "I don't mind doing the cooking."

"No, I'll do the cooking," Tucker said. "That's really not a problem."

"I don't mind. Really," she insisted.

"Neither do I. In fact, I'd prefer if you'd let me."

The exchange was interrupted by excited voices from the beach. They all looked down to see Lily squatting at the edge of the water, dipping Mimi's book purposefully in and out of the waves. Jamie and Brenna hovered over her, he laughing, she wringing her hands.

"I'm sorry, missus," Brenna called up.

Mimi groaned, but managed a smile. "I'd better go down and supervise. Ever since I got an au pair to help out, I haven't had a second's peace." She waved goodbye and descended the boulder stairway.

Phil said, "I'd like to go down there, too. I've been wanting to take a walk on the beach, but I want company. Harley—would you join me?"

She said, "Do you think I should? After the heatstroke?"

"As far as I'm concerned," Phil said, "if you feel up to it, you should do it. You'll know if it's too much. Besides, I'll be there if you start to feel sick."

She shrugged. "All right."

Phil shot a triumphant look in Tucker's direction, then added, "Too bad Tucker can't join us, but given his handicap, any kind of strenuous activity's pretty much out of the question."

Tucker rolled his eyes. "You *don't* play fair," he growled as Harley turned away and headed for the drop-off to the beach.

Phil grinned puckishly. "I warned you." He followed Harley to the beach.

Tucker lit another cigarette and watched them pick their way down to the shore. Phil assisted Harley with a hand on her arm, which probably served no purpose other than to slow her down, but annoyed the hell out of Tucker—no doubt Phil's sole intent.

Tucker reflected on that surprising openness in Harley's expression, which had turned out to be temporary. As quickly as it had come, it was gone, replaced by the old familiar distance.

He expelled a stream of smoke in a long sigh. It had been like a brief, unexpected thaw in the middle of January. It tantalized you with its warmth and then the cold set in again. The only thing that kept you going through the rest of the winter was the eventual promise of spring.

6

"TUCKER HALE HAS MARCHED to a different drummer from a very young age," Liz said.

Harley shifted the receiver to the other ear and turned her head to listen for sounds in the hallway outside the closed door to the study, but all she could hear was the light rain that had just begun pattering against the windows. Tucker was presumably in the kitchen, making a salad to go with the lasagna Mimi had brought over, but he might start wondering where she was and come looking for her. It would not be good for him to overhear her talking on the phone about him.

"He thinks, and will tell you, that his rebellion began at sixteen." Liz spoke the way learned people write, in complete and well-thought-out sentences, with no awkward pauses, not even the occasional "uh" or "um." She spoke slowly, and with a pronounced Hale's Point drawl that made her sound almost British.

"In fact," Liz continued, "he's been something of a wild card since much earlier—since the age of eleven, to be precise."

Liz loved to be precise—it was in the nature of statisticians, Harley acknowledged—but still . . . "Since the age of eleven?" Harley asked. "How did you pick that age?"

"I didn't just pick it," Liz snapped, and Harley realized belatedly what an insult that would be to a woman who had spent her career quantifying facts in order to prove how factual they were.

"I know, Liz," Harley began. "I didn't mean—"

"Tucker was eleven years old when he found out that his mother committed suicide," Liz said. "He hasn't been the same since."

It took several seconds for the older woman's words to sink in. Harley sat perfectly still with the phone to her ear, mentally replaying the words over and over to make sure she had heard them right: *His mother committed suicide... His mother committed suicide....* She was still a little dazed from the heatstroke, but she didn't think she had heard wrong.

Liz's voice snapped her out of it. "Harley? Dear?"

She said the words out loud. "His mother committed suicide?"

"Yes, of course. I assumed you knew."

"No. I knew she had died. When he was five, he said."

"It was suicide," Liz stated with finality. "Of course, he wasn't told the truth. He was deemed too young. R.H. told him her appendix had burst. Still, it affected him profoundly. He was despondent for quite some time. As he got older, I begged R.H. to tell him what really happened before he found out on his own, but unfortunately he didn't take my advice."

"How did he find out?"

"When he was eleven, he stumbled across her death certificate. The cause of death was asphyxiation by hanging."

Harley felt as if she had been kicked softly in the stomach. All the air went out of her lungs. "My God," she whispered.

There was a pause at the other end. Harley could sense Liz's puzzlement. "It does happen, my dear. People do kill themselves. It's a sad fact of life."

"I know," Harley said quickly. "I know. I just..." She closed her eyes and saw the darkly beautiful Anjelica as she appeared in the photograph on Tucker's desk, and the baby in her arms, the baby with her eyes. "Why? Why did she... Why would she—"

Liz's words were measured. "My understanding is that she was unhappy in her marriage."

Another face materialized over Anjelica's, also young, also sad-eyed, but fair and pale—Jennifer Sayers, Harley's mother. She rubbed her eyes to dispel the image.

"When Tucker found out," Liz continued, "he took complete leave of his senses. Children that age are notoriously irrational, especially the male of the species. He came to the conclusion that R.H. was responsible for her suicide, that he somehow drove her to it. He was also furious at having been misled for so many years about the cause of her death." She sighed. "He never did regain his trust in his father, and from then on, he pretty much went his own way."

"Which brings us around to his leaving home twenty years ago—"

"Twenty-one," Liz corrected.

"Twenty-one, and suddenly showing up now. Which, in turn, brings us around to the reason I called. Would R.H. approve of his staying on here for the summer? I pretty much invited him to stay, and I certainly don't want to have to take back the invitation, but this is R.H.'s home. If I have to, I will."

"You must understand, my dear, that in personal matters, R.H. has not always exercised the best judgment."

Harley marveled at Liz's diplomacy while deeply regretting the meaning behind the smooth words: R.H. would not want Tucker to stay.

"Therefore," Liz continued, "I suggest that you rephrase the question in order to inquire whether *I* would approve of Tucker's staying on."

"Oh." Was this strictly ethical? Harley quickly searched her conscience and concluded that it was close enough. "Then, is it all right with *you* if he stays?"

"But of course, my dear! I'm delighted if he stays! Tucker's happiness means more to me than my own. He's the son I never had."

"Oh. Good."

Several muted electronic beeps came from Liz's end of the line. "And now, if you will excuse me, it appears that my microwave has finished wreaking havoc with the molecules in my frozen veal marsala. Goodbye."

Harley dropped the receiver back in its cradle, slumped down in R.H.'s leather swivel chair, and rubbed her hands over her face.

His mother had committed suicide. She supposed she could have told Liz why that information had stunned her so, but although she liked Liz very much, their friendship had never been on that personal a level.

She uncovered her eyes. The study was a masculine enclave of leather, wood, and books, dappled with rain-silvered light from a big, multipaned window. Directly across from her, behind a tufted green leather couch on a table all its own, sat a large, exquisitely detailed model of a sailboat. Harley recognized it as an oversize twin of the one Tucker had been handling the other day in his room upstairs. It had been crafted of varnished wood with canvas sails, and she could tell from the scale that the boat it represented was a large one. It had two masts and four sails, and the word *Anjelica* was painted across the stern in neat maroon letters.

She looked at the two photographs on the desk, the photographs of Tucker, wondering why R.H. had kept them there, given their estrangement: the happy, clean-cut young boy at the wheel of the *Anjelica* and the worldly, disenfranchised teenager with the sailplane. Before and after.

She rose and walked around the room. The walls were covered in mustard-colored silk and crowded with framed pictures, a good half of them drawings or photographs of the

Anjelica. She knelt backward on the couch in order to face the model, and ran a finger along the hull. It was a beautiful piece of work.

The door opened and she jumped.

"Did I startle you?" Tucker said. "Sorry. The lasagna comes out in twenty minutes." He sat on the arm of the couch and nodded toward the model. "My father and I made that. I was seven or eight, I guess. It took months."

"It's beautiful."

"So's the original. The real *Anjelica.* She's an incredible boat. A forty-foot schooner, custom-made. The most perfect boat I've ever seen."

"Your father told me it was the *Anjelica* he'd be sailing in the Caribbean this summer, he and a friend of his, one of his retired law partners."

"She's a lot of boat for two men that age to handle alone. I'm glad to hear he's still sailing her, though. I'd wondered if she was still around—she's about thirty years old. But he always did take real good care of her." He reached over to touch one of the sails.

"I don't know much about these things, but are they going to actually *live* on it?"

"On *her.* Of course."

"And they'll be comfortable?"

He chuckled. "When he had her built, he was extremely particular about the living quarters. They're better-appointed than most people's homes."

"Did he have it—*her*—built for your mother? I mean, he did name her the *Anjelica.*"

His eyes grew opaque. "He built her after she—after she died."

"After?"

He was staring at the model. "He became obsessed with her after she was gone—when it was too late. If he'd paid that much attention to her while she was alive, she probably never would have . . ." His jaw clenched. "But that's in the nature of marriage, isn't it?"

She turned around, tossed her sandals off, and sat with her back against the other arm of the couch, legs stretched out and crossed. "What do you mean?"

He shrugged. "I mean, it's kind of a perverse institution, isn't it? You take two people who are madly in love, then they get married, and nine times out of ten, it goes sour. My parents were typical. The things he loved about her, that made her so different, suddenly looked like flaws that needed fixing. He took a quirky, artistic, impulsive Greek girl and tried to turn her into an uptight Hale's Point matron."

"Mimi's not uptight."

"She's the exception," he said.

"Do you really believe nine out of ten marriages are like that?"

Tucker kicked off his moccasins and slid down so that he was sitting against the opposite arm from Harley. He stretched his good leg out adjacent to hers, then lifted his bad leg next to it. The hair on his right leg softly tickled her left leg from thigh to ankle. "Enough of them are so you have to wonder why any sensible person would ever want to do it. The facts argue loud and clear against it. Marriage is for people who can't think straight."

"And you, of course, are a straight-thinking, sensible person."

"Absolutely."

"Much too sensible to be influenced by one bad marriage—your parents'—into condemning marriage as a whole."

Again he shrugged. "We are the sum total of our experiences. Our characters are forged in fires we didn't build, and there's little we can do to change them. Or, as Popeye so succinctly put it, 'I yam what I yam and that's what I yam.'"

She stared at him. "Popeye."

He grinned. "I don't just quote Thoreau, you know. I'm a well-rounded guy."

"You *are* well-rounded. Ridiculously well-rounded. That's a wonderful thing, and it's thanks to your father that you turned out that way. It was all his doing, you know. He wasn't all bad."

"He was just trying to make me like him. It backfired on him, though. We couldn't be more different."

"Except for this thing about boats, planes, and cars. You've both kind of got a fetish about machines that take you places."

He nodded grudgingly. "Boats especially." He turned to look again at the model of the *Anjelica*, and sighed. "I wouldn't want to be my father—I could never live my life the way he lives his. But I'll tell you, right now I'd trade places with him in a second. Sailing from port to port, dropping anchor occasionally to fish or swim or eat, then off again." He gazed at the model, but seemed to be looking at something very far away. "There's nothing better than a long sailing trip. It's the most relaxing thing in the world, *and* the most exciting, if you can imagine that. I'd give anything to be spending the summer that way." He looked at her. "Do you like to sail?"

She laughed. "I've never been on a sailboat."

He looked surprised. "Never? Not even once, the whole time you were growing up? You must have known somebody who owned a boat."

"There isn't a lot of room for forty-foot schooners in a trailer park, Tucker."

"I've made progress," he said. "I found out you lived in a trailer park."

Harley looked at the raindrops battering the window and made the decision to talk about the things she never talked about.

"It was ... I don't know how to describe it." The raindrops looked like hundreds of silver bubbles on the glass. "It was pretty low-end as those places go. A shantytown, really. Nothing more than a couple of dozen rusted-out old metal trailers on blocks in a field outside Dayton."

Just thinking about it made her throat tighten instantly. Maybe he could hear it in her voice. She looked at him. There was curiosity in his eyes—he undoubtedly wondered why she was suddenly willing to open up like this—but concern, also.

"The field was nothing but weeds and dirt," she continued. "There was this mountain of tires nearby, and that was our playground, the kids who lived there."

"Did you have any brothers or sisters?"

She shook her head. "It was just my mother and me. My father was long gone."

"Were they divorced?"

"I'm not even sure they were ever married, not legally. My mother used to tell me that someone named Swami Bob had officiated at some kind of ceremony in the desert somewhere. She wore a white sari, and my father wore cutoffs and a Harley-Davidson T-shirt. Supposedly they exchanged homemade vows and then chewed peyote and chanted and howled all night. Only I'm not sure whether that really happened or she just ... kind of made it happen in her head."

"Ah."

"'Ah' indeed."

"What did she do?" he asked. "Did she work?"

"She drank."

He waited for her to go on and then said, "She must have done *something* else."

"You're right—she took pills."

His big hand wrapped itself around her calf, and he shook his head. "Sorry," he said softly.

"The thing was, she was really sweet when she was sober. She *wanted* to be a good mother, and sometimes she tried real hard, but she was very young and completely aimless. I didn't love her any less because she tried and failed—maybe I even loved her more."

Tucker nodded encouragement, and Harley went on. "But when she wasn't sober—which was most of the time—she was just hopeless. I had this one little corner of the trailer that was all mine, and I kept it superneat. I tried to keep the rest of it picked up, too, but it was like living with a . . . a child, who had no sense of order or responsibility. I'd clean up in the morning and leave for school—I loved school, school was my salvation—and when I came home, I'd be wading through overturned ashtrays and dirty dishes and bags of pot and beer cans and piles of clothes and God-knows-what, halfway to the ceiling. And Mom would always be facedown on her bed, asleep."

"Did your father know how you were living?"

"He was off doing his biker thing, he didn't have a clue. I didn't even know what he looked like till . . . till I was nine."

"He came back?"

"He had to." She took a deep, shaky breath. "I came home from school one day . . . it was early May, and I was so happy, 'cause it was the first really warm day of the year. And the first thing I noticed when I walked into the trailer was this . . . this smell. I tried to wake up Mom to ask her what the smell was. I rolled her over, and—" Her voice caught in her throat, and her eyes burned with sudden tears. Tucker's eyes were enormous, his face ashen. She looked toward the window again, at the rivulets meandering down the glass.

She swallowed hard and continued. "Her face—" She swallowed again. There were some things she couldn't bring herself to relive. "The coroner said she'd been dead for four or five hours."

Hot tears spilled down her cheeks, and she covered her face with her hands and drew her knees up. She felt him shift position on the couch, and then he was beside her and around her, taking her in his arms, murmuring, "Shh, that's all right." He dried her tears with the hem of his T-shirt. She nestled into him, letting him stroke her hair and back until she felt limp.

"She did it on purpose," Harley said. "Barbiturates and alcohol. There was no note, but every single one of her pill bottles was empty. They were scattered on the floor around her, and she was lying on top of a half-full bottle of Southern Comfort."

She glanced up at him; he looked stricken. Laying her head against his chest again, she continued. "They sent me to a foster home, and then a couple of months later my father showed up—God knows how they found him—and threw me on the back of his Harley and took off with me. I spent ten months with him, on the road."

He absently stroked the nape of her neck. "You didn't go to school?"

"No, and that was the worst part of it. I loved school. My father was a stranger to me, and his friends scared me. People—regular people in towns we would go to—used to look at me, all dirty and ragged, and you could see it in their eyes, the pity and disgust. I thought it couldn't get any worse, and then I realized how he was supporting us. He was dealing grass and pills out of the saddlebags on the Harley. Not only was he a criminal, he was trafficking in the stuff that had killed my mother. I was horrified. Inside I was just a normal little kid, and I wanted my life to be normal. I'd look at other little kids, kids who had regular families and lived in houses, and I'd feel overwhelmed with envy. Despair, too, because I knew that kind of life would never happen for me—at least not until I was a grown-up and could make it happen."

He nodded again. Quietly he said, "Things do have a way of falling into place." He kissed the top of her head.

"Anyway, eventually my father was busted. It happened in Fort Worth, Texas, and they threw the book at him. He went to jail, and I went from one foster home to another. I won't bore you with the details. It was not a pleasant adolescence."

"How did you turn things around? How did you end up at Columbia?"

"Sheer force of will and about a hundred part-time jobs, plus the odd scholarship. I managed."

"Good for you. You should feel very proud of yourself. Whatever happened to your father?"

"Two weeks after he got out of jail, he was killed in a knife fight outside a bar in Oakland, California." He shook his head. "R.H. doesn't look half-bad by comparison, does he?"

He gave a long sigh. "No, I'm afraid he still looks pretty bad. There are things about him..." His gaze fell on the model of the *Anjelica*. "Your father destroyed himself. My father destroyed my mother. She killed herself, too. Did you know that?"

Harley nodded against his chest. "Liz told me just now. I called her. I—I wanted to make sure it was okay for you to stay."

"I was going to suggest that you do that, just to put your mind at ease. Did she tell you why my mother committed suicide?"

"She said it was an unhappy marriage."

He grunted dismissively. "Liz Wycliff, High Priestess of the Understatement. To R.H. it was an unhappy marriage. To my mother, it was a nightmare. Laura Tilton—the second Mrs. Tilton—was a close friend of my mother's, her confidante.

When I found out that my mother had died by suicide, I asked her to tell me why. She said the seeds were sown before my parents even met. Turns out she was already engaged, to a young cousin of hers named Anatole. The family had encouraged the marriage—practically arranged it—in order to unite certain business enterprises."

"What a cold-blooded reason to get married. She must have been dreading it."

"On the contrary, she was deeply in love with him, and he with her. They had grown up together, they were soul mates. She was a painter, he was a sculptor. They were going to let other people run the family businesses while they pursued their art."

Harley chewed this over. "Soul mates . . . I don't get it."

"You mean, why did she marry R.H.?" Harley nodded. "He swept her off her feet. He has a very commanding personality, and she was susceptible to it. She had a . . . a passionate nature. Lots of creative people are like that—emotional, impulsive. Of course, like I said before, it's the only impulsive thing *he* ever did."

"So she found herself in love with two men. She had to choose, and she chose R.H."

Grimly he said, "She chose wrong. From the moment she moved in here, her life was a misery. He didn't want her to paint, and he severed her contacts in the New York art world so she wouldn't have a career to distract her from hearth and home. He was busy with his law practice and didn't have much time for her. With what little time he had, he tried to remake her into a proper Hale's Point wife. He told her how to dress and what to order in restaurants. He told her how to make acceptable small talk. He monitored the books she read, the places she went, and the friends she spent time with. Laura Tilton was the only one they could agree on. She had no one else to confide in. Her father disowned her when she married R.H., and she never had any contact with her family after that."

"Then you came along."

"About five years into the marriage. I'd like to think I provided some comfort to her, but the truth is, I only made things worse. Soon after I was born, she started getting letters from Anatole. Secretly—he used a false name on the return address. He said he'd never stopped loving her, and he begged her to leave R.H. and marry him. She never returned his letters, although she shut herself up in her room and cried every time one came. She told Laura Tilton that she had responsibilities now. She had a baby, and was under an obligation to try and make the marriage work. So she toughed it out. Hale's Point syndrome is catching, you know. Of course, it was the worst thing she could have done."

"You're saying she should have bolted?"

"Absolutely. For five years Anatole wrote to her, but she never wrote back. She started hearing from friends in Europe that he was becoming self-destructive, drinking too much, doing reckless things. One day she got a phone call. He had driven his Lamborghini off the side of a mountain road in the Swiss Alps, and died."

"Oh, no."

"She sank into a deep depression. A week later she checked into a motel on the expressway and hanged herself with a length of sailing line. She didn't leave a note, but two days after that, Liz Wycliff received a letter from her, mailed the day she killed herself, asking her to look after me."

"Did she know how Liz felt about your father?"

"Undoubtedly. Everyone did." After a pause, he said, "You realize the only thing you and I have in common—aside from being driven, which we agreed on the other night, right?— the only other thing is that our mothers committed suicide. That's a heck of a comment."

"You're right," she said. "That's terrible. There must be something else."

"Name something." She couldn't. A bemused chuckle shook his chest. "Pretty scary, isn't it?"

They lay together quietly for a while, the only sound in the room the insistent pattering of raindrops on the window. They had settled together naturally and unselfconsciously, arms and legs comfortably intertwined. He continued to lazily stroke her hair, and she closed her eyes, thinking, *I could fall asleep like this.* Marveling at her ability to relax so completely in the arms of a virtual stranger, she realized it was because *he* was relaxed. He was a very physical person, touching her whenever the spirit moved him, taking for granted that it was okay to do so. From another man such familiarity might have seemed threatening, but Tucker had a kind of sincerity that put her at ease.

From the direction of the kitchen came the droning buzz of the oven timer. Tucker groaned. Harley began to disentangle her limbs from his, but he didn't budge.

"Let it ring," he said.

"I can't stand that noise."

He wrapped his arms around her and pulled her down on top of him. "I can live with it." He cupped the back of her head with his big hand, brought her face close to his, and gave her a quick but enthusiastic kiss.

She looked down at him. "The lasagna will burn," she said.

"Then you can make some gray stuff to take its place." His arms surrounded her, holding her tight.

"You're willing to eat gray stuff just so you can stay here with me?"

"Yes!" He loosened his grip to move his hands down to the small of her back, pressing her to him. When she felt his fingers slip beneath the waistband of her shorts, she pulled away and stood.

"Well, I'm not." She offered him a hand, which he took.

"You've got a hard heart," he said, gaining his feet and looking around for his cane.

"I've got an empty stomach. You're trying to keep me from my dinner. *You're* the one with the hard heart."

He followed her as she headed for the kitchen, and she thought she heard him mumble, "Right idea, wrong organ."

"What?"

"Nothing."

7

"YES, I *AM!*" Harley gave Mimi's lasagna pan one last scrub with the Brillo pad, rinsed it under the tap, and handed it to Tucker.

"No, you're *not!*" He dried the pan with quick, angry strokes and slammed it down on the counter next to the sink.

She felt around in the soapy water with a rubber-gloved hand—no more dishes, they'd done them all—and pulled out the drain plug. The gloves made a wonderfully angry snap when she peeled them off, the better to punctuate her wrath.

Wheeling to face him, she said, "Just because we're going to be living in the same house doesn't give you the right to run my life, like some kind of overbearing, know-it-all..." What was the word she was looking for?

"Paternalistic," he supplied.

"Paternalistic, full-of-himself, know-it-all..."

He leaned on the counter and grinned at her. "You're repeating yourself."

"*You* know what I mean!"

"God, you're beautiful. You *glow* with indignation."

She wasn't going to let him charm her out of her anger. "Phil said if I felt up to it, I should do it."

"He was talking about a walk on the beach, not swimming."

"He meant any physical activity. I need *some* kind of exercise, and I love my evening swim. Now that the rain has stopped, I intend to take it."

Tucker rubbed at his neck. "Look, I know you don't re-member yesterday very well, but you were very, very sick. I don't think it's a good idea to swim—not for a while."

"A doctor of internal medicine let me climb down to the beach and take a pretty long walk this afternoon."

He rolled his eyes. "That doctor of internal medicine hap-pens to have ulterior motives."

"Oh, please. First Jamie, now Phil. You think every man who knows me has designs on me, just because... be-cause—"

He leaned his cane against the counter and moved closer. "Because *I* have designs on you? I know what you think. You think I'm panting after you like a hungry wolf, that I'd do anything to get you into bed."

She took a step back and felt the sink behind her. "No, I don't."

He quickly closed in on her. "Well, I am, and I would." He took her face in his hands and kissed her, deeply and pas-sionately. When he released her, she gasped for air, and he murmured, "Anything. Just tell me what it'll take."

"You're *crazy!* Men don't just come out and *say* things like that. They, they finesse you, they—"

"Buy you flowers and take you to dinner and spend a lot of money on you and bring you home and turn off the lights and turn on some tunes and engineer some ridiculously ob-vious seduction, all the while pretending they're madly in love with you, and a month later you're history. Right?"

"I take it you're more into dragging them by their hair into the nearest cave. Right?"

He stood with hands on hips. "At least it's honest."

"And they're still going to end up history, only probably the next morning, not the next month, because you're heavi-ly into bolting. Am I on target?"

A slight pause on his part. "Pretty much."

She crossed her arms, looked down at the wide-planked floor, and shook her head. "The thing is, I know why you're coming on to me like this, and it doesn't have anything to do with me, really. I just happen to be the only woman around, and you're . . . Well, you know, you spent a year 'out of circulation,' as you called it, and you're—"

"Horny." She shrugged and nodded. He leaned toward her, one hand on the sink while the other lifted her chin, tilting her face toward his. She thought he was going to kiss her again, but he didn't. He just looked at her, his expression open and direct. "You're wrong," he said. His tone had lost its jocularity; he was quiet and sincere. "I don't just want a woman. I want you. Mimi and Brenna are attractive women, but they don't do anything at all for me. You do." He withdrew his hand, but she still didn't move her head; she couldn't take her eyes off his. "Frankly, that surprises me. You're fourteen years younger than I am, you're going for your M.B.A., and you iron your blue jeans, for God's sake. I wouldn't be surprised if you were a registered Republican."

"I *am* a registered Republican."

He blinked. "You *are?*"

"I thought you said it wouldn't surprise you."

"I lied."

She smiled. "I thought you said you never lied."

"You're a Republican? Really?"

"Yes. I am a member of the Republican Party. Not the American Nazi Party and not the Ku Klux Klan. The party of Abraham Lincoln. What's so wrong with that?"

"It's just that I never lusted after a Republican before. Not knowingly, anyway."

"Well, there's a first time for everything. Now, if you'll excuse me, I'm going to go change for my swim."

Exasperation clouded his features. "Harley...damn it. All right. All right. You can swim."

"Thanks for the permission, boss. I'll never forget this."

"But only with me there."

She swept past him, heading upstairs to change. "Are you going to swim, too?"

"Not a chance. I'll act as lifeguard. I'm very good at mouth-to-mouth resuscitation. Want a demonstration?"

"Not a chance," she echoed over her shoulder, grinning.

"Can't fault me for trying," he mumbled.

TUCKER RECLINED IN THE dark on a chaise longue, drawing slowly on his cigarette as he watched Harley's sleek form glide toward him beneath the water, brightly lit by underwater pool lamps. When she reached a point about ten feet from the end of the pool, she surfaced, skimming both hands back from her hairline to smooth down the slick tresses.

Tonight her swimsuit was a wisp of burgundy Lycra that clung to her as if it had been painted on. It was cut low front and back, and the whole thing was held up—rather tenuously, he thought—by spaghetti straps tied in bows on her shoulders. Suits like that were designed with bodies like hers in mind, he decided. He watched, mesmerized, as, head back and eyes closed, she twisted her hair to wring the pool water out of it.

Some might think her boyish, with her small breasts and slim hips. Tucker thought her anything but. Yes, she was strong and athletic, and no, she would never win any Dolly Parton look-alike contests. But she was incredibly nubile and, to his way of thinking, intensely female.

She stood waist-deep in the water and looked at him, and her pure, unadorned beauty took his breath away. The water's phosphorescent glow reflected onto her in quivering waves of light. With her gold-green eyes and sleek bronze hair, she looked like a virgin goddess emerging from the sea.

"Join me," she said.

Her words inspired an instant physical reaction in him that took him completely by surprise. Words—such innocent words, at any rate—had never done that to him before. To cover his speechlessness, he drew on the cigarette again, then tapped it into the jar lid he held in his other hand.

He cleared his throat. "Haven't we already had this conversation?"

She took a couple of slow-motion steps toward him in the water. "Come on. Let me see if you can swim a lap."

"Look, Harley, I'll save us both a lot of effort. I can't swim a lap. End of story."

"How do you know? You haven't tried."

He stabbed the cigarette into the lid. "Trust me, I know what my body's capable of."

"You don't have a clue what your body's capable of if you haven't even tried. I'd have a lot more respect for you if you tried and failed than if you didn't even give it a shot. That's like giving up without a fight."

He chuckled. "No offense, but that's a pretty lame excuse for inspiration. Your friend Eve what's-her-name had the right idea. What did she tell them? 'Catch me and you can have me?' *That's* motivation."

"Would that work with you?"

He met her eyes and smiled. "Try it and see."

There was a pause. She looked down at the bright water for a moment, and then she looked up and said, "All right. Catch me and you can have me."

He studied her eyes, trying to read her intent. "You're not serious," he concluded.

Her eyebrows drew together. "I'm always serious. And I always do—"

"What you say you're going to do," he finished. "Yeah, but . . . I know. You've got some loophole, some way of getting out of it if I catch you. That's exactly the kind of thing they teach you in business school."

"No loophole," she said. "Catch me and you can have me."

"'Have me,' meaning . . ."

"Have me for the night."

"For the purpose of . . ."

"For any purpose you want, although I've got a pretty good idea what that purpose will be. Even virgins aren't that dense."

He said, "Yeah, now that you mention that, are you sure you want to make deals like this, given your . . . lack of experience?"

"If it doesn't bother you, it doesn't bother me."

"Why would it bother me? Down through history, men have paid top dollar for virgins. And here I'll be getting one for the price of a lap."

"First of all, it's the nineties, and take it from me, virgins are no longer in such hot demand."

He allowed himself a slow smile. "Call me old-fashioned."

"Second, what makes you think you'll be getting me at all? By your own admission, you can't even swim a lap."

"Ah."

"Ah," she mocked.

He sat up and used his cane to help him stand. "Yeah, but like you said, how do I really know if I haven't tried?" He dropped the cane onto the chaise and whipped his T-shirt over his head. Tossing the shirt aside, he ran his hands through his hair, noting with amusement Harley's nonplussed expression. "So how does this work?"

"'This'? Oh, uh . . . why don't we just do it the way Eve did with her vets? You start at the shallow end, against the wall. I start at the drop-off to the deep end. When I say, 'Go,' we swim one lap. If you catch me before I touch the deck at the deep end . . . well, then—" she shrugged and spread her arms in offering "—one virginity, yours for the taking."

"Freestyle okay with you?"

"Whatever stroke suits your fancy."

"Mmm-hmm." He squatted at the edge of the pool. "You'll have a pretty big lead on me."

"You get to push off the wall," she told him. "You'll make up most of it that way."

He grimaced, trying to picture using his bad leg to push off the wall. "Right." Stepping out of his moccasins, he sat at the edge of the pool and lowered himself into the water. It was cold but not too bad. His baggy shorts were instantly waterlogged; they would weigh him down. He started undoing the fly. "Mind if I lose these?"

She glared at him. *"Yes!"*

He held up a placating hand as he rezipped with the other. "Just wanted to see you angry. For inspiration."

Who was he kidding, doing this? His trophy days were long past. Harley could swim circles around him. He honestly didn't know what he'd been thinking of, agreeing to this. It would be an exercise in humiliation.

"Ready?" Harley had moved to the drop-off, and stood facing him. He sighed and nodded.

She turned around. "One . . ."

He braced his good leg against the wall.

"Two . . ." She positioned her arms. Shaking his head, he did the same.

"Three. . ." She glanced back at him. As soon as he saw her face, he knew, hopeless or not, that he had to give it his all. He had to try. He had to have her. Against his better judgment, he braced his bad leg next to the good one for extra power in the push-off.

"Go!"

Her feet sprang up behind her and she flutter-kicked forward as Tucker pushed away from the wall. In his competition days, he'd shoot a good third of the length of the pool before he had to start stroking. This time, he made it just a few yards.

The pain—in his chest as well as his leg—began the moment he left the wall. He willed it from his conscious thought, as he had trained himself to do, but it wasn't easy. Every stroke, every kick, renewed it. His form was abominable, not only because of the pain, but because critical muscle groups in his left leg and chest were all but useless. Almost immediately he knew that there was no way he could possibly catch her. Lifting his head to take a breath, he saw her, reaching out to touch the deck at the deep end. He had only just entered the deep end.

Disgusted, he came to a stop and trod water, but that hurt almost as much as swimming. When she looked over her shoulder at him, he turned away and glided to the side of the pool. He held on to the deck and realized he was slightly winded, despite the brevity of the swim. He never used to get winded when he swam as a teenager. But he never used to smoke back then, either, except for the occasional Marlboro he and Phil would sneak from his dad.

Would he even be able to push himself up onto the deck, or would he have to use the steps? He growled a raw oath before he realized that Harley was coming up behind him.

She hung on to the deck next to him. "I don't generally hear you swear very much," she said. "Except for the occasional 'damn.'"

His smile was more of a grimace. "It's an absurd souvenir from my Hale's Point upbringing. I don't like to swear in front of women."

"I don't think it's absurd. I think it's sweet."

"Sweet?" Laughing wearily, he said, "I'm doomed. Not only am I a physical wreck and completely unlucky in love, now I'm sweet."

She said, "You made it halfway. That's not bad."

"How much of you do I get for halfway?"

"Well, none."

"Then it *is* bad."

He decided he had rested his body enough to try to get out of the pool. Pushing with both arms against the deck and grunting with the effort, he made it in one try, to his immense relief. Sitting on the deck, he felt something in his back pocket, groaned, pulled out his wallet, and shook its sodden contents out onto the concrete. His money, snapshots, licenses, and business cards were completely soaked and would have to be spread out somewhere to dry, or else discarded. Ironically, the only unaffected items were the ones he had the least use for: the two little square packets labeled Trojan. He noticed Harley's gaze linger on the condoms for a moment and then flick away. He stuffed everything back into the wallet, replaced it in his pocket, and leaned over to massage the aching muscles of his left leg.

"Are you in pain?"

"Don't worry about it."

"I didn't want this to hurt you," she said, her voice small. "Or depress you. I just wanted to inspire you. Maybe I'm just not as inspirational as Eve Markham—"

"Oh, honey..." A tendril of hair hung across her eyes, and he leaned over to tuck it behind her ear. "You are very inspirational. Trust me, my effort was heroic, even if the results weren't."

She propelled herself out of the water with fluid ease and sat next to him. After a few moments of silence, she wrapped her arms around her updrawn knees and said, "Maybe you'll have better luck tomorrow."

She was staring off toward the diving board. He strained to meet her eyes, then finally just took her by the chin and turned her head to face him. "Tomorrow? You want to do this again tomorrow?"

"Sure. This is supposed to be physical therapy for you. That's not just a one-shot deal, you know that. Improvement takes time. I figured we could do this every day, during my evening swim."

He searched her eyes. He was certain that she had originally intended this as a one-time-only challenge. "Why are you doing this? Really."

She seemed to be choosing her words carefully. "I want you to get better. Really. I like you. You've been good to me. You took care of me yesterday when I was sick. Let's just say I'm paying you back."

"Yeah, but aren't you concerned that I'll catch you and you'll have to pay up? Are you really willing to go that far in the interests of my rehabilitation?"

"Maybe I'm just dead sure you'll never catch me," she said smugly.

"Maybe you're dead wrong."

"Maybe I am. But don't worry. I know a deal's a deal. If I lose, I'll pay up."

"Do you really consider it losing?" He leaned toward her and murmured into her ear, "Who knows? You may like it." He took her chin again and turned her face toward his, but just as his lips brushed hers, she abruptly turned away.

"Probably not."

He paused. "Hey, I may be out of practice, but I still know how to—"

"I'm not talking about you," she said, without looking at him. "I'm talking about me. I just don't want you to get your hopes up, thinking it's going to be...I don't know, some kind

of night of unbridled passion. I don't think I'm very...
responsive."

He rested a hand on her shoulder. "I know you're inexperienced."

She shook her head. "I mean, I don't think I can..." She
sighed. "I had this boyfriend in college, Brian. He was always trying to get me to ... you know...."

"I can take an educated guess."

"But I just never wanted to, and he said I was, that I was
probably... that I couldn't—"

"He said you were frigid?" She nodded. "Oh, honey, that
word should be stricken from every dictionary in existence.
There *is* no such thing. Just men who don't know what they're
doing." He leaned toward her, kissed her throat, and said,
"I'm not one of them."

"I don't know. Brian said—"

"Brian's an idiot."

"No, he's not."

"Sure, he is. He let *you* get away, didn't he?"

A satisfied little smile slipped past her defenses. "Who said
you weren't smooth?" She rose to her feet and he struggled
to his, waving away her attempt to help. "I'll go get your
cane."

He draped an arm over her shoulder. "I can just use you.
If you don't mind." After a brief hesitation, she circled one
around his waist. The spaghetti straps of her suit were tied in
single-knotted bows, not double as he would have expected.
As they walked, he imagined taking one end of each bow and
pulling. In his mind's eye the suit peeled down like the skin
of a fruit.

When they got to the chaise longue, she extended her hand.
"So I take it we have a deal?"

He took her hand and drew her toward him, encircling her
with his arms and leaning down to take her mouth with his.

He kissed her with unthinking passion, tasting her ripe lips, probing between them until his tongue met hers.

After a brief hesitation, she returned the kiss, wrapping her arms around him and molding herself against him, her soft breasts crushed to his chest, her hips pressed to his. She was so warm and wet and sleek, she felt like no woman he had ever held. His hands traced hungry paths over her back, sliding down to cup her small, round bottom, pressing her toward him. Her nipples stiffened against his chest, and his body stirred in response. She felt it and broke the kiss, gasping, "Tucker..."

She tried to pull back, but he held her tight, murmuring hoarse words into her ear. "Forget the deal. Make love to me. Now." He tried to claim her mouth again, but she turned aside and pushed away from him. He let up on his grip and they stood for a few breathless moments in a loose embrace.

"It's best my way," she breathed. "It has to be my way or not at all. That's my only offer."

He emptied his lungs in a ragged sigh. "Wow, you drive a hard bargain."

She held her hand out. "Is it a deal?"

He wrapped his big hand around her small one and shook. "Deal."

HARLEY LOOKED UP from her book when she heard the telltale creaking stair. That sound was soon followed by others—the thump of the cane, the muffled footsteps in the hall outside her bedroom door.

Again? They had made their deal just that evening. Was he already tired of waiting?

But no, the footsteps passed her door and continued on down the hall. She heard another door open and close; its characteristic squeak told her it was the door to R.H.'s suite. What did he want in there?

After a few minutes of hearing nothing more, she settled back against her pillows, wondering what had possessed her to actually go ahead and make such a deal. Was it as simple as what she had told Tucker, that she wanted to inspire him to rehabilitate himself? Certainly she did want that, but she knew that she had also shocked the hell out of him, which was rather satisfying after all his comments about how uptight she was. On reflection, though, the most important purpose of the deal was to ensure that their relationship remained platonic. She certainly couldn't trust Tucker to draw that line, but neither could she trust herself. When he kissed her, she knew that she could give herself to this man, heart, soul, and body, despite her many misgivings about life-styles, values, goals, and dreams. And what then? He would bolt. Probably immediately, and probably without saying goodbye. And she didn't think she could bear that.

Hence the value of the deal. They both respected it; they would both abide by it. And, of course, he would never catch her. In September, when his father came home, he would leave, and she would probably never see him again. Because she cared for him, she would miss him. But missing him was better than hating him.

She closed her eyes and took some deep breaths to clear her thoughts, then opened her book and continued reading. This was a much more absorbing book than *Priorities for the Successful Manager,* and she found she didn't want to put it down and go to sleep. About an hour passed by, and then she heard the footsteps again. This time they did stop outside her door, and then came the two soft knocks.

Again she looked down at herself. Tonight an oversize T-shirt served as her nightgown. She adjusted it so that it covered her leopard-print panties, but stopped short at pulling up the sheet, remembering that he had, after all, seen her naked. How coy did she really need to be?

"Come in."

He didn't hesitate in the doorway this time, but walked right up to her and tilted his head to try to read the title of her book, which she immediately covered with her hand. "What is it tonight? *How to Make Enough Money to Pay for Your Therapy?*" He reached for the book and she held it away from him, but he snatched it out of her hand, laughing delightedly when he found out what it was. "The *Kama Sutra!* I *told* you you'd like it!"

He handed it back to her and she took it, feeling the warm blush crawl up her throat and over her face. "*You're* in a good mood," she said.

"Endorphins," he explained, sitting on the edge of the bed. "I've been working out in the gym."

"Ah!" That explained his appearance. He wore a gray T-shirt soaked through with sweat, navy gym shorts, and old running shoes. Strands of wet hair hung over his forehead, and he raked them back with his fingers.

He said, "The only way I'm ever going to make good time in the pool again is to develop the muscles that have deteriorated since the crash. Mainly my left pec and left quad. So I've tailored my workout for plenty of work in those areas— lots of leg extensions and leg presses, cross flies, bench presses. . . . You don't mind spotting me on the bench press tomorrow, do you? We can work out together. You spot me, I'll spot you."

She nodded mutely. She had never seen him so animated, and she didn't quite know how to take it.

He went on. "Of course, I can't just work those few muscle groups. I've got to get the whole body into condition if I want to be *really* fast. When I was competing, I was a *bullet* in the water. No one could touch me. I'm going to train the way my swim coach had me train back then. An hour of weight work a day, in split sessions, alternating upper- and lower-body work. Plus, every day, a hundred crunches and a hundred push-ups. He also used to have us run five miles, but I'm going to substitute forty-five minutes on the rowing machine. And, of course, laps, as many as I can manage. My goal is a hundred. So what do you think?"

"I think—I think you're going to be in pretty good—"

He took her chin in his hand. "I think I'm going to be a *monster.*" He gave her a quick, hard kiss, and stood. "Oh! I almost forgot why I came in here." He reached into the right-hand pocket of his gym shorts, pulled out a half-empty pack of Camels, and handed it to her. Then he pulled an unopened pack out of the left-hand pocket and handed that to her, as well. "I want you to hide those from me."

"You're quitting?"

"You need lungs to swim," he said, on the way to the door. "All the strength in the world won't help you if you can't breathe." He stood in the doorway and grinned at her.

Adopting what she hoped would pass for an unconcerned smirk, she reached behind her, grabbed the corner of a plump down pillow, and flung it as hard as she could in the direction of his cocky grin. He pulled the door closed, and it landed with a whump and dropped to the floor.

Harley fell back into her pile of pillows, forgetting about the gap left by the one she had just thrown. Her head slammed into the wall and she yelped at the sharp pain. She sat up and spent several minutes rubbing the back of her head, wondering just exactly what she had gotten herself into.

8

SHORTLY AFTER BREAKFAST the next morning, Tucker took a phone call from Phil.

"You know that old white Victorian house in the village, the one next to the bookstore?" Phil asked. "It was a funeral home when we were kids, then an antique shop?"

"Yeah. This doesn't have anything to do with my Jag, does it?"

"No, no, no. Doug Ralston bought it. You remember Doug."

"Sure," Tucker said. Through the open window facing the front yard, he watched Harley walk back from the mailbox at the road, flipping through a stack of letters and magazines. Her hair was still wet from her morning swim, which she had insisted on taking, and she wore her white terry-cloth robe and no shoes. She had a naturally graceful, loose-hipped walk that he found impossible to look away from. "Is he in the antique business now?"

"Doug? Not likely. No, he turned it into a club. Folk rock, mainly, but there's a jazz saxophonist who plays there on Monday nights."

"Hale's Point has a night-spot?" Tucker said. Harley dropped a letter and bent to pick it up. As she did so, the front of her robe gapped slightly, revealing the pale, rounded tops of her breasts. That she was naked under the robe came as a surprise; Tucker had assumed she still wore her swimsuit.

Phil said, "Yes, believe it or not, Hale's Point has a night-spot. It's a good one, too."

"And the point of all this . . ." Tucker prompted. Harley pulled out one of the magazines and smiled at the cover. Tucker ached with curiosity to know what had made her smile. He shook his head. Who cared? What was the matter with him?

"The point," Phil answered, "is that tonight's band has canceled, and seeing as how it's Friday, and the place will be packed, that's not a good thing. Luckily, he's got backup entertainment on reserve at all times. Bet you can't guess who that is."

After a moment's thought, Tucker said, "You're not serious. Not Rob and Jim and those guys? They can't still have that awful band after twenty years."

"Well, not Jim. He's doing entertainment law in L.A. But Rob and Larry are still here. Rob does environmental law and Larry teaches history at Stony Brook. They play together every chance they get. They're not awful anymore, either. Pretty good, in fact. Folk and blues. They even write some of their own stuff now. Why don't you come check them out tonight? Say, around nine? It'd be like a reunion. And ask Harley if she wants to come."

She was close now, on the front walk, her nose buried in the mail, completely unaware that he had been watching her. "Harley!" he called. He held the phone away from his mouth, but resisted the impulse to cover the mouthpiece; he wanted Phil to hear this.

She looked around briefly before squinting at the screened window. "Tucker?"

"Do you want to go to a folk-rock club with me tonight? As my date?"

"Damn it, Tucker!" came Phil's tinny voice over the line. "You know that's not what I meant."

After a pause, she shrugged. "Sure. That sounds like fun."

"Great," said Tucker. "I'll drive us there—" he held the phone close to his mouth and enunciated very clearly "—in my *new Jag.*"

Harley, looking puzzled, walked away, while Phil said, "You think you're so smart. You may have your *new Jag*, but I've got something better. I've got a *medical degree.* I am a *doctor!* A genuine, six-figure M.D. Ain't no car in the world can compete with that, even yours. Which is not to say I don't still want it. I definitely am still willing to trade you my house for it. I just want you to know it takes more than a great car to win over a girl like that."

"What does it take, Phil?"

"It takes a stack of credit cards so fat you could wrap both hands around them and your fingers won't touch. It takes Lord & Taylor, Bloomies, Saks, Bergdorf's, and about a zillion more. Oh, but I forgot! You don't believe in credit!" He laughed maniacally. "You lose!"

"Tell you what," Tucker said. "I feel sorry for you, so I'm going to find you a date. Matter of fact, I've already got someone in mind. You'll love her."

"Who? Not Mimi. She's cute, but she's not my type."

"Let *me* decide what your type is. I'm an excellent judge of these things."

"Tucker, don't go inviting some—"

"I've got to go now. Harley needs some help with the suntan oil."

"Tucker—"

"See you tonight."

After hanging up on Phil, Tucker looked up the Tiltons' number in R.H.'s massive black leather address book, the same one he'd had when Tucker was a boy.

"Mimi? Tucker Hale. Listen, some friends of mine are going to be playing at the club in the village tonight. Harley and

I are going, and we wondered if you'd like to join us. And there's someone else I'd like you to bring...."

AROUND ONE O'CLOCK, Tucker left for the afternoon, saying he had to finish his business with the Jaguar dealer and run a couple of other errands. While he was gone, Harley attended to the pool maintenance and briefly exercised R.H.'s eight sports cars, which he had asked her to do twice a week. Then she took her afternoon run, but her energy had been sapped by the heatstroke, and she ended up exhausted.

When she climbed up from the beach, his Jag was in the driveway. On the kitchen table she found a Vidalia onion, a head of garlic, a bottle of Tabasco, a bag of yellow cornmeal, and various other spices and canned goods. Passing by his room, she saw on his bed a scattering of bags and boxes.

Upstairs, the door to R.H.'s suite was ajar and she could hear a repetitive metallic scraping accompanied by labored breathing and an occasional grunt of effort. She closed the door to her room, stripped, slipped between the cool cotton sheets, and fell asleep.

A HAND GENTLY KNEADED her bare back. She opened her eyes to find him sitting on the bed, murmuring, "Wake up. Chili's ready." The sheet covered her only to her waist, but thankfully she was lying on her stomach. Even if she weren't, he'd seen it all before, she reminded herself. She had the sense of having slept deeply. "Come on, honey," he said, smoothing her hair off her face. "Up and at 'em."

"You leave and I'll get up and at 'em," she mumbled. She twisted her head to look at him. "And don't call me hon—" The rebuke stuck in her throat, and all she could do was stare dumbly. He looked completely different. He looked like a stranger. "You cut your hair," she finally said.

"There's a barber in the village." He ran a hand over it. It was very short all over; almost, but not quite, a crew cut. Most men looked awful in such an unforgiving cut, but Tucker wasn't one of them. The absence of hair showed off the pleasing shape of his head and the sharply carved bones of his face. He looked both aristocratic and military, like a young Roman emperor.

Standing, he draped her white robe over her inert form and headed toward the door. "Wake 'em and shake 'em, babe. Cold chili's a bummer."

Finding her voice as he closed the door behind him, she yelled, "And don't call me babe, either!"

THE CHILI AND CORN BREAD were ridiculously good, and Harley surprised herself by having seconds of both. She offered to clean since he had cooked. Tucker consulted the kitchen clock and said, "Okay. That'll give me some time to do a few laps before we swim. Then we should still make it to the club by nine. Can I, uh...can I borrow your... stopwatch?"

Harley allowed her stunned expression to metamorphose into a self-satisfied grin. "Of course," she said with mock graciousness, unbuckling the watch and handing it to him.

He accepted it with a sheepish grin and disappeared into his room. A few minutes later she heard the French doors open and close. When she looked out the kitchen window, she saw him standing in the dusk at the edge of the brightly lit pool, clad in a minimal black racing suit, which he must have bought that day. He had his back to her as he fiddled with the stopwatch, so she felt free to stare.

He stood with careless grace, his weight resting on his good leg. His shoulders were well muscled, squaring off a broad back that scooped down to narrow hips and a compact rear encased in the low-slung black Speedo. His short hair and long, powerful limbs completed the image: injuries aside, he looked not so much like a Roman emperor as a Roman god, carved in marble at the edge of a temple's reflecting pool.

He moved to the edge of the deep end, crouched in proper starting position, clicked the stopwatch, and sprang into the water. As he did so, she saw his grimace of pain, and winced.

She left him—swimming slow, laborious laps—to change into her white maillot, then joined him in the pool. For about forty minutes he continued his laps, checking the stopwatch periodically, while she lazily backstroked from one end to the other.

Now he's the driven one and I'm just hanging out, she thought as the stars drifted past overhead.

His voice interrupted her reverie. "Ready to try this again?"

They took their positions. "One . . . two . . . three . . . go!"

He made it a little farther into the deep end before she touched the deck, but not much. Nevertheless, he seemed exhilarated, which she knew owed less to endorphins than to anticipation, the prospect of catching her and collecting his prize. Shivering, she ran upstairs to shower and change for the club.

HARLEY HATED NOT KNOWING the right thing to wear. She had never been to a folk-rock club, or any other kind of club, for that matter. Did women wear jeans and T-shirts or nice dresses?

Scanning the half-dozen outfits carefully laid out on her bed, she chastised herself for her lack of self-confidence. *Wear whatever you want, for God's sake! Why should you knock yourself out, anyway? Imagine how Tucker will look.* The idea of walking into a public place on the arm of a man in faded army surplus only added to her distress, so she put it out of her mind.

In the end, she chose a white cotton peasant blouse and tucked it into what she thought of as her gypsy skirt. She had bought the skirt on impulse, having fallen instantly in love with its sheer, gold-flecked layers of teal, eggplant, and midnight blue. But she had never worn it, having had no place to wear it to—until now.

One of the advantages of being small on top was having the option of going braless if the spirit moved her. She exercised that option now, so that she could loosen the drawstring of her blouse and push the neckline down off her shoulders, as she had seen it displayed on the mannequin in the store. There. *Now* she didn't look like little Miss Republican M.B.A.

She rarely wore makeup, but tonight she thoughtfully applied some mascara, brushed on a light dusting of powder, and painted her lips shell pink. After brushing her hair out loosely, she put on her best silver-and-onyx earrings, then appraised the results in the mirror and smiled. She tossed a few things into her smallest handbag and went downstairs.

The door to Tucker's room stood open, and she saw that some of the bags and boxes that littered the bed had been opened. She didn't see Tucker himself until she stepped into the room, and the sight of him drew an astonished gasp from her.

He stood in front of the full-length, freestanding mirror, holding two linen ties up to his chest and frowning. One was floral, the other a pattern of free-form brushstrokes, both in shades of brown, gray, and a pale, muted green that exactly matched the green of his crisp, button-down shirt. He wore khaki trousers, and his belt and shoes were of soft, brown kid. A putty-colored summer blazer hung over the back of the chair in the corner. When he looked her way, all she could say was, "Wow."

His unblinking eyes took her in, head to toe, and then he smiled a smile of immense satisfaction. "That's *my* line. You look . . . Wow, you look outrageous."

Harley bit her lip, not wanting to look too pleased with herself. "So do you," she said. "You look so . . . different."

"I didn't want you to feel embarrassed to be seen with me."

"I—I wouldn't have."

He grinned skeptically. "Ooh, you're a *ba-a-ad* liar."

"I am not! I mean—"

"It's good to be a bad liar. It means you have an honest heart." He held the ties up for her inspection. "Which one?"

She considered for a moment, then picked the brush-stroke one. He tossed the other one on the bed and, turning back to the mirror, threaded it through his collar and swiftly tied it. When he was done, he loosened it and unbuttoned the shirt's top button, saying, "Mustn't get too carried away." He paused and reached a hand out to stroke her cheek. "You really look incredible." Tucking her hair behind one ear, he said, "Those are nice earrings, but with your coloring, you should really wear gold."

She shrugged. "I like silver. Besides, I can't afford gold."

His hand trailed down to her mouth, and he patted her lower lip gently with his index finger, then examined the little smudge of shell pink on his fingertip. "Do you ever wear red lipstick?"

"Ugh, no."

He took his jacket from the chairback and tunneled his long arms into it. "That's probably for the best. If you did, I think you'd send me *completely* over the edge."

9

HARLEY SPENT THE SHORT trip to the village holding her hair in a knot at the nape of her neck to keep the wind from whipping it into a rat's nest. Most of the trip from the house to the village was along one-lane private roads that twisted up and plunged down. Whenever Harley had to make this drive, she found the experience harrowing, especially in the dark, but Tucker seemed completely unperturbed. With one hand on the wheel and the other on the stick shift, he maneuvered the convertible smoothly up sharp inclines and around hairpin curves as if he were a part of the machine itself.

Harley found the antiquated buildings of Hale's Point very charming in a peculiar, off-kilter kind of way. Once a haven for sailors and smugglers, it was now peopled exclusively by the descendants of some of Long Island's oldest and wealthiest families.

Tucker drove up to a warmly lit ivory gingerbread Victorian built into a cliff overgrown with flowering vines. From the lamppost dangled a small wooden plaque with an infinity sign—a sideways figure eight—painted on it. He parked on the narrow street at an acute downhill angle and raised the roof, then came around and opened the car door for her. Another "absurd" souvenir from his Hale's Point upbringing? For a nonconformist wild card, Tucker Hale could be quite the gentleman.

No sooner had they entered the club than a deep male voice boomed, "Tucker Hale, you son of a bitch, where's my

Grateful Dead album?" A bearded, red-haired giant threaded his way toward them through the milling patrons.

"I don't *have* your Grateful Dead album, Doug, I told you that!" Tucker bellowed back.

"Then who does?" Doug demanded, looming over them.

"Ask Rob."

Harley's head spun. This man probably hadn't set eyes on Tucker for decades. As near as she could tell, the two men had just slid back into a twenty-year-old argument.

"Let's do that," the giant thundered, turning and motioning them to follow him to a large back room. She could tell it had once been a formal dining room, since a crystal chandelier still hung from its ceiling.

In the corner, on a small stage set up with a piano, two men, one blond, one dark, were testing microphones. "Rob," Doug roared, and the blond man looked up, grinning broadly when he saw Tucker. "Do you have my Dead album?"

Rob blinked. "Yeah. I thought you knew that."

Doug stopped in his tracks. "You've had my Dead album for twenty years, and you thought I knew?"

"It's a good album," Rob said, as he and the dark-haired man descended from the stage. "I was going to give it back."

Tucker punched Doug in the shoulder. "Don't you think you owe me an apology?"

Doug reared up like a bear. "*Hell* no! You don't call for twenty years, I don't owe you nothin'!" He and Tucker faced off for a moment, presently breaking into huge grins and wrapping their arms around each other. "I missed you, you bastard!" Doug said.

Phil appeared as Tucker exchanged hugs and backslaps with the other two men. When he saw Phil, Tucker drew Harley toward him with an arm around her shoulder. "Harley Sayers, this is Doug, Rob, and Larry. Dr. Zelin, you already know."

Now they think I'm his girlfriend, she thought, and she tried the idea on for size. Tucker's girlfriend . . . Her heart started rattling in her chest.

Phil took in Tucker from head to toe. "Trying to depunk your image? That's a military-school haircut if ever I saw one."

Tucker said, "I'm swimming again, and short hair helps to cut down on the resistance. I want to get fast." With a glance at Harley, he added, "*Really* fast."

Harley wondered if anyone noticed her blush as Rob and Larry went back to their onstage preparations and Doug led them to a large table near the stage. Harley ordered iced tea, Tucker beer, and Phil a Bloody Mary. The club filled up quickly, and before long the chandelier dimmed and stage lights snapped on, illuminating the little platform in the corner. Rob and Larry performed a set of mellow folk tunes, Rob on guitar, Larry on piano. They were pretty good, but she and Phil and Tucker seemed to be the only guests who had actually stopped talking to listen. The drone of conversation never let up, and it was fairly loud; the place was packed with people. Rob and Larry didn't seem to mind, and she figured that must be a drawback that club musicians just come to accept.

When it was time for their break, the two musicians joined the party at the table. Tucker sat on one side of Harley, a long arm draped over the back of her chair, Phil on the other, ignoring his friend's proprietary gesture by leaning toward her and touching her arm frequently as he talked. *Maybe Tucker was right*, Harley thought. *Maybe Phil is interested, after all.*

Grinning, Tucker announced, "Look who's here!" Mimi, Jamie, Brenna, and a blond woman came up to the table. Abruptly, as if she were suddenly hot to the touch, Phil's hand recoiled from her arm. What was *that* all about?

Like Harley, Mimi and the blonde wore skirts and blouses; Brenna had on a stretch lace minidress. Introductions were begun, but no one seemed quite sure who knew whom, and the identity of the blond woman remained a mystery to Harley. The men stood and pulled chairs out for the women—another remnant of chivalry quite foreign to Harley—and Tucker embraced the blonde, saying, "It's so great to see you."

"You, too," said the woman. "I'm glad you asked Mimi to bring me."

He asked Mimi to bring her? thought Harley, feeling a hard squeeze of jealousy. The blonde looked to be around Tucker's age, and was nothing short of striking. She exchanged greetings with Rob and Larry, but ignored Phil—rather pointedly, Harley thought.

Tucker said, "Harley Sayers, I'd like you to meet an old friend of mine, Kitty Zelin—Phil's wife."

"Kitty Acton-Kemp," the blonde corrected, holding her hand out for Harley to shake, as Phil shot a murderous look toward Tucker. "I've taken back my maiden name."

That Phil was married surprised Harley until she put two and two together—Kitty's coolness toward him, her returning to her maiden name—and realized that they must be separated, although probably not divorced yet, since Tucker had introduced her as his wife.

Another man who got the cold shoulder that night was Jamie, whose constant attentions toward Brenna were met with contemptuous disregard. Instead she flirted openly with Rob and Paul, who seemed entranced. She turned her Irish charm on Tucker and Phil, as well, but Tucker responded with distant politeness, and Phil didn't respond at all; he had withdrawn when Kitty showed up, saying and doing little except to stare balefully at her from time to time.

Doug appeared and motioned toward the crowd. "The natives are restless, boys," he said to Rob and Larry. "How about another set?"

"How about Tucker joins us?" Rob asked. "Like old times."

Tucker shook his head. "I'd need a guitar."

"Got one in back," Doug said.

"A twelve-string?"

"A twelve-string."

Tucker rolled his eyes. "Something tells me I've been set up." With his chair in one hand and his cane in the other, he mounted the stage and spent a few minutes conferring quietly with Rob and Larry while Doug went to fetch the guitar.

Jamie picked up his own chair and circled the table to set it down in the now-empty space next to Harley, with the back facing her. Straddling it, he reached out and fingered the ruffled neckline of her blouse. "This is nice. You look great tonight."

Of course, Harley knew exactly what he was doing—trying to make Brenna jealous. The au pair did glance in their direction briefly before returning her attention to the stage, where the four men—Doug was back with the guitar—huddled together intently. The only person who seemed bothered at all by Jamie's actions was Tucker, who frowned when he looked in her direction.

As Tucker demonstrated some piano business to Larry, Doug twisted a mike from its stand to address the audience. "If you can be patient for just a few more minutes, we've got a treat for you tonight, by the name of Tucker Hale. Anyone who was hangin' out in Greenwich Village twenty years ago probably heard him and Chet Madison play. They opened for major acts at The Bitter End and The Bottom Line. For the record, Tucker's the only guy I ever knew who actually *turned down* a record contract." There were murmurs from the audience. "He tells me he's got some new material he's written, seein' as how he's had a lot of time on his hands lately. In a minute, we'll see if it's any good."

Doug replaced the mike, descended from the stage, and came to stand behind Harley. Turning to look up at him, she said, "Tucker turned down a record deal? He told me things just didn't work out. He never said he was actually offered a contract."

The bearish man squatted down next to her. "From what I hear, the problem was Chet. Which wasn't really a surprise. That guy was always bad news."

"Wasn't he a good friend of Tucker's?"

"Friend? Yes. Good?" He shook his head. "He only brought Tucker down, and Tucker unfortunately let it happen."

"I don't understand," Harley said. "What happened?"

"You know they dropped out of school and left home at the same time." Harley nodded. "Then they played in the Village together. Started to get a following. One night this A-and-R man from Capitol caught their act."

"A-and-R man?"

"Stands for 'artists and repertoire.' They go to the clubs and scout new talent for the big record companies. Anyway, this one guy takes Tucker aside and offers to finance a demo—the first step toward signing him on—*if* he'll jettison Chet. Says Chet's not in the same league as him, which is true, and he'd be better off as a solo act." He shrugged. "Tucker wouldn't have it. Out of loyalty to Chet, he turned the deal down, thinkin' sooner or later someone would sign up the two of them. Course, he was just carrying Chet, and the two of them were never offered anything more than the occasional club gig. Eventually they quit the business and moved to Miami. Couple of years later, Tucker bought his Piper Comanche, and then . . . Well, I guess you know what happened after that." He shook his head.

"No, I don't," Harley said. "I know something happened, but—"

On the other side of her, Phil cleared his throat, and she turned to find him shaking his head at Doug. Avoiding eye contact with her, Doug stood. "I'd better go see if the guys are ready—"

"Tell me," Harley said.

He shrugged as he turned away. "Sorry."

She turned to Phil, who was motioning for the waitress. "Harley, I'm ordering you a Bloody Mary. Best you ever had, guaranteed."

"Phil, tell me about Miami."

"Shh," he whispered, as the chandelier dimmed and the stage lit up. "Show time."

The three men onstage took their seats, Larry at the piano and Rob and Tucker on hard wooden chairs with their guitars. Doug's voice filled the room: "Ladies and gentlemen, Tucker Hale." There was some polite applause. Rob and Larry looked toward Tucker, whose right foot beat out a rhythm that his guitar soon took up. When he nodded, the other two men joined in, their improvised accompaniment lending depth and complexity to the soulful melody. Then Tucker began to sing.

His singing voice had the same sandy quality as his speaking voice, but he interpreted the lyrics—his lyrics—with such restrained emotion that the result was mesmerizing.

When the waitress placed a drink in front of Harley, she became aware of the silence in the room. All faces looked toward the stage, their attention not just respectful, but enrapt. Harley was filled with awe at Tucker's power to so completely captivate an audience.

When the song was over, there was a hushed moment, as if every person in the club were taking a breath, and then came the thunderous applause, which Tucker seemed to find embarrassing. His next song had a more varied and complex melody. Again the audience was wildly enthusiastic, and again Tucker reacted almost shyly to the accolades. As the applause died down, Tucker leaned toward the mike and said, "This will be the last song." The audience groaned. "I didn't write it," he continued. "It's an old blues tune Rob and Larry and I used to play together."

The song was lively, funny, and very ribald. The audience seemed delighted and some began clapping to the music and whooping at the particularly risqué lines. Unlike the preceding songs, Rob and Larry had played this one many times. This familiarity showed in the way they wrapped it up, with a perfect synchronization of guitar and piano flourishes as Tucker held one endless final note.

Applause exploded from the audience, and many, including everyone at Harley's table, chose to underline it by standing. Doug's bellowed *"Yeah!"* was soon followed by cries of *"More!"* Tucker answered with a small shake of his head. He set his guitar down and reached for his cane, then looked directly into the audience for the first time, his eyes searching until they met Harley's. She made no effort to hide the pride that she knew must glow in them. Smiling, she nodded to him, as if to say he had done well. He smiled, too, for the first time since he took the stage, and Harley felt a warm and intimate connection between them, as if they were the only two people in the room.

That connection was broken when the house lights went up and people sat down again. Jamie relinquished his spot next to her, and Tucker took it back with a territorial glare at the younger man. Before she could say a word to him, Doug descended, leaning over Tucker with one beefy hand on the table and the other on the back of his chair. "Good set, man. You still got it. Can I book you for Fridays? You'll be here for the rest of the summer, right?"

Tucker rested his arm on Harley's chair and lightly touched her upper back, bared by her off-the-shoulder blouse. "Yeah, I'm staying till R.H. comes home. I'll play on Fridays. I'd like that."

As Doug left, Mimi and Kitty rose and headed toward the ladies' room. Phil took advantage of his wife's absence to hiss, "Tucker, damn you, what are you trying to pull, asking Kitty here? Is she supposed to be my date?"

"I told you you'd love her," Tucker said. "Have you talked to her at all?"

"I haven't seen her in six months!" Phil growled. "What the hell am I supposed to talk to her about?"

"Ask her if she's been needing any helium balloons." Harley didn't have the slightest idea what that meant, but apparently Phil did. He just shook his head and went back to his moping.

Rob and Larry played another set, which Tucker declined to join, and the outing broke up at about one in the morning. Harley and Tucker followed Mimi, Jamie, Brenna and Kitty out onto the downhill sidewalk.

"Poor Jamie," Harley whispered to Tucker. "I really like him, and I'd love for things to work out between him and Brenna, but she hardly looked at him. Even when he sat next to me and . . . and . . ."

"Started fondling you? He was being too obvious. She saw right through that. Now, if *you* had fondled *him*, that might have impressed her."

"You think so?"

"Trust me, I know her type. She wants his devotion just as much as she wants every other man's. The only reason she ignores him is because she knows she already has it. For him to come on to you only reinforces that knowledge, because it's just a transparent ploy for her attention. For you to come on to him, on the other hand, would be a genuine threat, because he might switch his devotion from her to you. Her only recourse would be to start responding to him."

"Sounds like you've made quite a study of the subject."

"I've known a few Brennas." He glanced at her, smiling, and it dawned on her that, despite his professed aversion to game playing, his comment was intended to make her jealous. Feeling slightly giddy from the Bloody Mary, Harley decided it was a game two could play.

"Thanks for the advice," she said, fluffing her hair and adjusting her blouse downward so that it revealed even more of her shoulders and chest. Jamie had parked his Saab two cars up from Tucker's Jag. He stood holding the door open for the three women as Harley and Tucker approached.

"What advice?" Tucker asked. "What are you going to do?"

Harley walked up to Jamie and put a hand on his shoulder as he closed the car door. She noticed that Brenna sat next to the front passenger window, where she would have a good view.

"Good night, Jamie," Harley said. Putting her arms around him, she whispered in his ear, "This'll give Brenna something to think about," then gave him a long, lingering kiss on the mouth. It seemed to take Jamie a second to realize what was going on, but when he did, he became an avid recipient, locking his arms around her and returning the kiss with enthusiasm.

When it was over, he gave her another kiss—a soft one on her cheek—and whispered, "Thanks," into her ear.

Brenna's blue eyes were as round as headlights when Harley turned away and walked down to the Jag. Tucker, eyebrows raised, held the door open for her.

"At least tell me you didn't enjoy that," he said, settling into the driver's seat and turning the key.

She smiled coquettishly. "But that would be a lie."

Yanking on the stick shift, he said, "*I'm* the one who doesn't lie, remember? You're allowed."

"You can't mean you *want* me to lie to you. You? Mr. Honest-as-the-Day-is-Long?"

The car squealed away from the curb. "There's a first time for everything."

It had become cool, so Tucker left the Jag's roof up for the drive home. They rode in companionable silence until he pulled into the driveway and killed the engine. Turning to her, he asked, "Did you have a good time tonight?"

She nodded. "It was great. *You* were great. I mean, you're a terrific musician. I had no idea."

It was dark inside the car, and his eyes were huge. That rare, shy look hid in them. "Thanks."

"Doug told me about Chet and the record contract. It's a shame things didn't work out."

For a long moment he stared at the windshield. Finally he looked back at her. "What else did Doug tell you?"

She met his eyes. "He didn't tell me what happened in Miami, if that's what you mean." Tucker's careful lack of response told her it was. "But I'd like to know. I'd like you to tell me."

There was another thoughtful pause. "Until I came back here, I hadn't thought about Miami in years. Or talked about it. I prefer it that way."

Deciding that wasn't exactly a direct refusal, Harley pressed on. "Whatever it was, don't you think I could understand?"

"Frankly, no. *I* still have a hard time understanding it. How could I expect you to? You're very bright, but you're also very young, and . . . I don't want to insult you, but you're kind of judgmental. I don't want you judging me and finding me lacking." He reached out and brushed his fingers across her temple and through her hair, leaving tingling trails of sensation. "I care what you think about me." He shrugged. "I don't know why I should, but I do."

She nodded. "Okay."

Tucker got out of the car and came around to open her door for her. Eyeing her intently, he took her hand to help her out, then shut the door, encircled her with his arms, and pressed her back against the car. His mouth found hers and closed over it in a deep, hungry kiss. This time, resistance never entered Harley's mind. With her arms around his waist, she returned the kiss with a hunger that equaled his.

I want him, she thought, in sudden amazement. *I want him to make love to me. How did this happen?* Crushed between his warm body and the smooth, cool car, captured by his strong arms and eager mouth, she went limp with surrender. *Am I weak? Have I lost control?*

Wasn't it all right to be weak sometimes, especially if it felt so good, so right? Wasn't she allowed to lose control once in a while? She couldn't go her whole life picking and choosing what happened to her. She had always wondered what it would feel like to get carried away by passion, to lose herself to it, to ignore good judgment and do something crazy. Perhaps tonight, for the first time, she would find out.

He tore his lips from hers and she felt them on her cheek, then her earlobe. His breath warm and rasping in her ear, he murmured, "I couldn't stop thinking about you tonight. I could barely stand to look at you, I want you so much. It's downright painful."

Spontaneously she kissed his throat, and a sound rose from it, a moan of pleasure. Then suddenly their mouths were locked together again, breathlessly, their tongues meeting in a flickering dance. With one hand he held her in a tight embrace; the other stroked her hair, her neck, a shoulder, then felt along the ruffled neckline of her blouse until it found, between her breasts, the drawstring bow.

Without breaking the kiss, he tugged on it. The drawstring loosened, and the blouse slipped down a bit. He lowered the fabric that covered her left breast, then paused for a moment, his hand hovering over it. Harley felt the cool night air on her bare flesh, and she swore she could hear her heartbeat, as well as his.

The coolness gave way to a delicious, spreading warmth as he caressed her, his large hand more than covering her small breast. Although his palm felt rough, he touched her with exquisite gentleness, as if he were afraid of hurting, or scaring, her.

Ending the kiss, he whispered, "You can't imagine what you do to me," and nuzzled her hair.

She didn't have to imagine. With his hips pressing her against the car, she could feel, even through the many layers of her skirt and the fabric of his trousers, how aroused he was. She wondered what it would feel like to take him into her. Would it hurt? Perhaps, but she knew in her heart that he would take great care to be considerate of her. He would be wonderful. He would be careful and tender.

She wanted her first time to be with Tucker, and she wanted it to be tonight. The deal they had made just the previous day barely entered her mind; her many misgivings evaporated in the wake of the sensations that enveloped her.

Yes. Tonight.

Her nipple tightened beneath his touch, and he moaned again. His thumb found the stiff little bud and brushed across it, sparking an electric thrill. She gasped in astonishment. "Tucker..." She needed him. "Tucker..."

He froze. "I know," he mumbled into her hair. "I know, I'm just... I'm sorry." He pulled back a bit, removed his hand from her breast, and pulled the white, ruffled cotton up to cover her. "I know we have a deal. I didn't mean to go this far, I just . . . I just wanted to kiss you, and . . ." He shrugged helplessly.

Harley was speechless to find him backing off, giving her the space he thought she wanted, doing the responsible thing. Now she was the impulsive one, and he was going by the book. Things were turning around, and Harley's mind reeled in confusion.

He began retying the drawstring that secured her blouse. "I didn't mean to take advantage of you or renege on our deal. It's just that you're so . . . God, Harley, I can't even think straight when I'm with you. I can't see you without wanting to kiss you, and I can't kiss you without wanting to . . . I've got no self-control with you. I'm like some goofy adolescent, all hormones and heat. I want you so much . . . too much."

She wanted to tell him that she wanted him, too. She wanted to tell him that he could abandon his self-control, abandon the deal . . . but she didn't. As ardently as she desired him, it was not in her nature to be the one to initiate things. She simply nodded and said nothing.

He took her face between his palms. "I promise you I'll keep to our deal. I won't try to rush things. We're doing this your way. I agreed to that. That's the way it'll be." His eyes were so enormous, so sincere. A lump filled Harley's throat and she nodded again. He kissed her forehead lightly. "It's late. You must be tired."

Taking her by the hand, he led her inside. At the bottom of the stairs they said good-night and went to their separate rooms.

10

DURING THE ENSUING weeks, Tucker fulfilled his promise. He rarely touched Harley, and his infrequent kisses were light. Even though she knew why he restrained himself, his doing so struck her as bizarre, considering how strongly he had come on to her at first. It was almost like being courted. He joked about their old-fashioned, platonic relationship, saying it was the first time he had actually been forced to get to know a woman before he could go to bed with her. Unaccustomed though he was to the role of gentleman suitor, he nevertheless played it well. Were it not for the transparent longing she occasionally glimpsed in his eyes, she might even have thought he had lost interest in her.

He spent a great deal of time with his guitar, working on new songs, and every Friday night he played at Doug's club, always to a large and enthusiastic crowd. He always insisted she accompany him, for moral support. He took her other places, as well; places she had never been, to do things she had never done. One day he rented a noisy little two-seater airplane and took her on a bird's-eye tour of Manhattan and the surrounding boroughs. The next week they went to a different airstrip and he took them up in a sailplane, which she found more to her liking; it was so quiet, so smooth, almost as if she herself had wings. But her favorite new activity was sailing, in Phil's little Flying Scot, the *Pacemaker*. She took to it instantly, and by the end of their first day out, was pulling her weight like a seasoned veteran, or so Tucker said. She loved it—the water, the wind, the freedom, even the hard work—and begged him to take her out whenever the weather permitted. Tucker said it looked like she was born to sail, and she couldn't disagree with him. She could easily understand his envy of his father for being able to spend the entire summer aboard the *Anjelica* in the Caribbean.

They orchestrated their chores around their workout schedules. Harley continued her daily swim and run, although she abandoned her original inflexible schedule—Tucker's influence. He adopted the routine he had outlined to her the night they shook hands on their deal. Although, like Harley, he did not adhere to a fixed schedule, every day he managed to work in about two hours in the gym and at least one in the pool, swimming laps. As time went on, Harley noted that not only did his form and speed improve considerably, he no longer swam in pain, or at least, none that showed.

Every once in a while Harley would find herself staring at Tucker as he crouched at the edge of the pool, stopwatch in hand, and thinking, *Is this the same raggedy, disheveled man who broke into the house at one in the morning and played the* Moonlight Sonata *on R.H.'s grand piano?* He remained clean-shaven, and although his hair quickly grew out of its severe cut, it was still very short. It took mere days for the sun to gild it, and to burnish his skin a golden brown. He credited his father's genes for the blond highlights and his mother's for the overnight tan.

As his conditioning improved, his body looked more and more like that of an Olympic swimmer—broad-shouldered, well muscled, but sleek. The wounds on his torso and leg became less noticeable as those muscle groups bulked up, and, more and more, he was able to do without his cane. It pleased Harley to see him walk unaided, his limp growing less pronounced as time went by.

Every evening after supper they met in the pool for their one-lap challenge. In the beginning, Tucker never came close, but as the weeks passed and he got faster, it became clear to Harley that it was just a matter of time before he caught her. By the beginning of August, he was finishing right on her heels. She would touch the deck at the deep end, and within a heartbeat he would appear next to her, grab the deck, grin, and haul himself out of the water. He would win any day now.

R.H. was not expected back until the first of September. Would Tucker bolt the morning after claiming his "prize," or would he wait for his father to return, and then leave? How would she feel when he left? With grim amusement she thought back to the time when she first made the deal, smugly certain that he could never catch her. Now that she knew he would, now that she eagerly looked forward to that day, to the prospect of sharing a bed with Tucker, she had to face the heartbreak that was certain to follow. He would leave—it was the only way he knew—and she would suffer. She tried to keep such thoughts from her mind, to enjoy her summer with Tucker and not think of its inevitable end.

AS HARLEY DRIED THE LAST of the supper dishes and put them away, Tucker opened up the fridge and withdrew the bottle of champagne that he'd been keeping cold for over two weeks now.

Harley's eyes widened. "You mean I'm finally going to find out what that champagne is for?"

"Yes, ma'am. You'd better put on something warm. I'm taking you down to the beach for a celebratory toast, and it gets cool down there at night."

She frowned. "Wait a minute. You can't get down to the beach. You've never been down there. I mean, not since you've been back."

He shrugged. "I'm going to give it a shot. I think I'm up to it now."

"And what about our evening swim? It's almost time for that. I'm surprised you'd want to miss that."

He smiled. "It's a trade-off, but tonight I'd prefer the beach."

"Yeah, but—"

"Look, I know you find it hard to be spontaneous—"

"No, I don't!"

"Prove it."

"Give me ten minutes to get into some jeans and a sweater."

Ten minutes later they were picking their way down the boulder stairway to the beach. Harley insisted on carrying the two blankets and the small knapsack that Tucker had filled. Even empty-handed, he found the descent challenging, although not as painful as he would have thought. His physical condition was light-years from what it had been six weeks ago, when he first came to Hale's Point. He hadn't picked up his cane in days, although his gait was still awkward and stiff-legged. The only real pain he still felt was when he crouched at the edge of the pool, waiting to spring. Any kind of kneeling or squatting was also problematic, but usually easy enough to avoid.

He was free of his cane and his cigarettes, he was strong, he was fast, and he was happy—and he had Harley to thank for all that. Thanking Harley reminded him of the little bag in the front pocket of his jeans. He patted it just to make sure—it was still there.

August had always been his favorite month. The beach was at its best in August; the water warm, and the sunsets, like tonight's, spectacular. Tucker and Harley paused at the bottom of the sandy precipice to admire the streaks of peach and gold and purple that stained the darkening sky to the west.

Giggles from behind the stand of pines separating the Hales' beach from the Tiltons' caught their attention, and they turned to see Brenna, completely nude, run out from behind them, toward the water. Jamie, also nude, followed her, and, overtaking her, tackled her to the sand. Their giggles turned to shrieks and then reverted to laughter when they realized they were being watched, and they jumped up and darted back behind the pines. Ever since the first night Tucker had played at the club—the night Harley had kissed Jamie for Brenna's benefit—the young couple had been inseparable. Tucker doubted the relationship would last beyond the summer. It certainly would not survive past Brenna's one year au pair's stint in the States. A relationship built on lust had its charms, but those charms were generally short-lived. Such a relationship was not worth salvaging or mourning, unlike, say, Phil's relationship with Kitty.

Phil had abandoned his pursuit of Harley the moment he saw his wife again, at the club. If only he would swallow his pride and throw himself at Kitty's feet. But he refused to give his wife the opportunity to forgive him, and as a result, a vital marriage was going down the tubes.

Tucker led Harley some distance to the east, past the jetty and well into the undeveloped, wooded part of the Hale property, to the piece of shore that had been his favorite as a boy—a patch of beach surrounded on three sides by a semi-circle of large boulders opening toward the Sound, which afforded almost-complete privacy. They would only be visible to someone walking along the water's edge, and given the hour and their remote location, Tucker thought that unlikely. Privacy was important to him tonight. He wanted to be alone with Harley, just the two of them in his favorite place—a place he had not seen for over twenty years. One of the disadvantages of his estrangement from his father was the possibility that he might not inherit this property. He cared nothing for its monetary value, immense though that must be. He cared about his favorite spot.

He spread one of the blankets, built a fire next to it from fallen logs, and lit it with the matches he had brought. Then, to Harley's obvious and very gratifying delight, he withdrew from the knapsack several pieces of antique cut crystal—a bowl, a vase, and two champagne flutes, each wrapped in dish towels to prevent breakage—and arranged them in the middle of the blanket. The bowl he filled with cherries and peaches, and the vase with lavender from the border by the stone wall. After opening the champagne, he filled the two glasses and, sitting close to Harley, handed her one. The firelight glittered on the crystal and danced in her eyes.

"Don't you think it's time you told me what we're celebrating?" she asked. He loved her smile. On a very serious person, a smile was especially precious and especially beautiful. "It must be something important. I mean, you climbed all the way down here, and that couldn't have been easy."

He said, "We're celebrating the fact that I was able to climb all the way down here, even though it wasn't easy. Cheers." He raised his glass. Harley, grinning incredulously, touched her glass to his; they rang like bells.

She took a sip. "Let me get this straight. You came down here so you could celebrate coming down here?"

He tilted the glass to his lips. The bubbles tickled his nose; the champagne was dry and delicious. "Yes." He looked around at the little protected stretch of sand and said, "This is a special place for me. I spent a lot of time in this one spot when I was a boy. Built a lot of bonfires here, spent a lot of nights sleeping out here under the stars, thinking about things, wondering what the future held. I wanted to bring you here. I wanted to share this place with you."

The leaping flames shimmered in her eyes. She swallowed. "Thank you."

"I'm the one who should be thanking you. If it weren't for you, I wouldn't have seen this place again. If it weren't for you . . . God, if it weren't for you, I'd be back up in Alaska wishing I was here, choking on cigarettes and stumbling around with my cane. I've been through a lot of changes lately, good changes, and they're your doing. So, thanks."

He took her by the chin and gently tilted her face up toward his. The kiss was careful, soft. He had promised her a long time ago that he would not allow himself to get carried away, and he intended to keep that promise. Setting his glass down in the sand next to the blanket, he reached into his front pocket and pulled out the little black velvet bag. He took her free hand and placed the bag in it. "I want you to have this."

She set her glass down also. Her eyes were unblinking, her voice, when she spoke, was high and childlike. "What is it?"

"Open it."

Tentatively she loosened the gold, tasseled drawstring and spilled the contents of the bag into the palm of her hand. When she realized what she held, she sat up straight with a startled intake of breath. "Tucker! Your mother's earrings!"

"I wanted you to have them."

She held one up. It dangled heavily from her fingers, ornate gold filigree surrounding a cluster of rubies. "These— these are four hundred years old!"

"Probably more like five." He picked up his glass and swallowed some more champagne.

"I can't accept them," she said, with conviction, returning them to the bag.

He said, "I'm not taking them back. Try them on. I want to see you with gold and rubies next to your skin. You were never meant to wear silver."

She looked at him. "Who owns these?"

He reclined next to her, enjoying her reaction. "You do."

"No, no, I mean—"

"I own all of my mother's jewelry. She left it to me in her will. It's spent the last three decades in a safe-deposit box in the bank in the village."

"You never wanted it?"

"What would I do with it?"

"Sell it to a museum. It must be worth a fortune."

"I'd never sell my mother's jewelry. Chet tried to talk me into it when I first left home. The idea made me sick."

"Donate it, then. Or lend it, for exhibits. I'll bet the folks at the Met would love to get their hands on that collection."

He thought that one over. "It never occurred to me. Maybe I will lend them out someday." He took the little bag from her hand and slipped it into the front pocket of her jeans. "Except for these. They're yours, whether you want them or not." He chose his next words carefully, and watched her closely for her reaction. "But maybe I'll take the rest with me...when I leave."

Her eyes darted to his and then quickly away. She studied the fire. "That seems wise. Keep them close at hand. There are safe-deposit boxes in Alaska, I'm sure."

"I'm sure there are, but I don't necessarily plan on going back there. I moved to Alaska because it was the farthest away from Florida I could get without leaving the country. I may be ready for a middle ground, now."

"Such as?"

He drank some more champagne and watched her over the top of the glass. "Long Island's nice."

She looked at him. "What would you do here? Something with airplanes?"

He shook his head. "I've had my fill of airplanes for the time being."

"Then what, if not music? Drive a forklift? Patch roofs?"

He put the glass down and lay on his back with his arms folded behind his head. The sky was an ever-deepening violet scattered with winking pinpoints of light. "Maybe I'll buy a sailboat and sail around the world and think about it for a while."

"Mmm." From the corner of his eye he saw her looking at him. "Nice work if you can get it."

They drank their champagne in silence for a while. When their glasses became empty, he refilled them. He tried to clear his mind of all thoughts. He listened to the waves and the popping of the fire, breathed in the salt air and the sharp woodsmoke. He ate a peach and reveled in its sweet perfume. He watched Harley's mouth—that amazing mouth—close over a cherry and nibble it off the stem.

He drained his glass and poured half of the remaining champagne into it, and the rest into Harley's.

"This is probably not a good idea," she said, between sips. "I don't hold my liquor very well. I'm likely to fall asleep on you." She did appear exceptionally relaxed.

"I'm not much of a drinker, either," he admitted. "Drinking and flying don't mix any better than drinking and driving. If anything, worse."

"You weren't drinking when you had your...when you crashed your airplane. Were you?"

"No way. I've never flown under the influence. That crash had nothing to do with alcohol. Mainly it just had to do with bad luck." She nodded and deposited a cherry pit into her hand, then flung it into the woods. There was an enormous boulder at the edge of the blanket, and he leaned back against it and looked away from Harley and the fire, toward the black waves slapping the shore. "Extreme bad luck." He tossed back the last of his champagne and set the glass aside.

She stared at him, her own empty glass on the blanket next to her. When he looked at her, she looked away, rubbing her arms.

"Are you cold?" he asked.

"A little."

He reached for the second blanket and unfolded it. "Come here. Sit next to me." He draped the blanket over their shoulders and wrapped his arms around her. She settled back against him, her head nestled against his chest, her small body curled comfortably into his.

"Extreme bad luck," she murmured, as if the words had an interesting sound.

"Mainly extreme bad weather," he said, and expelled a long, heavy sigh. "But there were other problems. Instrument failure nobody could have anticipated, plus I was flying at night, which never helps." Did she want to hear this? As if in unspoken answer, she nodded, and he continued. "I was on a routine cargo run between Anchorage and Fairbanks when it happened. You know Mount McKinley?" She nodded again. "Just down the block from there. All of a sudden this blizzard came out of nowhere. Totally unpredicted. Complete whiteout, high winds, no visibility. Suddenly I was shearing the tops off trees. I guess I hit the mountain at a pretty good angle—not dead-on, or I wouldn't be here to tell the tale. Kind of tumbled down, rolling over as I went. The fuselage broke up, my cargo went all over the place. Finally came to rest on a flat spot in the middle of all these fir trees."

She twisted her head to look up at him. "Were you able to get out, go for help?"

"Oh, no. Not a chance. The whole left side of the cockpit had gotten smashed up, and the whole left side of me with it. There were pieces of metal and glass sticking out of me." He felt her shiver, and held her tighter. "I was pinned in there like a butterfly in a box."

"Could you reach the radio?"

"Yeah, but it was out of commission."

"What did you do?"

"I watched it snow. I just stared out through the broken windshield and watched it fall out of the night sky. It never stopped, just kept coming, big flakes the size of my fist piling up outside. Piling up fast, in this deadly silence. The plane was getting buried under it. I knew by morning there'd be no trace of me. They'd never find me. I realized I was going to die. I didn't see how I could get to help, or how I could recover, if I did. My left leg was destroyed. And I knew that just about every other bone on my left side was broken. The bleeding wasn't very bad, but the pain was. It was overwhelming, but there was no way to make it go away, so I had to concentrate on denying it. I tried to think about other things—anything except the pain and the cold and the fact that I was going to die. Mainly I thought about my dad." He realized this was the first time in years that he had referred to his father as anything other than R.H. "I kept wondering if he'd ever find out I'd been killed. I don't think dying bothered me as much as his not knowing, which struck me as kind of strange, considering how long it had been since I'd even seen him. I thought about him and about my mother."

"Do you remember her very well?"

"Mainly bits and pieces. But I remember the Christmas before she died. She wore a green silk dress and her hair was in a braid down her back. I got my first guitar that year, a little one. I'm sure it was her idea. For a while I couldn't get that Christmas out of my mind. I think it was the smell of all the broken fir trees around."

"Were you awake the whole time?"

"No, eventually I lost consciousness, but apparently I was awake until dawn. The snow completely covered the plane by then, but I remember seeing the glow of sunlight through it, and I thought, this is the last sunlight I'll ever see. Now that there was some light, I could see my cigarettes, just out of reach. Drove me crazy, not being able to get to them. I thought, damn, I won't even have to feel guilty about smoking, 'cause I'm dying anyway. Then I was out of it for a while, and I woke up to the sound of a shovel scraping against the windshield. Then this face looked through the glass and smiled at me, and I realized they'd found me, after all. I don't remember, but they said I asked for a cigarette before I passed out again. I came to in the hospital a week later."

"You were unconscious for a whole week?"

"More or less. They said I came out of it once in a while, but I don't remember. The first couple of days they thought I was going to die, and they wanted to notify my next of kin. They asked my pilots and my friends, but all they could say was they didn't know. I had never gotten close enough to any of them to tell them who my father was or where he lived. I pictured the funeral, if it had come to that. Some small, generic ceremony at some funeral home in Seward with about a dozen people, tops—my pilots and a few buddies, guys I hung out with. They would have said, 'Wasn't Tucker Hale a swell guy and aren't we lucky it happened to him and not us?' The only women there would have been Molly Little and maybe a few of the girlfriends and wives. No other woman knew me well enough to come. No one would have cried."

Harley murmured something. It sounded like, "I'd have cried."

Tucker was seized with desire for her, but it was more than the simple physical desire he had felt a thousand times before. He wanted to feel her beneath him and around him. He wanted to be a part of her, he wanted to lose himself inside her. At that moment it took all of his self-control not to lower her to the blanket and make love to her.

He took a deep, shaky breath. He had to wait. For one thing, she had drunk half a bottle of champagne, and he drew the line at taking advantage of an inebriated woman. For another, they had a deal. In a day or two she would be his, on her own terms. She had to know that, and it didn't seem to bother her—in fact, he sensed that she looked forward to it as much as he. He had often speculated on her motives for initiating the deal in the first place. She had to know she might lose. She had seen his trophies. Of course, she had wanted to rehabilitate him—and it had worked—but he suspected she had another, perhaps subconscious, motive. It was possible that she had simply wanted to enforce a waiting period before they consummated their relationship. She knew that he had no interest in waiting; he had made that clear from the beginning. But she did. Hence the deal. Hence six weeks of being with her, taking his time with her, getting to know her. He felt as if he knew her as well as he knew himself. She had changed him. She was a part of him now. That felt both comforting and frightening.

He closed his eyes for a while and listened to the reassuring rhythm of the waves. Quietly he said, "I did a lot of thinking in the hospital. Nothing had really mattered to me for a long time. Then I cracked up the plane and things started to matter. People...my father. I came back here because, no matter what he did or didn't do, he's my father. He matters. And now...I don't know how this happened, but...you matter, too. You matter a lot. I think I've fallen...I think I'm..."

He shook his head. "I've never said this to a woman before. It's hard. How do people do this? Help me out, Harley. Tell me you want me to say it." Her breathing was very regular and she felt warm and heavy against him. "Harley?"

She was asleep. She had warned him that might happen. He kissed the top of her head. Now what? Wake her up? He didn't have the heart for that. And he certainly couldn't carry her back up to the house. Carefully he laid her down on the blanket, curled on her side, then fit his big body to hers, spoon-style, and covered them both with the second blanket. It wouldn't be the first time he had spent the night on this beach—in this very spot, in fact. But it would be the first time he'd have someone to hold while he slept.

11

LATE THE NEXT MORNING, Harley opened and closed drawers in R.H.'s desk, idly searching for stamps, her mind preoccupied by three conflicting forces: the warm afterglow of having awakened on the beach in Tucker's arms, the nausea and pain of her first hangover, and the knowledge that the phone bill was due in two days.

She remembered R.H. taking a sheet of stamps from one of the drawers and placing it on top of the desk, saying, "That should be enough, but if you need more, get them from the drawer." Well, now she did need more, but she couldn't remember which drawer he stored them in. She began searching them one by one, finding them irritatingly neat and organized, everything in tidy stacks at right angles. Or maybe she was just irritated because of the hangover. Everything ached. Her *eyes* hurt. It hurt to *think*—just to string one thought onto another.

She came to a drawer containing a monogrammed leather photo album, which she lifted without opening. Beneath it lay a yellowed newspaper folded to reveal a particular article. The article was illustrated by a photograph of two policemen flanking a young man in handcuffs.

The young man was Tucker.

She blinked several times in an effort to clear her eyes and mind. Tucker in handcuffs.

She took the newspaper from the drawer. It was an old copy of the *Miami Herald*, and paper-clipped to its edge was a business card engraved "Charles Madison, Jr., Attorney at

Law," giving a Wall Street address. There was a message written in fountain pen, beginning on the front of the card and continuing on the back: "R.H.— A friend in Fla. sent me this. Read it. It should cure you of the notion that it's my Chet who's the bad influence. —C.M."

Boldface words above the article read: Feds Crack Down On Drug Smugglers.

Tucker Hale, twenty, was arrested at 5:30 a.m. today, charged with transporting cocaine and marijuana....

Her stomach did a slow flip, and she suddenly felt starved for air. Lurching to the window, she raised it and tried to breathe deeply, but found herself gasping in time to her runaway heartbeat.

She looked at the photograph. It had been taken indoors and lit with the glare of flashbulbs. Tucker, his hands cuffed in front, towered over the two burly policemen. His uncombed hair brushed his shoulders, and he wore jeans and a dark sweatshirt. He still had some adolescent lankiness, and his face looked smooth, unscarred and very young. Despite the indignity of the situation, he stood tall and looked straight ahead, his expression grim but calm.

She skimmed the article, then reread it slowly. It described how, shortly after midnight, federal drug-enforcement agents aboard a surveillance vessel off the Florida coast had observed seven plastic-wrapped bundles being dropped into the water from a Piper Comanche.

The agents intercepted the drugs as they were being loaded into a powerboat by an as-yet-unidentified accomplice. The accomplice opened fire and was killed in the ensuing exchange. The plane had been identified and was located two hours later at the Opa-Locka Airport just outside Miami. Tucker Hale was registered as the owner. The agents, accompanied by Dade County Police, went to Mr. Hale's home, and he and his housemate, Charles Madison III, were taken to the police station for questioning. Following lengthy interrogations, Mr. Madison was released and Mr. Hale was arrested and taken into custody.

Harley's head throbbed as if it were being squeezed repeatedly by a giant pair of hands. She felt woozy, faint. A movement from outside the window caught her eye: the black Jag pulling into the driveway. Tucker emerged, carrying a bagful of bagels. She slammed the window shut and went back to the desk to return the newspaper to its drawer.

When she lifted the photo album she noticed something else beneath it, another folded newspaper with Chet's father's business card clipped to it. The headline announced Tucker Hale Guilty on All Counts, and beneath it, Street Value of Drugs $1.2 M, and, Maximum Sentence Expected. The picture showed Tucker in a suit, his hair conservatively shorn. Other men in suits surrounded him, all of them walking down the steps of a courthouse. Reporters crowded around, raising cameras and thrusting microphones at him. He ignored them, his eyes again directed straight ahead, strangely dignified despite the circumstances.

Hearing Tucker in the hall, she quickly slipped the first newspaper in its place and shut the drawer.

He appeared in the doorway and opened the bag. "Did you know they made blueberry bagels? You didn't tell me what kind you liked, so I got one of everything."

An image of Tucker in handcuffs superimposed itself on the man in the doorway. Harley turned away and leaned on the desk.

He approached her. The aroma of warm yeast mingled with onion and garlic, raisin and blueberry, caused a swell of nausea to rise in her throat. She closed her eyes and swallowed hard. Feeling his hand on the small of her back, she jerked away, then the hand was gone.

His tone softened. "What's the matter? Still hungover?" Without opening her eyes, she nodded. "Have you eaten anything?" She shook her head. "Dr. Hale recommends a poppy-seed bagel with cream cheese and lox, followed by as many laps as you can manage, to burn the toxins out of your system. I swam, and I feel great now."

How nice for you, she thought. *How nice that you can feel great while I'm twisting inside.*

"I can't eat," she managed to say.

"Nothing?" He replaced the hand on her back. "You'd really feel better if—"

She opened her eyes. "I'm going for a run." She shook off the hand and darted from the room, leaving him staring after her.

TUCKER HALE GUILTY on all counts. She repeated the words over and over in her mind as she ran. They became her mantra. They seared themselves into her consciousness. They were hard words. They were painful. It hurt her to think them, yet she forced herself to think them over and over again.

"Tucker Hale guilty on all counts." She whispered the words out loud to reinforce them, to underline their truth. Tucker Hale had been found guilty on all counts. A court of law had determined that he had attempted to smuggle cocaine and marijuana into Florida in his Piper Comanche. That was the truth. She couldn't afford to flinch from it.

He had taken her in, charmed her, made himself a part of her life, all under false pretenses. Refusing to tell her what happened in Miami amounted to a lie by omission. So, technically, he had lied to her, despite his pious insistence that he never lied. She remembered his excuse when she had asked him directly about Miami and he had declined to answer. He was worried that she would judge him and find him lacking.

Damn *straight*, she would find him lacking.

He had been a drug dealer, just like her father. Well, not *just* like her father. Her father had been small potatoes compared to Tucker. Her father had peddled nickel bags of pot and the occasional Quaalude to his fellow down-and-out biker hippies, making barely enough to keep them both fed. Tucker, on the other hand, had smuggled millions of dollars' worth of drugs into the country, or had attempted to.

Harley tried to piece it all together, struggling to remember the things he had told her about his past and his business, and reconstruct the things he hadn't. After his music career had fizzled out, he'd moved to Miami—he and Chet— and saved up for a Piper Comanche. She couldn't recall his saying exactly what kind of cargo he had intended the plane for, although now it was clear enough. The shipment that the feds intercepted might have been his first, or he might have been doing it for a while and had millions in a Swiss bank by the time they caught him. Harley didn't know or care; a drug dealer was a drug dealer.

Apparently they had sent him to prison, and when he got out, he moved to Alaska and saved up for another plane. He'd started as a humble bush pilot, he said, parlaying that into an air cargo business so successful that he had a staff of pilots, half-a-dozen planes, and enough pin money lying around to drive Jags off the lot when the spirit moved him.

Harley began to wonder just what kind of cargo he'd built his business around. Granted, to her knowledge, Alaska, unlike Florida, was not exactly a hub of international drug trafficking. But she did recall having heard about some kind of special, superpotent marijuana they grew in Alaska's Matanuska Valley, which sold for astronomical sums. The possibility that he had returned to the same risky, but superprofitable business for which he had once been sent to jail could not be discounted.

Did he really intend to give it all up and move back to Long Island? Maybe. Maybe the crash had convinced him it was time to retire. He was a wealthy man; he could certainly afford to.

"Tucker Hale guilty on all counts," she whispered again. It didn't matter if he *was* getting out of the business. It didn't even matter if he hadn't been in the business since Miami. That he had been in it at all condemned him for eternity as far as she was concerned.

She closed her eyes as she ran and saw her mother's once-pretty face, made monstrous by an ugly, drug-induced death. No prison term could make up for the crime of preying on the weakness of people like Jennifer Sayers. Tucker had not paid his dues, and she could not forgive him.

She opened her eyes to erase her mother's image. He had kept the truth from her because he knew that, once she learned it, she would never want to have anything to do with him again. He had tricked her, ingratiated himself with her, and it shamed her that she had let it happen.

She stopped running and looked around, chest heaving. Neither this stretch of beach nor the houses above it were familiar to her. She had never run this far before.

Tucker Hale guilty on all counts.

She had even begun to think she might be in love with him. A sob rose in her throat and she choked it back. *He's not worth crying over,* she thought. *Don't let him get to you any more than he already has.*

She turned around and headed back, grimly whispering her new mantra over and over: *He's not worth crying over. Don't let him make you cry.*

HARLEY THOUGHT UP a number of unnecessary errands that would keep her out of the house all day. When she came home late in the afternoon, Tucker told her that Phil had invited them, along with Rob and Larry and their wives, to his place to boil some lobsters. She declined, citing her hangover as an excuse. The truth was that her morning run had cured her of it. But she insisted that he go without her, that she was going straight to bed.

There were things to think about now, decisions to make. Should she ask Tucker to leave? That would be hard to do. This was his father's home; she was just an employee. R.H. obviously knew about his son's arrest and conviction. Did Liz? She doubted it, given Liz's obvious affection for Tucker. Probably R.H. had kept the truth from her to protect her, just as he had kept the truth of Anjelica's suicide from Tucker to protect him. A mistake in both cases. Ignorance wasn't bliss, it was just ignorance. As Harley had found out that morning, when the truth finally came to light, it was all the more painful for having been kept a secret.

As darkness fell, Harley decided to take advantage of Tucker's absence and go for her evening swim. She wouldn't have dared it had he been there, given their deal. But he was gone, and she could use the relaxation. Soon—by this time tomorrow at the latest—she would have to develop a strategy for dealing with Tucker. That strategy would certainly involve a confrontation with him, and she dreaded the idea of that. But she didn't have to confront him tonight. She didn't even have to think about it tonight. Tonight she would swim.

She changed into her burgundy suit with the bow-tied spaghetti straps, and slipped into the cool, comforting water. For about ten minutes she backstroked slow, relaxing laps, watching the night sky and purposefully occupying her mind with trying to make out the constellations.

A sound from the shallow-end deck startled her; she coiled up like a spring and trod water. Tucker stood there, kicking off his moccasins.

He said, "I thought you were going to bed."

She willed calm into her voice. "I feel better now."

"Really?" He grinned. "Then you won't mind my joining you." He pulled his T-shirt off over his head and tossed it aside. Dressed only in khaki shorts, he lowered himself into the pool.

The blood roared in her ears. Taking a deep breath, she said, "Why aren't you still at Phil's? This is kind of early to be leaving a dinner party."

"All Phil can talk about is Kitty. It seems she went on a date last night with the head of cardiology at the medical center. Phil's turned into a raving basket case over it, but that's good. Maybe now he'll be desperate enough to finally take my advice and let her know how much he wants her back. Anyway, it was a pretty tiresome evening, but that's not the only reason I left. You weren't feeling well, and I wanted to check on you." He smiled again. "I'm glad you're feeling better. And I'm glad I came home before you left the pool."

"I was just about to get out," she lied.

"You wouldn't deny me my nightly shot at the big prize," he said. "It won't take a minute."

Unless you win, thought Harley. *Then it'll take all night.*

She could not go to bed with Tucker Hale—not knowing what she knew now. But she wasn't prepared for a showdown, either. She hadn't even decided which of them should be the one to leave. Confronting him without knowing what she wanted would put her in a position of weakness. She needed time. She needed until tomorrow. Biting her lip, she calculated his chances of catching her tonight at thirty, maybe forty percent, thinking, *Wouldn't Liz be proud of me for reducing this situation to numbers.*

"Okay," she said, positioning herself at the drop-off. *Let's get this over with.* "Ready?"

"Am I ever. I'm really up for this tonight."

Harley recalculated his chances at closer to fifty percent.

"I'm feeling *fast.*"

Maybe sixty. Tops.

She inhaled deeply and let it out. *Got to pull out all the stops tonight. Whatever you do, don't let him catch you.*

"One . . . two . . . three . . . go!"

Go-go-go-go-go! Harley surged forward, a lightning-fast, unthinking machine. *Kick-kick-kick-kick-kick, go-go-go-go-go!* She could hear him pursuing her through the water, his strokes quick and powerful. Her heart raced with the panic of the chased animal. He was closing in on her. She could feel the turbulence of the water as he neared. Was he doing the butterfly? She pictured the trophy in his room, inscribed Tucker Hale, 200-Meter Butterfly, First Place—

The big hands wrapped around her waist just a split second before she touched the deck. *He did it! No-no-no-no—*

She grabbed the deck with both hands to pull herself up, but he pressed down on her shoulders, halting her efforts to rise. He was behind her, very close to her. She could hear his ragged breathing, she could feel his heat through the water that separated them.

What could she say to him? How could she get out of this?

He gathered her wet hair to one side, and then she felt his lips, warm and gentle, on the back of her neck. His kisses sent shivers down her spine, and she closed her eyes, thinking, *I don't want this, I can't let this happen.*

Abruptly she gripped the deck and pushed herself up and out of the pool, but he was right behind her, leaping up like a big cat. Before she could rise, he lowered her to the deck, covering her body with his.

Maybe she could tell him they had to wait until tomorrow. She could claim she still felt unwell. That would give her the night to think of what to say to him. But when she opened her mouth to speak, he leaned down and closed his own over it. He kissed her with a deep and urgent passion, the culmination of six weeks of aching need. His hands traced restless paths over her breasts, down to her waist and hips, and back up to her shoulders.

Impatiently he untied the straps of her swimsuit and peeled it down to her waist, cupping her breasts with his hands. She broke the kiss, gasping. *This can't happen, this can't happen.*

Lowering his head, he took one taut nipple in his warm mouth. She groaned as he kissed and suckled her, a groan of both despair and yearning. She wanted to feel his lips on every inch of her body, she wanted him inside her, she wanted to give herself to him.

How could this be? How could she still want him, knowing what he was? He had the power to make her forget herself, that's why. When he touched her, she dissolved.

Summoning all her strength, she pushed him away. Released of his mouth and hands, she quickly turned and sprang to her feet before he could stop her. Standing with her back to him, she pulled up her suit and retied the straps.

He sat up. "Harley? What's going on?"

Without answering him, she walked around the pool to the shallow end, feeling Tucker's eyes on her the whole time. She lifted her robe from the chaise where she had left it and put it on as he gained his feet and walked toward her. "Come on, Harley, talk to me."

She tried to walk away, but he stepped in front of her and grabbed her arm. She tried to shake him off, but his grip tightened. "Don't freeze me out, Harley. Talk to me. What's the matter?"

She looked away from his huge brown eyes. "I just ... I don't want to ... to be with you that way. I just don't want to."

"I can see that. You mind telling me why?"

"Look, I know we had a deal—"

"Forget the deal. This isn't about any deal. This is about you and me."

She straightened her back. "There's never been any 'you and me.'"

"Then what's been going on here all summer? You mind telling me that?"

She met his eyes. "I've been getting conned all summer. That's what's been going on."

"What?"

She grabbed his hand by the wrist and flung it away. "But it's over."

"Harley, I don't—"

"Save your breath. It's over." She circled him, opened the French doors, and went into the house. Glancing back, she saw him reach into his back pocket, pull out his wallet, grimace, and hurl it angrily across the patio.

She ran to her room, closed and locked the door, then curled up on her bed, shaking from head to toe.

It took about half an hour for the tremors to cease. She got up and went to the window. The patio was dark. She stood still and listened for a minute; the house was quiet. Carefully opening the door, she walked down the hall to the bathroom, dropped her robe and swimsuit onto the tiled floor, and took a long, hot shower.

Wrapped in a towel, her wet hair combed straight back, she returned to her room. Tucker was there. She froze in her tracks, staring from the doorway.

He stood at her dresser, opening the top drawer, which was about chest-high on him. He had traded his wet khaki shorts for olive-green fatigue pants and a white T-shirt. When he saw Harley, he looked up, his eyes lowering automatically to the towel and her bare legs, then returned his attention to the drawer. He felt around inside, lifting a stack of scarves and looking under it. Closing that drawer, he opened the one beneath it.

"What are you looking for?" Harley asked.

"My cigarettes." He pushed aside a jumble of socks.

"You can't be serious," she said. "You haven't smoked for six weeks. You're going to start again now?"

"My motivation for quitting is gone."

"You don't want to be healthy anymore?"

He slammed the drawer closed and yanked another open. "I didn't quit for my health. I quit for you." He glanced at her and then back at the contents of the drawer. It was her underwear drawer, and he blinked at the display of patterns: zebra, leopard, tiger, Dalmatian, snakeskin.

"They're not in there," she volunteered.

He shut that drawer and opened another. T-shirts. He pawed through them freely. "I wanted to get into decent enough shape to win you. I knew I couldn't just have you. I had to earn you. I thought, this woman is special. She deserves the best."

Finished with the T-shirt drawer, he squatted down and opened the bottom one, hesitating at the neat piles of bras and stockings.

"They're not in that one, either," Harley said.

He closed it, stood, and looked around. Zeroing in on her night table, he slid open its single drawer, finding it filled with odds and ends: memorabilia, buttons, sewing things, pens and pencils, safety pins . . .

"I tried to be the best for you," he said. "I made myself over for you. I reinvented myself just for you. And meanwhile I waited for you. For six weeks I kept my distance from you, and don't think for a second it was easy." He pushed the drawer back in and looked at her. "I thought you understood why I was going to all that trouble. I thought you wanted me as much as I wanted you."

He turned away again and went to her dressing table, which also had only one drawer. Rummaging through her modest collection of makeup and toiletries, he said, "I guess I was pretty naive. You're in the market for some doctor or lawyer, just like Phil said. Not some crippled high-school dropout who makes his living hauling stuff from one place to another."

"Oh, please. I *never* thought of you that way."

"Didn't you? I mean, *I* know I'm more than that, I know I deserve you. Maybe I didn't six weeks ago, but I do now. Only now you don't seem to know it."

He looked around in frustration. No more drawers. Without thinking about it, Harley glanced toward her bed, and Tucker noticed. His eyebrows shot up. "You're kidding," he said. Lifting the mattress with one hand, he snatched the two packs of Camels from beneath it with the other. "Is this what they teach you in business school? To hide your valuables under the mattress? I thought that was out of style." He pocketed the cigarettes, except for one, which he placed between his lips.

"Tucker, don't." Harley walked over to him and grabbed the cigarette away from him.

His hand closed around her wrist. "The first time you did that, it was kind of cute. It's lost its charm." He took the cigarette back and released her wrist. Producing a pack of matches, he lit up, grimacing as he inhaled. He sat on the edge of her bed and rubbed his neck, then looked up at her, his eyes briefly drawn again to the towel in which she was wrapped. "So, what now?" he asked, leaning forward, elbows on knees. "What do you want? Level with me this time, Harley. Tell me what you *really* want. You want me to get lost? Just tell me the truth this time."

The truth. "I know you want to see your father. And this is more your house than mine, so I'd feel funny asking you to leave. I don't mind if you stay. As long as . . . as long as you understand—"

"That I'm to keep the hell away from you," he finished, meeting her eyes. "That I'm not to call you honey, that I'm not to touch you or tell you how much I want you. I'm not to think about you every waking hour, imagining what it would be like to take your clothes off and make love to you. I'm not to wake up in the middle of the night in a sweat because I've dreamed about you again. Right?" Harley just stared at him, unable to speak. He closed his eyes, lowered his head, and sat that way for a few moments, the ash growing longer on his unsmoked cigarette. "The thing is—" he looked at her, and she saw the honest confusion in his eyes "—you just didn't seem like the kind of woman who would let things get this far and then yank the rug out from under me."

Her response was immediate. "And you didn't seem like a drug dealer. I guess we're both full of surprises."

His gaze never left hers. The ash from his cigarette dropped onto the rug, but he didn't notice. Finally he said, "That's what this is about?"

She said, "I found two articles from the *Miami Herald* in your father's desk this morning—"

He stood. "Show me."

After a brief detour to the bathroom to substitute her robe for the towel, Harley led him to the study. She opened the drawer and pulled out the first newspaper. Sitting in the leather swivel chair, he crossed his legs with graceful ease— something that would have been impossible for him six weeks before—and read the article in its entirety with no change in expression. When he was done, she handed him the second article, and he read that, as well. Still holding the newspapers, he sat back and studied her for a minute.

When he spoke, his voice was a soft rasp, and his words seemed to have been chosen with care. "I can understand how this must have made you feel, finding all this out. Your childhood was ruined because of your parents' dependence on drugs, I know that. That's a big part of the reason I didn't want to tell you about Miami. I didn't want you to think I was connected in any way with drugs, and I certainly didn't want you to know I'd been in prison. Something I found out after I got out was, people aren't interested in why you served time, whether there was any justice in it or not. The very fact that you were in there at all, brands you as a criminal permanently. The stigma is almost impossible to erase."

She folded her arms. "You're assuming I'll agree with you that there was no justice in your being sent to jail. That's assuming a lot."

He nodded slightly, as if he had expected her to say this. "I was convicted on the basis of Chet's testimony. He swore in court that I'd been away from the house all night, that he'd heard me return half an hour before the police got there. I swore that I'd been asleep since eleven o'clock. It was a little more complicated than that, but that's the gist of it. As soon as Chet's father found out what happened, he arranged for this high-powered, silk-suited lawyer to coach him through his testimony. I was represented by this overworked young public defender who didn't seem to know a damn thing about me or the case except that I had to be guilty as hell or they wouldn't have arrested me in the first place. Anyway, the jury believed Chet, and I was convicted on all counts and sentenced to spend half of the rest of my life behind bars."

"You're saying you were innocent?" He nodded. "I'd find that a little more plausible if there was any reason for Chet to have invented that business about you being gone all night. But why would he have lied? You and he were friends. You turned down a record deal for him. If anything, he would have been grateful. He would have felt like he owed you."

He sighed wearily and looked at the floor. "You'd think so. But some friendships are more...one-sided than others. People always tried to warn me about Chet, but I was...I believed in loyalty. And I never thought he'd actually do anything to hurt me." He absently patted the pocket of his T-shirt, seeming vaguely surprised to find the cigarettes there. He pulled out the open pack, looked at it for a second, then tossed it in the trash. Then he did the same with the full pack.

He said, "I'd served seven months of my sentence when they called me down to the warden. Seems Chet was at the controls of a Beechcraft Sierra filled with cocaine and heroin that lost power somewhere over Texas. He tried for an emergency landing, but ended up hitting this grain silo dead-on. The engine went up in flames, and the cabin with it. They got him out, but he was...He lived for six hours. He was conscious most of that time, but he knew he was dying. He talked nonstop, they said, and he was surprisingly coherent. He told them about the night he borrowed my Piper Comanche without asking, for that drug run that got intercepted, and about how he set me up for the conviction to protect himself. The police tape-recorded his confession, the investigation was reopened, and I was completely exonerated. They released me on Christmas Eve, sixteen years ago."

He took a deep breath and met her eyes. Unsure what to say, or what to believe, Harley just stared back. He opened the drawer and replaced the two newspapers, saying, "Apparently Chet's father didn't see fit to fill R.H. in on the final chapter. For all I know, he thinks I'm still in prison. He's probably glad people think I'm dead. He probably wishes I were."

Still, Harley couldn't think of anything to say. Rising, Tucker walked to the doorway. "What I just told you is the way it really went down, Harley. You can believe it or not, it's your choice."

He turned and was gone.

IF ONLY THE TRUTH WERE a matter of choice, but it wasn't. It was a matter of facts.

The next morning, Harley drove to the library of the State University of New York at Stony Brook, in search of the facts.

"Do you have back issues of the *Miami Herald* on microfiche?" she asked the clerk, an emaciated young woman with black-dyed, buzz-cut hair and a pierced nose.

The clerk turned a page of her magazine. "Year?"

"Uh . . . sixteen years ago. December twenty-fourth."

Seven minutes later the clerk handed over the microfilm, saying, "You gotta return it to the desk when you're done."

Harley sat down at a microfiche reader and inserted her film. Clutching the knobs, she leaned forward to inspect the miniature white-on-black pages as they scrolled down the screen. Nothing on page one, nothing on page two, nothing on page three . . . Surely there would have been some kind of public statement about his release. If it had really happened, that is.

Finally, after ten minutes of searching, she found what she was looking for, was hoping to find but fearing she wouldn't—a small item with no picture, buried dozens of pages into the paper. The words leapt out at her: Tucker Hale Released From Prison Today.

Frantically she twirled the focus knob, squinting to make out the story: "Tucker Hale, twenty-one, falsely convicted on five counts of drug trafficking, was released from prison this morning...."

She slumped in her seat, resting her forehead against the screen. "Thank God," she whispered. "Thank God."

Her chair tipped over and clattered to the floor as she stood, but she barely noticed. Grabbing her purse, she jogged toward the door.

The clerk's voice followed her as she sprinted from the building. "'Scuse me. Miss? Hey! You gotta return that film to the desk. I *told* you!"

HALF AN HOUR LATER, Tucker sat next to Harley on the stone wall overlooking the beach, numb from emotional overload. First, the phone call that had come while she was gone, leaving him reeling. Then Harley's return and unexpected apology. He wanted to accept it graciously, but he wasn't feeling particularly gracious at the moment.

He spoke slowly. "I just wish . . . I don't know. I wish you hadn't found it so easy to believe the worst about me. I know it's hard to discount something you read in black-and-white, but a *little* doubt would have helped."

She nodded, staring glassy-eyed over his shoulder at the sun sparkling on the corrugated surface of Long Island Sound. "I'm sorry I didn't question it. I jumped to conclusions. I think I did it because I was scared."

"Scared of what? Me?"

She transferred her gaze to her hands, clenched tightly in her lap. "You hit the nail on the head that first night, before you left, when you said I was afraid of anything messy or unexpected in my life. I didn't expect you in my life. And I sure didn't expect to . . . to grow to feel anything for you. I'm sorry I couldn't handle it. I messed everything up. I'd like to . . . to wipe the slate clean and start over, if we could. I promise I won't bring my preconceptions and prejudices into our relationship. I mean, now that you've explained how it was, what really happened—"

"You mean, now that you've had a chance to go to the library and research my explanation like it was part of some thesis you were working on?"

Clearly stung, she reddened and looked away.

He said, "Honey, I'm sorry, too. I'm sorry you couldn't accept my version of things on faith." He saw her swallow hard as she nodded again. Softening to her, he added, "But I'm also sorry for the part I played in all of this. I shouldn't have kept Miami a secret from you. I realize that, now. And for that I apologize. I guess we've both been partially to blame."

After a long pause, he said, "Maybe it's best that this happened when it did. I mean, what do we have in common— *really* have in common—besides the fact that our mothers killed themselves? Maybe you and I just weren't meant to . . ."

She bit her lip, and he knew she was struggling to hold her emotions in check. He resisted the impulse to take her in his arms and comfort her, much as he wanted to. If he held her, he would want to kiss her. And if he kissed her . . .

No. There had been enough complications, enough confusion, for one summer. Why add pathos to what should be a clean end to things?

A minute or more ticked by. He turned and gazed out at the Sound, trying to follow her line of sight. Near the horizon, the tiny silhouettes of two sailboats drifted slowly toward the east, and the Atlantic.

"Liz called," he said, his eyes following the boats' stately progress. "While you were at the library. R.H. had a series of angina attacks and decided to cut his sailing trip short." From the corner of his eye, he saw her turn to look at him. "He's in Fort Lauderdale now, but he's booked a morning flight. She'll meet him at La Guardia and drive him back here. They'll be arriving around one, tomorrow afternoon."

12

TUCKER SPENT THE afternoon and early evening in the black Jag, touring Long Island's back roads for hours, with no particular purpose or destination. A long drive usually relaxed him, distracted him from his troubles, but this one just felt pointless. The only thing that kept him behind the wheel was the knowledge that if he went back to the house, he would have to interact with Harley. Psyching himself up to leave, getting used to the idea so he could find the strength to do it, was hard enough. If he had to look at her while he thought about it, it would be impossible.

It was dark by the time he pulled the car into the driveway. The lights were on in the house, and he saw shadowy movement behind the kitchen curtains. He sat in the driver's seat for a minute and then got out and walked across the brightly lit patio and the dark lawn to the low stone wall overlooking the Sound. He sat facing the inky, moonlit water and breathed deeply, imprinting in his mind the distinctive fragrance that existed in this one spot and no other—lavender and thyme, salt air and seaweed.

The fragrance of Hale's Point. He would miss it.

He patted his T-shirt pocket and sighed. That was a reflex that would take some time to lose, but one that was worth losing.

The waves were unhurried tonight, a steady *hush...hush...hush.* There were other sounds, a lazy summer symphony carried on the warm breeze. He heard the distant drone of a powerboat way out on the water.

The ambient light behind him disappeared, leaving the yard that much darker; she must have shut off the patio lights. He turned around just in time to see the sudden appearance of a glowing blue rectangle in the darkness as the pool lights snapped on. Where was she? Ah, there...walking across the patio to the shallow end, wearing that white terry-cloth robe of hers. She started untying it, and he turned back to face the Sound, leaning forward, elbows on knees, concentrating on the ceaseless, comforting *hush* of the waves.

Their uneven rhythm was soon accompanied by gentle splashes from the pool as Harley took her evening swim. It was a short swim; he soon heard a different kind of splash and knew she was climbing out onto the deck. He glanced back over his shoulder and froze, staring.

She was naked.

Her lithe body shone like wet marble as she walked over to the outdoor shower and turned it on, testing the water.

She had swum in the nude. Did she know he was there? The Jag sat in the driveway, and she would have heard him drive up. Still . . .

She stood beneath the spray and rinsed off, her back to him. Then she turned toward him, tilted her face up, and let the water flow through her hair as she ran her fingers through it.

She was perfect. He had never seen anyone like her, so flawlessly proportioned, tight and firm, with no excess anything. Tucker had always admired simplicity of design, a by-product of his love for cars, boats, and planes. Sighing with regret, he turned back toward the water.

Presently he heard the soft whisper of footsteps on the grass. Looking back over his shoulder, he saw her walking toward him, complete with robe, her wet hair slicked back. The robe was very white in the dark, and she had both hands in the pockets. He lifted his legs over the stone wall and sat facing her as she approached.

She came to stand before him, withdrew one hand, and held it out to him. He took it in his. Her eyes beckoned him, a silent invitation, breathtaking in its frankness. He instantly grew hard.

When he found his voice, he said, "I'm leaving tomorrow."

Her expression carefully neutral, she nodded. She had clearly expected this. Without releasing his hand, she took a step forward and knelt before him, his long, jeans-clad legs flanking her. Softly she said, "Then we should make the most of the time we have." They had been his words. He had said them to her that first night, when he had come to her room, reckless and overeager. Overeager for her body, not for her. That was before he had fallen in love with her. Before everything had gotten so thrilling and wonderful, so full of potential . . . and so ultimately impossible.

He realized he was staring at her, overwhelmed and uncertain. It was she who acted, she who let go of his hand to reach up with both of hers and guide his head down, meeting his mouth with her own in a deep and passionate kiss. She had never taken it upon herself to kiss him before, and after a moment's stunned hesitation, a flood of longing washed through him, like a dam breaking somewhere deep inside.

His arms encircled her; he couldn't have stopped them if he'd wanted. He held her tight, clamped between his legs, his mouth crushed to hers, her scent and her warmth filling him, consuming him. She wrapped her arms around him, pulling him closer. The kiss was blindingly intense. When his lungs were searing and his heart ready to explode, he tore his mouth away, gasping her name.

He watched in slow motion as she fell back onto the grass, and realized as he followed her, settling onto her and fitting his body to hers, that she had pulled him down with her. Their mouths found each other's again as they molded together in a hungry embrace.

They rolled to the side; he stroked her wet hair, her shoulders and back, cupped her bottom through the terry cloth and pressed her toward him so she could feel the effect she had on him. She slipped a leg between his and moved her hips, and he moaned, pulling her hard against him and guiding the rhythm of her movements with his hands. All his reservations evaporated in the wake of his overpowering need.

Too overpowering. He was too close, it was happening too fast. It was her first time, he would have to go slowly, but at this rate that wouldn't be possible. He drew away from her and lay back on the cool grass, his chest heaving. Closing his eyes, he willed control over himself.

Her fingertips, cool and soft, brushed his hair, his face, his throat. He opened his eyes and saw that she was sitting next to him, looking down. Her moonlit face was clouded with sadness, and he knew she already grieved for tomorrow. He took her hand, pressed her palm to his lips, and kissed it.

"Don't think about it," he murmured. "Think about now."

She banished the grief from her eyes. "I don't want to think at all." She reached for the sash of her robe, fumbling with its double knot. Instantly his hard-won control vanished, replaced by unstoppable desire. Impatience drove him as he grabbed her shoulders and pushed her to the ground, straddling her and yanking at the knot until it loosened.

A heartbeat's pause . . . *Slow down, Tucker, take it slow.* The robe—that damn robe that had taunted and teased him all summer—was unbound, but unopened. *Slow, now. For her.*

Harley sensed his inner struggle. She looked up at his face, incandescent against the night sky, as he slowly parted the robe and gazed down at her. Surprisingly, she felt not the least embarrassed under his rapt scrutiny, just as she had felt no shame earlier, swimming in the nude, hoping he would see her, come to her, join her. She had been forced to come to him, but that was all right. That was good. After the way she had screwed things up, that was as it should be.

He touched a finger to her brow; she must have been frowning. "No thinking," he reminded her softly.

She forced a smile. "I forgot."

He buried his hands in her hair and massaged her scalp until it buzzed with pleasure and her eyes closed of their own accord. Lowering his touch, he traced light, feathery paths across eyelids and cheekbones and lips. She found it oddly moving for him to devote this kind of attention to her face when her body lay exposed beneath him.

He did not ignore it for long. Her throat was next, and his delicate ministrations drew a purr from her. He ran a finger lightly back and forth along each collarbone, and then paused. Her breasts felt warm from his nearness even before he lowered his hands to lightly rest on them. When he caressed her—gently, as if he were testing fruit that he didn't want to bruise—she moaned, and felt her nipples tighten. He grazed them with his palms, then captured one and leaned down to take it in his warm mouth. His teeth lightly scraped the tender flesh, igniting currents of pleasure that shot through her like lightning.

She opened her eyes. He was still fully dressed. That wouldn't do. She sat up, pulling at his T-shirt, which he whipped over his head and tossed into the darkness. She kissed his throat and those impossibly wide shoulders, her hands exploring him eagerly, while his tangled in her hair. When she reached the scar tissue on his left side, she paused. She considered his leg, his chest, his back, the terrible wounds.

"Tucker . . . this won't hurt you, will it?"

He chuckled disbelievingly. "You're worried about hurting *me*? I'm terrified of hurting you." His brows drew together. "The first time . . . it could hurt."

She felt a curious thrill at this acknowledgment that they were actually going to make love. "Then we're both terrified," she said. "You're terrified that you'll hurt me, and I'm terrified that I'll disappoint you."

"How could you possibly—"

"I don't know if I can . . . I mean, Brian always said I was probably fr—"

"Brian's an idiot! I told you."

"But—"

He eased her back down and hovered over her. "You're not only thinking too much, you're talking too much." His mouth closed over hers in a deep, delicious, thought-erasing kiss. He followed that with a series of licks and nibbles along her jaw that ended at her ear, into which he whispered, "I'll show you how wrong Brian was."

Reclining on an elbow, he watched his hand trace a warm path down her chest and abdomen to her lower belly. He paused briefly before continuing, his fingers brushing ever so lightly. . . . She gasped and stiffened, clutching a fistful of grass in each hand.

"Easy," he whispered hoarsely.

"I know, but—" Her words caught in her throat as he intensified the caress, stroking her in a tantalizing, languid rhythm. The sensation was hypnotic; she closed her eyes and lay still, paralyzed by his touch. She heard his breathing, and hers, and felt the prickle of the grass beneath her open robe, but otherwise her senses were focused exclusively on that place between her legs. Her hips rose without her willing it. As if that were his cue, he slipped a finger deeper into her moist heat. Jolted, she drew in a sharp breath and opened her eyes to stare into the smoky depths of his.

His smile was reassuring, his raspy words almost inaudible for the blood roaring in her ears. "Easy," he repeated. "Give in to it. Go with it." He leaned over her, his mouth descending on hers for a remarkably tender kiss, his intimate caress never pausing. "God, you're so beautiful," he murmured.

Suddenly self-conscious, Harley turned her head, trying in vain to hide her face even as she writhed beneath his touch. As if sensing that she didn't want him watching her, he lowered his head to her breast, where he bestowed flickering little licks on an ultrasensitive nipple. Drawing it into his mouth, he sucked, hard this time, using his sharp teeth and the dancing tip of his tongue to escalate the torment.

The hand that played between her legs grew bolder, the skilled massage of his fingertips generating an itch that grew into a kind of exquisite agony, grew and grew until she thought her heart would burst if she had to endure another second of it. *Close... So close to...something.* He found the tiny, hidden source of her pleasure, and one fleeting touch was all it took to draw a startled cry from Harley. Her back arched, and she grabbed his arms, her fingers sinking deep.

He withdrew his hand. "No!" she groaned.

"I want to be inside you when it happens," he rasped. Rolling to the side, he reached for his fly, but she got there first, unbuttoning with a lust-induced haste she had never felt before. Raising his hips, he swept jeans and shorts off in one swift motion.

Harley stared. He noticed, and lay still, giving her time to look. She sat up straight and closed her robe around herself, feeling the same incredulous fear that she had felt once as a child, when a doctor whipped out a hypodermic about twice the size she'd thought it would be. He reached out and gently stroked her arm through the rough terry cloth. Trailing his fingers down to her hand, he took it and pulled it toward his erection.

"Tucker, I don't think—"

"Shh." He brought her hand to rest on the rigid shaft, which jerked at her touch. "Don't think, remember?"

She hadn't expected the tightly stretched smoothness of it, the heat, the little pulses that quivered within. He closed her fingers around it, drawing her fist slowly along its length.

His breathing quickened. "I told you a long time ago that it would be great between us, and it will. You trust me, right?"

"Yes, but . . ." *But that will never fit inside me.*

He sat up and lowered her onto her back. "Trust me," he whispered, one hand cupping her face while the other once again sought out that place of torment and ecstasy. This time he slipped a long finger inside her.

"*Oh!*" she gasped as he gently probed. "What are you doing?"

A second finger followed the first. "Stretching you just a bit. I don't want to hurt you. I'll be as careful as I can."

He leaned down for a lingering kiss as he slowly drew his fingers out. Then he reached for his wadded-up jeans. "Speaking of being careful . . ." He withdrew his wallet from the back pocket, slid the little square packet out, and ripped it open.

Wanting to prove that her attack of nerves was behind her, Harley said, "Let me help with that."

He positioned the condom and showed her how to unroll it over his penis. She smoothed it up and down with firm strokes, as if trying to make it perfect, pleased that she could feel his heat through the latex. He seized her by the shoulders, inhaling sharply.

"Am I doing it wrong?" she asked, her wicked smile belying the innocence in her voice.

"Absolutely not," he growled, but his hand clamped over her wrist and pulled her hand away. "It's *too* right. You're a quick study."

She lay back in the grass and opened her arms to him. "Always have been."

He eased himself down onto her, took her in his arms, and brushed his warm lips across forehead and eyelids, nose and cheeks and chin. Maneuvering himself between her legs, he rose onto an elbow, took her right hand in his, kissed it, and brought it down between them. "You guide me."

He gazed directly into her eyes as she took somewhat tentative hold of him, tilted her hips, and led him to her narrow entrance. Her breath caught as he pressed inward. So warm and hard, so much to take in . . . She stretched to accommodate him, her flesh burning.

"You're so tight," he breathed. "Are you all right?"

She nodded, relieved, but then she reached between them with her hand and felt that he had barely entered her.

He kissed her eyelids and whispered against them, "Relax completely. And trust me."

She felt his long arms tighten around her, holding her still, and she wrapped her arms around his back. Murmuring reassurances, he pushed into her, very slowly, paused, and then pushed again, and again. Despite the discomfort, it was a strange and wonderful feeling, to be penetrated by this man, possessed by him. She wanted to remember everything about it.

When it seemed as if he could make no further progress, he moved his hands to her hips, slid them beneath her, and pulled her toward him. He pushed harder this time, and she winced, but with the second thrust she felt something give way inside, and he collapsed on her with a groan.

When he lifted his head to look at her, his eyes were smiling. He guided her hand to the juncture of their bodies, where they were intimately connected. All she could feel was a tangle of hair, his and hers. He was completely inside her now.

"How does it feel?" he asked.

Enormous and hot and hard. "Amazing," she whispered.

He rested his forehead on hers. "It feels amazing to me, too. I've wanted this for so long. So many times I've wondered what it would feel like to be buried inside you. I never dreamed it would feel this good."

Rising over her, he braced himself on one arm and reached down to gingerly touch her aching flesh where they were joined. The touch galvanized her, sweeping her back into a state of high arousal. His nimble fingers increased their tempo, spiraling her to the edge of something dark and extraordinary before retreating to a gentler caress. Again he picked up the pace, and again backed off, denying her release.

She writhed unselfconsciously, clutching his arms, her robe, the grass. She yanked two fistfuls right out of the ground. He drew himself gradually out of her, just a bit, and then pushed back in. Again, and then again, slowly, carefully... It was torment. It was unendurable. His ragged breathing and the quivering strain she felt in the hard muscles of his arms and back betrayed his own frustration, and the control she knew he struggled to maintain.

The hell with control. She pressed her hands to the small of his back and arched. "Please," she moaned.

He fell on her, driving himself in to the hilt, pressing her into the ground with his weight. He pulled out and then plunged in again, deep.

"Yes," she breathed, rising to meet the slow, penetrating thrusts that were as maddening, in their own way, as his teasing touch. *So close . . .* She heard him murmur her name, tell her she was beautiful, and that he wanted to feel her come.

He took her hands in his and held them near her shoulders as she threw her head back. Nearly insensible, she thrashed beneath him as he pumped faster, in an urgent rhythm, straining with her toward release.

Just as she reached the precipice and teetered off, he covered her mouth with his and captured the animal cry that rose within her. The explosive pleasure detonated where their bodies were joined, then coursed through her like rolling thunder, rocking her with its power. He clenched her hands in a painful grip and groaned into her mouth, shuddering violently as his own pleasure overtook him. Together they rode out the aftershocks, moaning as the spasms subsided, then holding each other in a limp, breathless embrace.

He stroked her hair with a shaking hand. Her ears rang.

"Wow," she whispered.

"That's my line, remember?" he whispered back. He lifted his face to look at her, and a drop of sweat fell from his forehead onto her cheek.

She said, "You know what I think?"

"What?"

"I think Brian was an idiot." He laughed, and she felt him throb within her. "I didn't know," she said. "I had no idea it would be . . . like that."

"It's not," he said. "I mean, it's not usually. It's never been like that for me. Never." He enclosed her in his arms, buried his face in the crook of her neck, and kissed her throat. "I don't guess it ever will be again."

13

TUCKER SAW HARLEY in the window of the study, watching him toss his modest possessions into the trunk of the Jag. She was talking to someone on the phone, but her eyes followed his every move.

It was noon already, but it felt later. The night before, by unspoken agreement, he and Harley had retired to their own rooms. To share their bodies was one kind of intimacy, to share a bed, another. Tucker couldn't imagine waking up next to her, all warm and soft and sleepy, and then having the courage to leave. So he had slept in his own little bed in the maid's room, although he'd actually done a lot more tossing and turning than sleeping. He'd awakened exhausted, then spent a long morning trying to avoid Harley as much as possible. To be with her, knowing he had to leave, filled him with a pain more severe in its own way than anything he had suffered after cracking up the Skywagon.

R.H. had made it clear, through Liz, that he would prefer Harley to stay on until September, as originally planned. The maid wouldn't be returning until then, and he needed someone to look after things, especially given his precarious health. Liz had confided to Tucker that she had offered to stay there herself, but R.H. had declined, preferring not to inconvenience her. Tucker had sensed Liz's disappointment.

Liz had stressed that Harley would not be expected to wait on R.H. hand and foot. She would be regarded, not as a domestic servant, but more as a guest who'd agreed to help out.

Unsurprisingly, no such offer of hospitality had been extended to Tucker, although Liz had told him that he was there.

The job of packing and loading his things took less than ten minutes. He sat in the driver's seat and pondered whether this was a good thing or not. Harley disappeared from the window and reappeared a few minutes later in the passenger seat next to him. So much for trying to avoid her.

She said, "That was Phil. He said to tell you you're not so dumb, after all."

Trying to match her studied nonchalance, Tucker said, "What does *he* know?"

"He said he was calling from the ... It sounded like the *castle?*"

"That's Kitty's parents' house," Tucker explained, suddenly interested. "It's about a quarter mile from here."

"He said he wishes you could see it. All twenty-two rooms are literally filled with multicolored balloons saying, I Love You, Kitty.' Every ceiling is covered with them. Kitty's parents are not amused, but the boys are thrilled. Kitty, too. She's calling off the lawyers and going back to him. He said it was like she was just looking for an excuse."

"It worked! Wow."

"That was your idea? I guess you're *not* so dumb."

He couldn't stop the grimace. "Oh, I don't know about that."

There was an uncomfortable moment. Pressing on in her attempt to make normal conversation, Harley said, "I asked Phil if this means the trade is off now—your Jag for his house? And he laughed and said, 'You didn't really think I meant that, did you? Can't you take a joke?' And I said I'd never been able to, but I was working on it." Tucker couldn't help smiling. "His sons are begging him to let them release the balloons over the Sound. He's making them wait all day in order to annoy 'Lord and Lady Acton-Kemp' as much as possible. I'm to tell you to watch the sky around sundown."

He couldn't look her in the face. "I'm afraid I won't be here then."

There was only a brief pause. "You're going to leave right after your father gets home? 'Hi, Dad, bye, Dad'?"

"No. Probably before."

A longer pause this time. "*Before?* They'll be here within the hour."

He inhaled deeply. "I'm sorry, Harley. It's time to cut my losses."

She nodded slowly. "That's what you said that first night, when you walked away in the rain. That you knew how to cut your losses. If you had followed your instincts then and bolted, you'd still be in Alaska."

"And I'd still walk with a cane and I'd still be smoking and I'd still be in constant pain. I know. I'm glad I stayed and I'll always feel indebted to you for what you've done for me. I'll always love you." He spoke the words without intending to, but there they were. She stared at him. "I love you, Harley. I do. You're the first woman I ever loved, and the first one I ever waited for, ever struggled for, ever tried to become a better person for. I wanted things to work out between us, but when push came to shove, we just fell apart. Maybe we're just too different to make a relationship work."

"Phil and Kitty are different, and their relationship works. They weathered a crisis and overcame it because Phil followed your advice. He didn't give up. That's what you do when you're in it for the long haul. You make it work. You fix it. You don't bolt. I know you don't know any other way, and I know you're afraid—"

"Afraid?"

"Of commitment. But you can't just walk away and pretend nothing happened. Not this time, Tucker. It's not fair. You can't make me fall in love with you and then..." Her chin trembled, her eyes were filled with sudden tears. Tucker took her hand. Seeming angry with herself, she rubbed the tears from her eyes. "And then just leave!"

Tucker sat wordlessly for a moment, awed by her teary declaration of love. *So this is what it's like when two people are in love,* he thought. *This is pretty scary stuff.*

Softly he said, "I'd drive you crazy. Just like I drove my father crazy. You're a lot like him. You like things just so. I like them pretty much however they fall."

"Don't underestimate your influence," she said. "I don't iron my blue jeans anymore."

Tucker smiled. "Gee, and I was kind of getting used to those creases."

She said, "Well, they're history. And if I can change, your father can, too. At least stay till he gets here. He'll be expecting you. Liz will have told him you're here."

"He'll consider himself lucky not to have to confront me."

"Confront you? You're his son."

Tucker rubbed the back of his neck. She just didn't get it. "He thinks I just got out of prison, Harley. He thinks I made my living selling dope. He's undoubtedly ashamed of me and horrified that I've spent the past six weeks living in his home."

"So this is your opportunity to set him straight. Try telling him what really happened. There's no reason to think he'll be as dense about it as I was. Give him the benefit of the—"

"I'm telling you, it won't work. We're two personalities that just don't mix. And now that I've done time, justified or not, there's that stigma on top of everything else. He hated me then, and he'll hate me even more now."

"*Hated* you? Did you ever stop to wonder why he kept your room the same for twenty-one years? Why he's got two pictures of you on his desk?" Tucker had no instant answer for that. She curled around in the passenger seat to face him. "Obviously he missed you. He probably regretted having made the mistakes that forced you to leave."

"It would have helped if he hadn't made them in the first place."

"Look, I wasn't there, and I don't know what really happened, but I can't help but draw certain conclusions based on what I do know. I know that your mother took her own life, and I know that your father was at least partially responsible. It's doubtful that he ever acknowledged that responsibility to himself. People tend to protect themselves by denying that they caused something terrible to happen—in your father's case, the suicide of a woman he seems to have truly loved. So he convinced himself that the fault lay not with him, but with Anjelica—in other words, that she was unstable. Given her impulsive, creative nature, so different from his own, that was an easy mental leap for him."

"And an unfair one."

"Possibly. Then there was you. He worried about you while you were growing up. You were creative, like her. You were also angry, once you found her death certificate. He didn't understand any of it, and it scared him to think how you might turn out. You could destroy your life, too, unless he did something to stop it. He had to discipline you, to correct you, for your own good. Because he loved you. Not because he hated you. I think you know in your heart that he loves you, despite everything. Why else would you have thought about him like that after your plane went down, worrying that you'd die and he'd never know? Why else would you have come all the way back here? You wanted to patch things up with him."

He said, "Well . . . I wanted to see him. It would be great to patch things up, but I never really thought that was possible."

"It's not, if you leave before he even gets here." After a moment of silence, she withdrew her hand from his and pulled something from the pocket of her shorts: the little velvet bag. "I can't keep these now."

"Like I said before, I'm not taking them back."

"Tucker—"

"Can't I make just this one small gesture to thank you for everything you've done for me? Don't deprive me of that right. Accept them. Please." He could see the hesitation in her eyes, and then the small nod. "I'd like to see them on you. Would you mind?"

Shaking the little bag into the palm of her hand, she inserted the earrings and looked at him. He had to tuck her loose hair behind her ears in order to see them. He'd been right; she was meant to wear gold and rubies next to her skin. She looked like a beautiful statue cast in bronze, with sparkling green jewels for eyes.

He leaned over and kissed her lightly on the forehead. Her arms wrapped around him and her mouth found his. She kissed him with a sense of urgency and passion that overwhelmed him. He returned the kiss unthinkingly, his senses rioting.

Releasing her mouth from his, she held him tightly. He felt the hot tears on her face. "I want you to be more to me than just a summer romance, just a beautiful memory. I want you to be a beautiful future. Nothing I say or do can force you to stay. Leave if you have to," she said in a faltering voice, "but I can't stand here and watch you drive away. I don't think I could take that." She pulled back and looked up at him, her image wavering through the glaze of Tucker's own unshed tears. He brushed the wetness from her cheeks with trembling fingertips. "I'm going down to the beach. I'm going to run." He nodded, swallowing hard, not knowing what to say. She stroked his face with her hand, and he leaned into her palm, his eyes closed, not wanting her touch to end. "I hope you're here when I get back."

Hearing the car door open, he rubbed his eyes, struggling to maintain his composure. When he opened them, she was sprinting away, toward the beach.

HARLEY CLIMBED the boulder stairway and went directly to the front of the house. Her heart pounded wildly, not from exertion—a half-hour run was little more than a warm-up to her—but from anticipation. Would Tucker's black Jag be sitting in the driveway when she got there?

It wasn't.

"No," she whispered, the word catching on the sob that convulsed her chest. *No. No.* She sank to the grass and buried her face in her hands, giving herself over to despair. Her whole body shook as she cried; she was beyond self-control.

You blew it. You blew it. You stupid idiot. How could you have let him leave? Why did you make him leave? You blew it.

The sound of a car on the road made her look up. A blue Volvo—Liz's Volvo—pulled into the driveway. Harley jumped to her feet and darted into the house. Hurriedly she dried her face with a dish towel and located her seldom-worn sunglasses. It wouldn't do to let them see she'd been crying. Walking out the front door, she met them on the porch.

It was hard to believe R.H. had cut his trip short for health reasons. He looked remarkably fit for a man pushing seventy, but that was probably just the tan. His resemblance to his son struck Harley immediately. His white hair was as short as Tucker's, and he was nearly as tall. Against the tan, his silver-blue eyes glared like two tiny hundred-watt light bulbs. He was not happy.

Liz, tall and slender with a regal bearing, looked like R.H.'s twin sister, albeit in a better mood. She wore a linen pants outfit, and her short gray hair was concealed beneath a straw gardening hat. The pants surprised Harley; she had never seen her former professor in anything but Chanel suits. Retirement seemed to have taken the starch out of her wardrobe.

Liz kissed her on both cheeks. R.H. shook her hand and looked around.

Harley cleared her throat. "How was your flight, Mr. Hale?"

"They're all the same."

"Have you eaten? I can make you some—"

"Don't bother," said Liz. "We stopped on the way." She looked around, too. They were looking for Tucker.

"Iced tea?" offered Harley. "Or lemonade. I have some fresh lemons, I can make you some—"

Liz touched her arm. "We're fine, my dear. Tell me, where's Tucker?"

They both looked at her. Summoning a steady tone, she said, "Tucker's gone." The exact same words R.H. had used when she had asked *him* about Tucker, shortly after he hired her. *Tucker's gone.* A statement both accurate and vague.

Liz hesitated. "Gone. Do you mean he just stepped out for a moment, or—"

Gravel crunched at the end of the driveway, and all three heads turned to watch the vehicle that pulled up and parked behind Liz's blue Volvo.

It was Tucker's black Jag.

Harley stared, wide-eyed, as Tucker emerged, his own eyes riveted on his father.

"Here he is!" Liz crowed, descending the porch steps to kiss his cheeks. "Look at you! You look wonderful! Where have you been? I began to worry you'd gotten cold feet."

Tucker's eyes met Harley's for a fleeting second. "I had an errand to run. I had to go to the bank in the village."

His words extinguished the tiny flicker of hope that had sparked within her breast at his reappearance. He had gone to the bank, obviously to empty out his safe-deposit box so he could take his mother's jewelry with him. He would be leaving, after all, although apparently he had taken her advice and decided to see R.H. first.

R.H. studied his son from the porch. "Tucker."

"Sir."

No one spoke for a moment, and Harley swore she could hear the electric crackle of tension in the air.

Finally, nodding toward Tucker's car, R.H. said, "Is that the XJR-S?" Slowly he walked down the steps and over to the car.

Tucker met him there. "That's right."

R.H. ran a respectful hand over the front fender. "What's she got inside?"

"Six-liter overhead-cam V-12."

R.H. nodded thoughtfully. "Horsepower?"

"Three-eighteen."

"Pop the hood." Both men spent a minute admiring the gleaming new engine. Their resemblance was enhanced by their identical attire: chinos and dark, weathered polo shirts. "How does she ride?"

Tucker took the keys out of his pocket and handed them to the older man. With R.H. behind the wheel and Tucker in the passenger seat, the Jag tore out of the driveway and disappeared.

Rejoining Harley on the porch, Liz said, "Men have this absolutely amazing capacity for superficial communication in even the most emotion-charged circumstances." She used the same measured tone with which she used to deliver her statistics lectures. "They do it because they're frightened, poor things, and they usually use sports or toys as props to facilitate the process. With R.H. and Tucker, vehicles are the toys of choice. Let's have a drink."

"Iced tea or—"

"I don't know about you, but right now my nerves are shot. Do you have any single-malt Scotch?"

The liquor cabinet was in the study, so that's where Harley led Liz, then excused herself to shower and change into a sundress before joining her. For an hour or so they made preoccupied conversation while they waited for the men to return. Liz nursed two single-malts straight up; Harley, two iced teas. They spoke briefly about R.H.'s aborted trip. Liz told of R.H.'s anguish at feeling compelled to put the *Anjelica* up for sale, since the strain of sailing her appeared to be more than his heart could stand.

When they finally heard the Jag slowly pull up, they each took a window, shamelessly peeking through the closed curtains. R.H. turned the engine off and sat quietly for a moment, listening to his son talk. Nodding thoughtfully, he responded. This went on for some time, none of it audible to the two women.

For the most part their conversation seemed eerily restrained, but from time to time one or the other of them would betray his emotion with a forceful gesture or intense expression. Anger occasionally surfaced, but was quickly extinguished with calming words.

R.H. rubbed at his eyes. Tucker put a hand on his shoulder and said something; his father nodded in response. When R.H. spoke, Tucker nodded. For several more minutes the exchange continued this way, hinting at reconciliation and agreement.

They got out of the car. Tucker offered his hand, and R.H. took it in both of his. Each gripped the other's shoulder, and when they spoke, there was conviction and sincerity in their eyes.

Emotion welled within Harley. When she sniffed back the tears that threatened, Liz snapped, "Don't you *dare* cry! If you do, then I shall, and I refuse to allow it!"

As DINNERTIME APPROACHED, Harley scanned the cupboards, wondering what she could dream up to feed four people, when she had only shopped for two. Improvising with what was at hand, she picked some of the basil that had been planted among the lavender, tossed it together with hot fettuccine, olive oil, and sun-dried tomatoes, and served it on the patio. R.H. ate with gusto and several times mentioned how pleased he was that she would be staying on until September. Not wanting to put a damper on things, Harley smiled and pretended that her heart was not filled with anguish at Tucker's imminent departure.

The only awkward moment occurred when, halfway through the meal, she carelessly pushed her hair behind her ears, freezing when she noticed R.H. staring at her with narrowed eyes. *The earrings!* She wore his dead wife's five-hundred-year-old earrings! What would he think? What should she say?

To her amazement, his expression softened into something almost like a smile. With a brief glance in his son's direction, he said, "Those earrings are most becoming on you, my dear. I wonder if I might have another serving of that fettuccine?"

When the sun had sunk low in the sky, R.H. suggested coffee and liqueurs in the study.

"Can we meet you there in a little while?" Tucker asked. "I was hoping I could talk Harley into a walk on the beach before night falls."

"YOU'RE NOT SO DUMB, either," Tucker said, breaking the silence in which they walked.

The waves alternately slapped Harley's ankles and sucked the sand from beneath her feet. Up ahead she saw the giant boulders that defined the secluded little spot where she and Tucker had spent the night in each other's arms. The sight should conjure up happy memories, she thought, not sadness. Everything had gone wrong. Most of it was her fault, and now he was trying to tell her she wasn't so dumb?

Stealing his line, she said, "Oh, I don't know about that."

"I'm talking about the things you said when we were sitting in the car earlier today, before you went for your run."

"About you and your father?"

"About everything. You can be pretty persuasive when you put your mind to it."

All Harley could take credit for persuading him to do was talk to his father. "I take it you explained things to him?"

"We each explained things. A *lot* of explaining went on. And a lot of promises to make things right. I must say he wins the prize for the most impressive gesture of good faith. He gave me the *Anjelica*."

"*Wow!*"

"That's my line. Don't make me tell you again."

Despite everything that had happened, she was unreservedly thrilled for him. The *Anjelica!* "Where is it now?"

"*She. She's* dry-docked in Fort Lauderdale."

"How are you going to get it—*her*—up to Alaska?"

He said, "I'm not. I'm going to fly down to Lauderdale and get her out of dry dock and sail her."

"In the Caribbean?"

"To start with, but I've always been kind of curious about the South Pacific, too. I think I'll just leave it open-ended. Start sailing and not worry too much about where I go or how long it takes. It could be two months or two years."

Two months or two years. She missed him already. Not that she could ever expect to see him again if he went back to Alaska, but at least then, she would know where he was. In her mind, he would have a distinct location. Sailing off to nowhere like this was like falling off the edge of the earth. But that was just like Tucker. No itinerary, no expectations. Still, even he had obligations. "What about your business?"

"I'm going to make Molly happy and sell it to her."

"Then what? After your sailing trip is over, I mean."

"I don't know. I figure I'll have plenty of time to decide that during the trip. That's one thing about long sailing trips, you've got plenty of time to think."

They approached the semicircle of boulders and Tucker led her to a low one with a flattened top. They sat side by side, facing the water, still holding hands. In the distance, silhouetted against a sky the color of apricots, a single large schooner sat motionless.

Harley said, "The *Anjelica's* a forty-footer, isn't she? Can you handle that much boat alone?"

"Not a chance," he answered lightly. "I was hoping you'd come along and give me a hand."

She regarded him in stunned silence.

He said, "You love to sail, and you're damn good at it. A trip like this is just what you need to shake out all that chaff your life is so filled with."

Struck dumb, she just sat there.

He lifted her hand to his lips and kissed it. In a quiet voice he said, "Please say yes. I won't want to go without you."

He wanted her with him! But... "What about all those things you said about us being too different, and—"

"And what about all those things *you* said about weathering a crisis? I compared the things you said to the things I said, and you won. You're right, it's fear that drives me to bolt. That and the fact that I've never done anything else. But I don't want to bolt this time. This time I'm in it for the long haul."

"The long haul means the long haul, Tucker. Are you saying you're not going to panic two weeks from now and—"

"Not two weeks or two months or two years. I know what the long haul means. It means a commitment. I never wanted one before, and I can't believe I want one now, but I do, with you. More than anything. I can appreciate your skepticism, though. I anticipated it." He reached into the front pocket of his rolled-up chinos and handed her another little black velvet bag. "My Dad's not the only one who knows how to make a gesture of good faith. This is mine, to you."

"Tucker, no. I really can't keep taking—"

"Open it."

"Tucker—"

Impatiently he took the little bag from her, opened it, and shook it into his palm. Something rolled out: a gold ring set with a cabochon emerald held in place by two tiny hands.

"Tucker! That's your mother's—"

"Engagement ring," he finished. "Now I'd like it to be yours."

She was breathless. Hers? He couldn't mean... "This is why you went to the bank? To get this? For me?"

"Of course."

"I thought... I thought..." What did this mean? Did this mean... "Why are you giving this to me?"

He sighed, but he was smiling. "Honey, I'll get down on one knee if I have to, but you know that kind of thing still hurts like a son of a—"

"But I just don't under—"

"All right, here goes." He got up and awkwardly knelt in the sand at her feet, his weight on the good leg.

She could tell the position was painful for him. "Tucker, get up."

"Not until you agree to marry me."

"What?"

"I want you to marry me." Taking her left hand in his, he slid the ring onto her finger. It fit perfectly. "I've thought it all out. R.H. has invited me to stay as long as I like, but I think three days is all the state requires between the blood test and the marriage. My father's minister can do the honors, or we can use a justice of the peace, whichever you prefer. Then, that same day, we fly to Lauderdale and sail the *Anjelica* into the Caribbean."

"But—"

"But who'll take care of my father? Somehow I suspect Liz'll be more than happy for the opportunity to prove how loving and nurturing she really is under all that frost."

"Yeah, but—"

"But what about your M.B.A.? Take a leave of absence. I'm sure Liz will be happy to arrange it for you. Then, when we come back, you can complete it."

Harley couldn't think. She could barely breathe. "But, Tucker, you don't believe in marriage. You said it was for . . . for people who couldn't think straight."

"It is. I'm a case in point. I'm way too crazy about you to think straight. All I can think about is spending the rest of my life with you. You're all I want anymore. You're the only thing that's really important to me. Please say yes."

Harley looked down at her hands, enveloped in both of his. She looked into his eyes, deep and translucent.

"Come on, Harley. Say yes."

He was all she wanted anymore, too. More than anything. Suddenly all her careful plans and well-thought-out schedules and inviolable rules seemed petty and unimportant. The only important thing in the world was Tucker—her life with Tucker.

"Say yes, Harley. Please. My leg's killing me."

She took a deep breath. "Yes."

"*Yes!*" Seizing her around the waist, he pulled her down onto the sand, rolled on top of her, and covered her mouth with his. With no reservations she gave herself over to the pleasure of the kiss, to the feel of his body pressing her into the sand, his hands stroking her face, caressing her breasts. . . .

Her desire for him was sudden, overwhelming, almost painful. Senseless with need, she clutched him to her, instinctively parting her legs. He moved against her, and she could feel his need, equal to her own. When he lifted her skirt and fondled her through her thin cotton panties, she pressed her hand over his and moaned his name. He knelt over her and swiftly unbelted his chinos. Sitting up, she unzipped them and reached in to torment him as he had tormented her.

He yanked her panties off and tossed them aside. She grabbed his wallet out of his back pocket, ripped open the little packet with frantic haste, and expertly sheathed him, all in a matter of seconds.

Too impatient to undress further, Tucker threw her on her back and rose over her, lifting her hips and driving himself into her. They coupled with unthinking urgency, moving together in a primal rhythm, like a single, struggling creature.

On the verge of climax, she froze at a sound from beyond the boulders. Tucker heard it, too, and turned his head to listen. A jangling...panting...a man saying, "Catch, Rusty!"

With a mumbled curse, Tucker quickly rolled them onto their sides and adjusted her skirt—to give the impression, she realized, that they were merely locked in an innocent embrace.

"Good evening," the man said as he passed the semicircle of boulders.

"Good evening," Harley and Tucker said in unison, not too breathlessly.

The man walked on a few yards, until he was out of sight but not out of earshot, and proceeded to toss whatever it was he was tossing to his dog.

They still lay side by side, intimately joined. "Shh," Tucker whispered, as he closed his big hands around her hips and rocked them slowly.

"Oh my God," she breathed. She locked her legs with his and slid her hands beneath his shirt to grip his back. "I'm so close."

"Me, too." He was trembling.

Harley thought she was going to explode, to fly apart in a million shivering pieces. She felt Tucker's body go rigid and flex as his fingers dug into her hips. A strangled sound escaped his throat, and the skin on his back erupted in goose bumps. The convulsive throbbing within her sent her over the edge, into a heart-stopping orgasm of excruciating intensity. The struggle not to cry out only magnified its force. He held her tight as it ran its course, and for some time afterward.

Eventually they drew apart and set about adjusting their clothes. Rebuckling his belt, Tucker peered over the boulders. "That guy is gone. It's about time."

Harley slipped her panties back on and smoothed down her dress. "I don't know. I thought it was kind of exciting having him there, kind of dangerous."

"Exciting? Dangerous?" He sank down next to her and took her in his arms. "I've created a monster."

"An insatiable monster," she said. "Come to my room tonight."

She could see his eyes light with anticipation, but after a moment's thought he said, "Not here, not in R.H.'s house with him down the hall. We'd have to sneak around like teenagers. And not out here anymore, for the amusement of the neighbors. Let's wait until we're aboard the *Anjelica*."

"You want to wait until our wedding night?"

He chuckled. "It does seem out of character, I know. But yes, I want to wait. The next time we make love, it's going to be on the deck of the *Anjelica*, under the stars. I want to feel the ocean swell beneath me while I'm inside you. I want to make you insane with pleasure. I want us to lose ourselves in each other, in the middle of nowhere, where no one can hear us or see us."

"Yes," she whispered, gripping his head to pull it down until their mouths met in a deep, lingering kiss.

Tucker broke the kiss and pointed to the sky. "Look."

Harley sat up and looked. Against a sunset of fiery brilliance, tiny spheres floated up and drifted out over the sound. "Phil's balloons," she said. "Phil's and Kitty's."

"Ours, too," he said. "They were my idea, after all. And now that they've been set free, I think we have as much of a claim to them as anybody."

Tucker put his arms around her and held her in a silent embrace as the balloons rose higher and higher, floating wherever the breezes took them. First there were dozens, then hundreds, in every hue of the rainbow, scattering across the sky, filling it with color.

They watched, transfixed, until the last balloon rose into the darkening heavens and disappeared, a fleeting testament to lasting love.

HARLEQUIN®
Temptation®

Secret Fantasies

Do you have a secret fantasy?

Willow Evans does. But it involved independence
and solitude at the Cape Cod house she'd inherited
from her grandmother. Not being torn between two
men...who look identical...neither of whom can really
exist...who both want her. One man loves her...the
other needs her. Discover a tale of impossible love by
Lynn Michaels in #542 NIGHTWING, available in
June 1995.

Everybody has a secret fantasy. And you'll find them
all in Temptation's exciting new yearlong miniseries,
Secret Fantasies. Beginning January 1995, one book
each month focuses on the hero or heroine's innermost
romantic desires....

MILLION DOLLAR SWEEPSTAKES (III)

EXTRA BONUS PRIZE DRAWING

SWP-H595

MOVE OVER, MELROSE PLACE!

> Apartment for rent
> One bedroom
> Bachelor Arms
> 555-1234

Come live and love in L.A. with the tenants of Bachelor Arms. Enjoy a year's worth of wonderful love stories and meet colorful neighbors you'll bump into again and again.

When Blythe Fielding planned her wedding and asked her two best friends, Caitlin and Lily, to be bridesmaids, none of them knew a new romance was around the corner for each of them—not even the bride! These entertaining, dramatic stories of friendship, mystery and love by JoAnn Ross continue the exploits of the residents of Bachelor Arms and answer one very important question: Will Blythe ever get to walk down the aisle? Find out in:

NEVER A BRIDE (May 1995) #537

FOR RICHER OR POORER (June 1995) #541

THREE GROOMS AND A WEDDING (July 1995) #545

Soon to move into Bachelor Arms are the heroes and heroines in books by always popular Candace Schuler and Judith Arnold. A new book every month!

Don't miss the goings-on at Bachelor Arms.

HARLEQUIN® *Temptation*

THREE GROOMS:
Case, Carter and Mike

TWO WORDS:
"We Don't!"

ONE MINISERIES:

GROOMS ON THE RUN

Starting in May 1995, Harlequin Temptation
brings you an exciting miniseries called

GROOMS ON THE RUN

Each book (and there'll be one a month for three
months!) features a sexy hero who's ready to say,
"I do!" but ends up saying, "I don't!"

Watch for these special Temptations:

In May, I WON'T! by Gina Wilkins #539
In June, JILT TRIP by Heather MacAllister #543
In July, NOT THIS GUY! by Glenda Sanders #547

Available wherever Harlequin books are sold.

In June, get ready for thrilling romances
and FREE BOOKS—Western-style—
with...

WESTERN *Lovers*

You can receive the first 2 Western Lovers titles FREE!

June 1995 brings Harlequin and Silhouette's
WESTERN LOVERS series, which combines larger-than-
life love stories set in the American West! And WESTERN
LOVERS brings you stories with your favorite themes...
"Ranch Rogues," "Hitched In Haste," "Ranchin' Dads,"
"Reunited Hearts" the packaging on each book
highlights the popular theme found in each WESTERN
LOVERS story!

And in June, when you buy either of the Men Made In
America titles, you will receive a WESTERN LOVERS title
absolutely FREE! Look for these fabulous combinations:

♦ Buy ALL IN THE FAMILY
   by Heather Graham Pozzessere (Men Made In
   America) and receive a FREE copy of
   BETRAYED BY LOVE by Diana Palmer
   (Western Lovers)

♦ Buy THE WAITING GAME
   by Jayne Ann Krentz (Men Made In America)
   and receive a FREE copy of
   IN A CLASS BY HIMSELF by JoAnn Ross
   (Western Lovers)

Look for the special, extra-value shrink-wrapped
packages at your favorite retail outlet!

HARLEQUIN® ✦ *Silhouette*®

Announcing
the New Pages & Privileges™ Program
from Harlequin® and Silhouette®

Get All This FREE
With Just One Proof-of-Purchase!

- **FREE Travel Service** with the guaranteed lowest available airfares plus 5% cash back on every ticket

- **FREE Hotel Discounts** of up to 60% off at leading hotels in the U.S., Canada and Europe

- **FREE Petite Parfumerie** collection (a $50 Retail value)

- **FREE $25 Travel Voucher** to use on any ticket on any airline booked through our Travel Service

- **FREE Insider Tips Letter** full of fascinating information and hot sneak previews of upcoming books

- **FREE Mystery Gift** (if you enroll before May 31/95)

And there are more great gifts and benefits to come!
Enroll today and become Privileged!

(see insert for details)

 PROOF-OF-PURCHASE

Offer expires October 31, 1996

HT-PP1